The School Gates

Nicola May

D1581767

Published by Accent Press Ltd 2015

ISBN 9781783758944

Copyright © **Nicola May** 2015

First published by Nicola May 2012

Acknowledgements

I wrote most of *The School Gates* while recovering from a hysterectomy. I had no choice but to have the operation. I have no children so it wasn't an easy time.

My heartfelt thanks go to:

My selfless sister Sara – who quietly came in every day and did everything for me so I had no worries.

My beautiful nieces, Georgia and Trinny, for sleeping by my side and making me lots of tea.

My steadfast brother Mark, for the best homemade mackerel paté ever.

My funny sister Fiona for cleaning and carrying on demand.

And, of course, my lovely dad, who supported me throughout, when I couldn't work.

Dear Harry, for driving my car every week so the battery didn't go flat.

Joan, Emma, Philip, Scott, Jeff, Liane, Jules, Lucy, Charlotte, Kia, Kate, Sophia, Bird, Hannah, Ralph, Jacqui, Marlene and Fiona for being just downright lovely friends really.

And always in my heart, my baby angels whose little souls will never ever be forgotten.

For Fiona, Mark & Sara

'No woman can call herself free until she can choose consciously whether she will or will not be a mother.'

Margaret Sangar

– Autumn Term –

'The decision to have a child is to accept that your heart will forever walk outside of your body.'

Katherine Hadley

Prologue

– Eliska's Mum –

'Joshua P said if I give him a pound, we can kiss at playtime,' the red-headed six-year-old announced at the breakfast table.

'Did he indeed?' Alana Murray sighed, wishing that after several years of abstinence, it could only be that easy for her too.

'So?' Eliska continued, bashing her spoon annoyingly against the cereal bowl.

Alana Murray straightened down the skirt of her smart black suit.

'Come on, Eliska, please be a good girl. Mummy has got a really important meeting today.'

'You always have important meetings.' The little girl stuck out her bottom lip.

'And where's bloody Inga? She should have been here an hour ago,' Alana barked.

'So, can I have a bloody pound?' Eliska suddenly screeched at the top of her little voice, pushing her chair back violently.

'No!' Alana shouted back, pushing her hands through her sleek blonde bob as the doorbell rang and her daughter tore past her and ran up the stairs.

Then: 'Thank God, Inga,' she said weakly. 'I thought you were never coming.'

Inga Gowenska, current au pair to the Murray *famille-à-deux*, was a stunning, waif-like Polish girl of eighteen.

'I am so, so sorry, Alana. My bus it didn't come so soon. Did Eliska have her breakfast already?' She looked at the mess in front of her.

'Yes, yes. Look – I have to go. I'll be home seven-ish.'

'No, you will be home at seven exactly,' Inga stated sternly. 'It is my night off.'

Alana went upstairs to find her red-haired, red-eyed daughter lying on her bed sucking her thumb.

'Darling, I'm sorry I shouted.' She kissed her lightly on the cheek. 'You know Mummy can't be late for work. I'll bring back a new computer game for you.

'Promise it will be Make-up Studio.' Eliska jumped up in excitement.

'Yes, yes, of course. Now come on down and let Inga sort your ponytail before she takes you to school.' Eliska ran towards the stairs. 'And young lady,' Alana added, 'don't ever let me hear you swear again.'

Alana pulled into the Chiswick courtyard and turned off the ignition. As she stepped out of her sporty Mercedes, the wind suddenly gusted, sending colourful autumn leaves swishing around her legs.

Stephen McNair, the proprietor of SM Public Relations, greeted her in the plant-laden reception with a kiss on both cheeks.

'Look at you, Ms Murray, arriving all windswept and sexy. It's been far too long.'

'That's not really appropriate talk for one of your key clients, now is it?' Her heels clicked on the polished floor as she followed him to his office.

Facing him across his green-leather-topped desk, she sat back comfortably whilst crossing her legs to reveal a little too much thigh.

Her motive – distraction. It was getting so much harder now to keep him off the scent. If he started questioning her about her daughter again, what on earth would she say?

Joan Brown jumped as her husband of ten years lightly patted her on the bottom. 'Stop that, you silly old sod,' she laughed, balancing her eleven-month-old daughter on her fleshy hip, whilst stirring a big saucepan of beaten eggs.

'Mum just swore,' seven-year-old Clark said without changing expression, knife and fork held high in anticipation of his breakfast.

'What does sod mean anyway?' Kent, his nine-year-old brother questioned.

'It means a piece of earth,' Colin intervened quickly.

'So, that means Daddy is a silly old piece of earth then?' Skye, their six-year-old daughter, added quizzically.

'Something like that,' Joan replied, spooning fluffy scrambled eggs on to hot buttered toast. 'Now eat your breakfast, or we'll be late for school as usual.'

She put Cissy in her high chair and wiped her hands down her apron, assessing her brood and feeling a deep sense of love as she did so.

'You'll need to check their barnets before school. I saw Clark scratching like mad upstairs earlier,' Colin told her.

'Did we really sign up for all this?' She smiled and took off her apron.

'What – recruitment for Michael Bentine's flea circus?' Colin joked as he headed to the loo, newspaper in hand.

The three older Brown children stood dutifully, heads down in front of their mother as Cissy, now free from her high chair, crawled over to Squidge the dog's food bowl, and unbeknown to all, started munching on a bone-shaped chew.

All of the children had been blessed with mad mops of curly blond hair, just like their mother. Unfortunately, they had also been blessed with attracting the nit population of Denbury; twice already this year.

'Right, Skye, looks like you've just got eggs. Clark, they're having a right old party in your hair. Kent, lucky you. You're fine this time.'

'Ha. Ha. No smelly shampoo for me.' Kent mocked his younger siblings.

'Cissy, you little tinker.' Joan placed the baby back in her high chair, prised open her chubby hands and deftly replaced the dog chew with a digestive biscuit.

Appearing from under the table, covered in toast crumbs and tomato ketchup, Squidge, the black and now slightly greying Labrador flopped down with a grunt into his basket.

Balancing a piece of cold toast in one hand and his briefcase in the other, Colin leaned down and kissed his four children one by one, totally oblivious to the affray around him. Then it was his pretty wife's turn for a kiss.

'Another day, another dollar, my sweet,' he sang and headed for the front door. 'Oh, how I wish I had the easy life of being a full-time mum,' he added, deftly ducking to avoid a wet dishcloth hitting him on the head.

'Don't forget to see if you can find any fortieth birthday invites in your lunch-hour,' she shouted after him as he walked past their caravan parked on the drive.

'OK, see you later, you lovely lot. Be good for your mum,' he grinned and waved wildly.

However, on rounding the corner his smile faded. He had never lied to his wife once in all of the twenty-three years they had known each other, and he wasn't sure how long he could keep up the pretence.

'You're a fat, lazy bitch, that's what you are. All I want is four cans of lager – not much to ask, is it?' Ron Collins lit another roll-up, flopped his beer-bellied carcass on to an armchair and switched on to breakfast television.

'I literally haven't got the money until I collect the Child Benefit later.' Mo Collins knew she should keep quiet, but her anger overrode her inner voice of caution. 'If you got your hairy arse off that chair and went to look for a bloody job, you could buy your own beer.' Her voice dropped another octave. 'And for the love of God, will you please stop smoking in the house!'

She yelped in pain as the remote control hit the top of her left shoulder.

Her husband began to bellow, 'Nag, nag nag. Job! Fucking job! It wasn't my fault I was made redundant and you know that. Blame the bloody government for taking the bottom out of the car industry if you're going to blame anyone.'

He started coughing uncontrollably.

Mo noticed her daughter cowering at the bottom of the stairs. She put her finger to her lips to make sure the six-year-old remained silent and gestured for her to go back up to her room. She then went to the kitchen, got a glass of orange juice and loaded up a tray with some toast and Marmite to take upstairs.

Her baby girl was now sitting on her bright pink duvet shaking. Pressing her to her large bosom, Mo rocked her gently.

'It's OK, angel. Daddy's just angry that he hasn't got a job. He's not cross with us.'

'Tell him not to hurt you again, Mummy.'

'Oh darling.' Mo kissed her only daughter on the cheek. 'Come on, eat your breakfast up here, and we'll get you ready for school.'

Mo heaved her body up off the bed. Her husband was right about her being overweight. Their lives had become unbearable since he had lost his job five years ago.

Ron Collins had turned to drink for solace. Mo had found comfort in food.

'Good girl,' Mo said as Rosie handed her mum the empty plate and glass. 'Now, let's get your shoes on, shall we?'

'Do you think I could have a new pair, from Father Christmas maybe?' the little girl asked.

Tears pricked Mo's eyes. She pushed on her daughter's scuffed school shoes and felt her toes press against the end.

'Let's see, darling.' Mo wasn't sure where on earth she'd find the money. Even the benefits her good-for-nothing husband used to get had stopped, as he was either too drunk or too lazy to go and sign on.

Mo and Rosie started their walk to school, bumping into the now fairly nit-free Brown clan as they did so. Clark and Kent were in the front of the group, pedalling their little legs furiously on their bikes, school bags flung clumsily over shoulders and wearing matching blue cycle helmets. Skye sat in a seat on the back of her mum's bike, and Cissy lay regally in a customised cat basket on the front handlebars.

'Morning Mo,' Joan greeted her neighbour cheerfully, then realised she looked even sadder than usual.

'Boys, come back here a minute,' she commanded. As her sons pedalled back to her side, she murmured, 'Are you OK, love?'

'Fine, fine,' her friend replied, already puffing from such a short walk.

'Now, I know that means you're not. You off to work

this morning?'

'On a morning shift. Supposed to be at the surgery for eight-thirty,' Mo sighed.

'You've still got fifteen minutes, so why don't you head straight there and Rosie can come to school with us. How about that, Rosie? You can sit on my seat and I'll push you all along.'

'Yeah! Can I, Mummy? Please, can I?'

'Yeah, yeah!' Cissy gurgled, trying to copy her.

'As long as you're sure, Joan.'

'Don't be daft, of course I'm sure. One extra makes no difference to me. I'll see you at the school gates later. We can have a proper catch-up then.'

'I'm out for dinner with clients tonight, so can you drop me at the station before taking Tommy to school?' Mark asked, putting his newspaper down and pushing back his dark floppy fringe. His evident crow's feet betrayed his thirty-five years but he was still a very handsome man.

'Course I can, but we'd better get a move on. Tommy, you ready, my darleen?' A glimmer of Dana's Czech accent could be heard as she shouted up the stairs.

Her son appeared, long mousy locks needing a brush, grey school jumper on back to front, his head in his portable computer console.

'Here, let me brush your hair. I don't think Mr Chambers will like you looking like a hippy.'

'But, Mum!'

'Yes, Mum, don't you mean?' Dana swiftly turned his jumper around the right way and combed through his hair.

'Right, coat on, Tommy Knight. No packed lunch today as you said you fancied school dinner this week. Chicken pasta – yum, sounds nice.'

'Sounds yuk, but Joshua P is having it too.' Tommy stuck his finger in his nose, and his mother immediately pulled it away.

As Dana revved up the 4 x 4 on the drive, she lamented the fact that their car was so eco-unfriendly, but Mark insisted on the recommendation of a Top Wheels television presenter that this was the car to be seen in, so he just had to have it.

'Hurry up, Daddy,' the six-year-old piped up, as his father dived into the passenger seat, briefcase in hand. Then, 'Mummy?'

'Yes, darleen?'

'Eliska told me yesterday that her mummy has an old pear, and that you used to be an old pear once too.'

Mark laughed. 'It's au pair, Tommy – and yes, Mum did used to be one.'

'What does an old pear do?' the inquisitive little boy continued.

'Looks after children and cleans the house. Not much different from being a mum really,' Mark chipped in.

'Oi, you.' Dana poked her husband in the ribs, feeling slightly narked at his comment, and even more so that the snooty Alana Murray should be discussing their private lives.

'So whose children did you look after then, Mum?'

Dana raised her eyebrows. This was getting far too complicated and she didn't feel that her son was quite ready to know the ins and outs of how her parents had got together. Just then, they arrived at the train station.

'Right, we're here now,' she said, relieved to put a stop to the conversation.

'Have a good day, angel cheeks. Don't do anything I wouldn't do,' Mark Knight said to his pretty petite wife, kissing her on the forehead as he did so, then adding, 'And don't forget to pick up my dry cleaning, will you. Oh, and I need a couple of shirts ironed.'

He went to the back door of the car and opened it. 'And as for you, mister, be good at school.' He reached in and tweaked Tommy's cheek.

Old pear, Dana thought as she drove away. More like des-pair, at her boring day ahead.

The radio in the smart chrome-and-black kitchen blared out the latest and greatest hits from Madonna. Gordon Summers, a well-groomed thirty-year-old with wavy dark brown hair and pecs to die for, began to dance around the kitchen.

'Oh Lily! Oh Lola!' he called. 'Daddy Gordy has got the best breakfast ready for you both – pancakes and maple syrup and a strawberry smoothie, no less.'

While he was wondering how Mads could possibly look so good in her fifties, he heard the feet of his six-year-old twins running towards the kitchen of the modern three-bedroomed flat. He turned the radio down.

'I knew that would get you moving,' he laughed as the four blue eyes, one pair encased in bright red spectacles, looked back at him over the breakfast table.

'This is toast and honey,' Lily said sternly.

'And this is strawberry milkshake out of a bottle,' Lola added. 'You lied; we're not allowed to lie.'

'OK. So it's nearly your favourites.'

'Soooo not funny,' Lily remonstrated. 'But on this occasion you're lucky, as I like toast and honey.' She pushed her glasses up on to her nose.

'Where's Daddy Chris this morning anyway?' Lola asked

'He's gone to look after the passengers on the planes, today and tomorrow.'

'Oh OK,' the twins said in unison.

Gordon looked at them lovingly as they munched on their toast. His girls were easily distinguishable, as bespectacled Lily insisted on a short-fringed crop like her favourite television character, and Lola wanted 'the longest hair in the world'.

'Now, I've made you your packed lunches.'

'If you haven't been shopping, please don't tell us it's peanut butter and jelly sandwiches again,' Lily smirked.

'Jam, not jelly, Lily. You've got an apple and yoghurt too, though,' Gordon replied hurriedly. 'But I solemnly promise I will go to the supermarket later, and we'll be back on our "five a day" as usual. And before you say it, I know you're not allowed peanut butter at school, but just eat them discreetly and stay away from Ralph Weeks. If you set off his allergy we'll all be in trouble.'

Lola got up from her seat and walked round to where her father was packing their school bags. She put her arms around his legs and squeezed him tight.

'I love you, Daddy Gordy. Even if we have only got stinky sandwiches today.'

'And I love you too, Lola and Lily Summers.'

'Erg. You're both so soppy,' Lily interjected.

Gordon, ever the emotional, sniffed loudly and dabbed his eyes with some kitchen roll.

'Right, you ready for school, ladies?'

'We haven't cleaned our teeth yet,' they said in unison.

'Oh yes, silly Daddy Gordy. Use your teeth-timers, then we must get going.'

Gordon looked at the clock; it was time to leave for school. No doubt all the usual gang would be there – his favourite and not-so-favourite mums and dads – and there might just be time for a chat at the school gates.

Chapter One

Gordon, Lily and Lola were singing and gyrating along to a Top Ten girl-band track, when they pulled up at the school gates.

Eliska Murray banged on the car window and stuck her tongue out at the twins. Lily pushed her face right up against the glass and poked hers right back.

'Eliska called me "four-eyes" yesterday,' she grumbled.

'Did she indeed?' Gordon replied. 'Well, if she says it again, tell her you've only got to wear glasses till you're ten, but sadly, she'll always be a ginger.'

The twins giggled, and pushed their way out of their dad's blue and white Mini Cooper.

It was a windy day and some of the children were already running around the playground throwing big handfuls of red and golden leaves at each other. Eliska had already charged up the drive towards school.

'Morning, Inga sweetie – and how was the wicked witch this morning?' Gordon greeted the pretty au pair.

'Witchier than usual, if that's possible. Luckily my bus didn't come so soon, so I only was with her for five minutes. You work today?'

'No. Two days off now. Bliss.' Gordon smiled broadly, showing off his perfect set of white veneers.

'Doing something nice?'

'Chores, darling, chores,' he waved his arm in the air.

'Elocution lessons, then supermarket, then the gym to pump up the pecs, then back to pick up the munchkins.'

He realised the girls were still at his legs, waiting for

him to say goodbye. 'Bless you, gorgeous ones. Now kisses for Daddy Gordy before you go.' He leaned down and planted a smacker on them both.

'Yuk!' the girls said in unison, wiping their mouths with the back of their hands.

'Year Two is great – so much better not having to take them right up to the door if we don't want to. Soon I'll be pulling up and just throwing them out of the car,' Gordon joked, but watching that the twins reached their class safely.

'You are a naughty man. But yes, we wouldn't have to talk to anyone we liked not a lot either. Talking of which...' Inga faked a wide smile at the approaching whirlwind.

'Oh Gordon, so glad I've caught you,' gushed Emily Pritchard – Head of PTA, Netball Coach and Mother of Joshua P, seven, chief swot and playground kisser. She flicked back her hair, so that Inga noticed the effects of further Botox in her forehead, before the dyed blonde locks bobbed back around her face.

'I was helping out at netball yesterday and noticed that Lola showed great promise.' She batted her false eyelashes and continued: 'We need a new team for this term and I would love her to join in.'

'What about Lily?' Gordon asked.

'Oh, I think she would be far more suited to something a little less active, like Reading Club maybe.'

Inga disguised her snort of laughter as a cough.

'Well, ya know, Emily, that's just great news,' Gordon humoured the woman. 'I'll see what Lola says tonight and let you know. Maybe I can get Lily to read up on it too.'

'Lovely, perfect. By the way, great hair, Inga! Did you cut it yourself? Toodle oo!' And with a flick of her hair and a wobble of her bosom, Emily headed off to her convertible which was parked in its usual prime position, near to the school gates.

'That fuckeeng bitch,' Inga spat, but then had to laugh as Gordon was in hysterics, saying, 'I guess at least she makes your Alana look like an angel.'

Gordon loved Featherstone Primary and all it stood for. Situated in a residential No Through Road on the outskirts of the town of Denbury, it retained a village 'small school' feel. With just the one set of school gates and a fairly long drive, he felt it was a safe haven for his precious girls.

The building itself was nothing spectacular – brick-built, on one level only; modern and open-plan. It was home to just 150 pupils based in six classes, with a headmistress, seven teachers and four teaching assistants.

As well as the teaching areas, the school housed a multi-purpose dining/assembly/sports hall and a quiet playroom for the little ones. Sport was high on the agenda, and outside there was a playground with a netball court and two large fields for other outdoor sports. Plus, after many successful fund-raising efforts by the active Parent Teacher Association, the children were also lucky enough to have use of a swimming pool in the summer. It was as good as any private school in the area, and everyone who lived in Denbury wanted their children to go there.

One minute to spare before assembly, and there was the commotion of the Brown family arriving. Joan cycled as fast as she could up the drive with her boys pedalling furiously behind her.

'Quick! Helmets off, boys, and bikes in rack. Here are your bags. We'll be in trouble if we have to sign the late book again. Skye, just look at your face.' She spat on a tissue and wiped remnants of breakfast from her daughter's chin. 'Rosie, you OK?' Rosie nodded. In lifting the tiny girl off her seat, Joan noticed her badly scuffed shoes. Cissy, a shock of fair hair poking out of her blue beanie hat, snored in the customised cat basket. All four

17

children ran to their respective classes.

'Love you all. Be good!' Joan shouted after them.

Rosie smiled and felt warm inside. She loved being ensconced in the family madness that was the Browns.

Joan got on her bike as Dana and Tommy Knight were pelting towards her. 'Makes a change for me not to be the last,' she said, cycling gently past.

'I know. Hopefully I can sneak him in the back door,' Dana panted.

'Glad it's a school day. They'll all be going crazy in this wind,' Joan added and sped off, leaving the pretty Czech completely perplexed.

Then, all of a sudden, as if she had broken free from greyhound traps, Eliska Murray was running as fast as her little legs would carry her, back out of school and back down the school drive. Luckily, Inga was such a bad driver, she was still trying to do a U-turn in the road outside. She looked in horror at Eliska tearing out of the school gates, with Miss Bradshaw, one of the teaching assistants, in hot pursuit.

The panicked au pair hurriedly got out of the car. 'Eliska, are you OK? Did you forget something?' 'Yes,' Eliska puffed. 'Can I have a pound, please?'

Alana sat at the boardroom table in Stephen McNair's spacious, bright office overlooking Chiswick High Road. He was looking particularly sexy today, in a sky-blue shirt and grey suit.

When all six-feet-four of him got up to go and fetch a cup of coffee, she suddenly had a clear vision of him ripping her clothes off all those years ago in that fancy London hotel.

It had been a typical one-night stand, if ever a one-night stand can be classed as 'typical'. It had happened like this:

Company Christmas party

Invite the PR agency along

Drink too much

Hotel bar closes

'Come to my room for a night-cap from the mini-bar?'

Drinks in – wits out

Wake up in the morning, regretting mixing rum with vodka and also business with pleasure

However, the untypical thing about this one-night stand was that Stephen McNair wasn't normally a philanderer, and even Alana, with her insatiable desire for sex, realised that he was actually a decent bloke.

In her alluring black dress and high heels, the attractive blonde fox had lured the prey back to her lair and a full mini-bar, and then pounced.

Yes, he had shown weakness, but if Stephen McNair hadn't been such a nice person, he actually could have won a case of rape against her.

They had met a week later at this very office and she solemnly promised him that nothing would ever be said about the matter. She realised just how much he loved his wife and that was it. The case of Murray v. McNair – *closed.*

One sip of coffee down and *the* question immediately arose though. 'So, got any pictures of that wee bairn of yours?' The word 'bairn' emphasised his brusque Scottish accent.

'No, no.' Alana swallowed hard. 'New term, new school pic. I'm waiting to upgrade.'

'Typical – Alana Murray even upgrades her photos,' Stephen laughed. He still found her very attractive. 'How old is she going to be this month? I forget now.'

'Seven this year.' Alana wanted to slip under the chair.

'And will she be seeing her daddy on her birthday?' Stephen continued to dig.

Of course she bloody won't, Alana felt like saying. Now that Eliska was older she was even more adamant that she shouldn't meet her father. It would just cause too much complication in her little life and she was a difficult enough child already. Was Alana being selfish? Yes she was, but at the moment it was the way she wanted it. If Stephen or Eliska asked her, Daddy was 'always away on business'.

'No, not this year. He's away. Sri Lanka, I think he said.'

'And he's still looking after you both?'

'Stephen! We don't need looking after.' She bit her lip.

He swiftly changed the subject, with, 'Quarterly reports – then lunch, I think.'

'You think well, Mr McNair,' Alana beamed, suddenly recalling the sight of Stephen's large cock and cursing the butterflies in her stomach that had suddenly awoken.

Mo sped up the steps to the doctors' surgery and headed to her desk. Not having had time to wash her hair that morning, she quickly wound it into a bun and smudged on some clear lip gloss. The waiting room was already heaving. The supervisor, Grim Lynn, was such a grumpy old bag that it wasn't worth even being a nano-second late and suffering her bitter wrath.

Puffing and panting, Mo peeled off her old coat, relieved to see that all of the three desks in the small room behind the main reception counter were empty. She could hear cups clanking and smelled fresh coffee from the kitchen and knew that it must be her colleague Ffion, as the grim one 'didn't do caffeine'.

As Mo went to sit down, she noticed that on her swivel chair was an oblong of cardboard with a chain attached; she turned it over to see the words 'Nil by Mouth' on it. Normally she would have laughed, but feeling particularly sensitive after her already terrible morning, she choked back the tears.

Ffion appeared with two steaming cups of coffee.

'Morning, my lovely. The grim one has had to go and take Dr Jennings on a house visit, since her car wouldn't start. I'd like to say we'll have an easy time of it, but it's a full pen of 'em out there today.'

She stopped as Mo sniffed loudly and a tear rolled down her cheek. Ffion quickly shut the reception hatch, ignoring a patient who'd just come in and was waiting to see her.

'What on earth's the matter?'

Another sniff and Mo pointed to the Nil by Mouth sign.

'Oh, cariad, I'm so sorry. It was just a joke. Dr Delicious left one for each for us, thought it would stop us both eating so many biscuits. Look, mine's up already,' Ffion gestured at her desk, where the offending article was hanging in pride of place behind her flat screen.

Just five feet tall, with a petite frame, designer glasses enhancing her big brown eyes and shoulder-length thick auburn hair, Ffion was Little to Mo's Large.

The annoying thing was that her twenty-year-old metabolism allowed her consistently to eat crap and down at least a bottle of wine a night, without her gaining a gramme. However, Mo didn't hold this against her. Ffion Jones was a lovely, thoughtful girl and thankfully kept her sane enough to stop her putting morphine into Grim Lynn's Elderflower and Burdock herbal teas.

'Look, give it here.' Ffion took the sign back. 'Swap it with these.' She handed over a pack of chocolate Hobnobs. 'Now, get that hatch open and give us a smile.'

At that moment, Dr Noah Anderson, a.k.a. Dr Delicious, sounded his buzzer. 'Mrs Rachel Smith for Dr Del- – I mean Dr Anderson, please,' Mo announced to the waiting room, jumping into action.

A red-faced man was shifting with agitation on the other side of the reception counter.

'I am so sorry for the delay, sir,' Mo said briskly. 'Now, how can I help?'

The morning flew by in a blur of snuffles, urine samples, smear tests and screaming babies. Both Ffion and

Mo breathed a sigh of relief when lunchtime came.

'You are so lucky that you're done now,' Ffion said as the last patient left. 'I've got another four hours of this.'

'If it wasn't for collecting Rosie, I could do with another four hours of money myself, to be honest. It's Charlie's birthday on Saturday and I want to send him a present.'

'Charlie?'

'My son.'

Ffion looked perplexed. Just as Mo was about to explain, Dr Delicious appeared, causing Ffion to turn the colour of her hair.

The sexy doctor had not long been a GP at The White House practice in Denbury. In fact, he had arrived six months ago, the same month that Ffion replaced old Betty on her retirement. Mo had worked there part-time for eight years, just having a break when Rosie was born and then going back when the little girl started nursery.

All the time she had been there it had just been Dr Amanda Jennings and Dr Paul Stevens. That was, until Dr Stevens had a terrible accident with his ride-on lawnmower and had suffered permanent injuries, poor man.

Dr Noah Anderson looked young for a GP. Ffion guessed thirty, Mo guessed thirty-five. Both ladies thought that he would be far more suited to a role in an American hospital soap opera. Jaw-droppingly handsome, with black cropped hair and chiselled features, he had such a soft voice and calm demeanour that Mo was sure that half the female population of Denbury who claimed breast or vaginal problems were lying!

'So how is my conscientious double act today then?' he asked pleasantly.

'It's OK, you can say Little and Large,' Mo said tongue in cheek, looking towards Ffion's 'Nil by Mouth' sign.

Dr Delicious put his hand to his forehead, stuttering,

'I... I... it wasn't...'

'We're knackered,' Ffion announced, shielding his embarrassment.

'Me too,' the doctor replied, glad of the interruption. 'What time's my first one of the afternoon anyway?'

Mo looked at her computer.

'Two-thirty. It's Hypochondriac Hilda too, so go and put your feet up till then.'

The delicious one laughed, relieved that Mo really wasn't too offended.

'Right – I must go.' Mo suddenly realised the time. 'I've got to get to the postoffice, shop for dinner, then go and collect Rosie.'

'No time for a quick sandwich with me in Rosco's then?' Ffion asked, itching to find out more about Mo's son.

'Sorry, love. Maybe tomorrow. Enjoy your afternoon and remember...'

'Patience with the patients, ladies,' Ffion intervened with her finestimpression of Grim Lynn, sticking two fingers up in jest at Mo as she did so.

Chapter Two

A tear ran down Dana's face as she pulled away from the school gates. She ignored the scathing glance of Emily Pritchard – who had quite clearly stated her dislike of women who drove 4 x 4s.

Dana's husband Mark had told her that the only reason old Preachy Knickers (Mark's words) protested, was that she really wanted one herself and couldn't afford it.

Dana was sure that the fact that they lived in a big house up Bramwell Hill and drove a fancy car had stopped her making friends. She quite often thought that some of the other mothers were whispering about her at the school gates, and it made her really sad. She should make more of an effort, but she was really quite shy – and Mark's insistence that she didn't work, and his dislike of her not being home with him in the evenings had made it nigh-on impossible for her to start building relationships outside the family unit.

She was lucky to get a parking spot in Denbury High Street, since the 'Ladies Who Latte' (LWL) Brigade usually grabbed all the places. Talking of the LWL Brigade, Dana fiercely rejected any idea of her belonging to the same category as them.

She could have a facial, pedicure, manicure or back massage every day of the week if she wanted, and Mark wouldn't bat an eyelid. But that wasn't her. She was a natural beauty, with her cropped blonde hair and big blue eyes in a heart-shaped face. Her beauty regime was soap and water and a supermarket own-brand moisturiser. Her generous nature was much bigger than any whims or fancies. In fact, she hated the fact that she did not earn any money of her own. Mark had always lavished on her expensive gifts of brand-name cosmetics but she usually sneaked them to the women's hostel in the next town, soon after receiving them.

She picked up the dry cleaning and laid it neatly on the back seat, her tears replaced with a smile as she saw Tommy's favourite bear propped up on his booster seat. Noticing half a sticky lollipop wedged in its hand, it reminded her that she needed to get some after-school snacks for him.

She crossed the road to the newsagents. The outside hoarding screamed its news – Denbury Vicar in Summer Holiday Collection Scam.

Hilarious, she thought. She picked up a paper. She must see what he'd done, plus there was no harm in looking at what jobs were around, now was there?

She crossed back over the road to the car and seeing Rosco's on the corner, thought she would treat herself to a cream doughnut to have with her morning coffee back at home. The café was packed with an eclectic mix of business people having breakfast meetings, workmen and, of course, the LWL Brigade.

Suddenly feeling bold, she stepped out of her place in the take-away queue and sat down at a small table in the corner. Using the local paper as her companion, she spread it in front of her. A good-looking young waiter approached, looking slightly harassed. Dana flashed a smile at him and he managed a weak one in return.

'You OK?' she asked kindly.

'We're rushed off our feet! Have been trying to fill the vacancy for a waitress for two weeks now. You'd think in these tough times, people would be crying out for jobs.' He took her order and hurried away.

Dana picked up the newspaper and swiftly flicked to the Jobs Section. 'Anything to fit in with school,' she said under her breath, using her finger as a guide. Now what could she do? Her written English wasn't great. Maybe shop work? Nothing. Garage forecourt attendant? No – the shifts wouldn't fit with school.

When her cappuccino came, she took a sip of it and looked around her. At the table where the Ladies Who Latte congregated, she observed how the women dripped in designer clothes and jewellery and lifted their cups cautiously with perfectly manicured hands.

Two 'suits' staring into a laptop, slurped black coffees and droned on about the falling Euro. Three decorators discussed the mid-week football results, whilst tucking into hearty bacon rolls.

Dana caught the waiter's eye. He must only be about twenty-one, she thought, assessing him as if she was far older than her own twenty-five years. Italian maybe. Long, dark wavy hair, tied back in a ponytail, and limpid brown eyes. He scurried over with the bill, saying, 'Here you are, signorina. Is that all?'

'This job here,' Dana blurted out.

'Yep?'

'What are the hours?'

'Eight-thirty till two.'

'Oh.'

Almost seeming to read her mind, he said, 'But we're so desperate, I'm sure my brother would negotiate on hours if he had to.'

'I happen to be interested. Do I need to fill out an application form?' The handsome young man took in her pretty face and pert little figure.

'No, in fact, *grazie Dio*, you've got the job. When can you start? And perhaps you should tell me your name.'

'I'm Dana, and I can start tomorrow – at nine.' She grinned excitedly. 'But I'll work till two-thirty.'

'Great. Right – must get on. It's thirty quid a shift, by the way, plus tips. We'll need you on Wednesdays,

27

Thursdays and Fridays. My name's Tony. I'll show you the ropes. See you tomorrow.'

He winked and Dana was surprised to feel herself blushing. She almost skipped back to her car, feeling more alive than she had done in years. Then, as she got behind the wheel, her smile dimmed slightly. How on earth was Mark going to take this news...?

Chapter Three

Joan panicked slightly as her vision became blurry. She leaned her bike against the front wall of her house and steadied herself. Cissy woke up and started screaming.

'Now, now, little lady. Let's get you out of here, shall we?' she cooed, shaking her head to try and clear her sight that way. It was the second time this had happened this month.

As she unlocked the front door, Squidge the dog tore outside and promptly squatted in the middle of the front lawn to do a wee. Joan sighed. She was sure Colin had taken her for a walk earlier. Now she was getting older, the poor old bitch's bladder wasn't what it used to be. Come to that, nor was hers after giving birth to four children.

She changed Cissy's nappy, then placed her in her walker. After making herself a cup of tea and some toast, she sat down at the dining table for a few minutes. She really ought to change the beds today, she thought, as it was a perfect drying day what with all the wind and sunshine. A strong feeling of tiredness suddenly overtook her and she struggled to keep her now clear-sighted eyes open. Yawning, she got Cissy out of the walker and took her upstairs to her cot.

'Just a little sleep, angel,' Joan soothed the whimpering child. 'Mummy has to have a little lie-down too.'

Joan awoke with a start at midday, her frizzy blonde hair all over the place. Cissy was screaming. She rushed to lift her from her cot and immediately took her down to the kitchen, put her in her high chair and gave her a beaker of juice while she prepared her lunch. She stuffed down a

29

cheese sandwich herself and, suddenly feeling very thirsty, drank a whole pint of water in one go.

Feeling so much better for her nap, Joan tidied herself up for the afternoon ahead. She decided that the beds could wait. Instead, she would head into town to get something nice for dinner. She dismissed that morning's episode. No one ever said that looking after four kids was easy. She just needed to get some early nights.

Cissy screeched in joy from the cat basket on the handlebars as Joan rode out of the council estate and coasted carefully down the big hill to the High Street. She tied her bike to a lamp-post and put the baby in a sling on her hip. She loved going into Fishers, the posh delicatessen. Colin's accountancy salary was fair, but with the outgoings that four children brought, her food budget wasn't big. Still, there was no harm in her having a look now was there? She took in the smells of the cold meat counter and her mouth watered at the selection of cheeses on display. She selected a few jars of pickled delights, winced at the cost and put them down again.

Coming back out into the fresh air empty-handed, she felt sated by her Fishers fix and pleased with herself for resisting temptation.

Veronica Glancy, the vicar's wife, was behind the counter of the charity shop. Her mauve twinset and pearls didn't sit right on her square, manly figure. Her posh deep voice boomed at one of the charity-shop volunteers, who was looking at crystal jugs before getting ready to work her afternoon shift.

'Well, of course, you can imagine my shock when my poor dear Henry was accused of creaming off thousands from the collection. I've never heard of anything so ridiculous in all my life! My Henry, a pillar of society – a thief? We're suing, of course.'

The volunteer nodded wildly. Her beige Chanel suit clung to her skeletal frame, making her look like a whippet.

Joan carried on perusing the clothes section, ignoring the sneers of both women as Cissy decided at that moment to start filling her nappy.

'Just what I was looking for!' Joan exclaimed, evoking further eyebrow-raising. She went up to the counter, where the LWL was now in situ.

'Do you have some sort of box I could put them in?' she asked politely, handing over a pound coin.

'This is a charity shop, dear, not Jimmy Choos. Here.' The beige LWL thrust a red carrier bag into Joan's hand as Cissy trumped loudly.

Veronica Glancy's Bentley roared into life outside.

'I'm guessing they have a very good lawyer,' Joan said, smiling sweetly, leaving eau-de-baby-poop and a grinning whippet in her wake.

'The rain in Spain stays mainly on the plain,' Gordon Summers recited. 'Jeez, this is harder than I thought. Can we take a break please so I can get a glass of water?'

'Wort A, tA, tA!' Mrs Burrows, the elocution coach, accentuated.

Gordy sipped some cold water, then slumped back in his chair. He was doing this not only for his girls, but also for his dear departed sister, so he had to persevere. Surely it wasn't that difficult to lose an inherited Canadian accent?

'I would like a cup of breakfarst tea, please.'

'Perfect, say it again,' Mrs Burrows encouraged, her tight white perm nodding of its own accord. She moved closer to him and he felt slightly uneasy as he smelled her coffee breath against his face. If her saggy breasts so much as touched his arm again, then he was sure he would scream like a girl.

Once his hour was up, Gordon ran outside into the fresh air. He was ten miles outside of Denbury, and he took a deep breath at the beauty of the wild countryside and rolling fields around him.

He looked at his watch, got into his car and began to check his Things to Do Today list, which was stuck to the dashboard. It always made Chris laugh that his wacky partner used the Mini as his office. Gordon checked his diary and as he noticed the date, he felt tears prick his eyes. He couldn't believe that a whole three years had passed since the accident. The drunk driver would soon be out of prison, but the suffering of Gordon's family would continue for a lifetime.

In recognition of the anniversary, he scrabbled about in the glove compartment and pulled out a battered pink envelope. Unfolding the letter, he began to read.

Dearest Gordy,

Hopefully nobody ever has to find this letter, but if they do I know it will be you reading it first as you will have been drawn to the colour of the envelope!

He smiled through his tears; it was as if Jessica, his vibrant, beautiful sister, was in the car with him again.

As you know, the guardian information is all in the will, but if something was to happen to both Peter and myself – yes, I know it's highly bloody unlikely as we rarely go out on our own since the twins. But IF it does and you are reading this, then as agreed, you and Chris are my first choice to bring up the girls. I have total trust in you to let them grow as I would. We share values and you are everything anyone could want in a brother and a father.

Gordon sniffed back his tears.

But there are just a few little things I'd like to note.

Laughter is paramount: a happy house is a healthy house.

Try not to inflict your accent and Canadian quirks on them. I want them to know the difference between a fanny and a butt, thank you very much. I can imagine you thinking, How dare she! I know, I know you were the brave one who broadened his horizons!

Manners, manners, manners.

Five a day! Limit those take-aways. Thank goodness Chris can cook!

If God forbid, for some reason you and Chris split, you have to make sure you find someone who will love them as much as he does.

And finally, just lots and lots of love forever, please.

It is so doubtful you will even be reading this. So much so that I don't think I need to be so organised as to write a separate letter to the girls. However, if you are, then please just tell them just how much I/we both loved them. Show them photos. Talk about the past. I want them to be saturated with memories of their mummy and daddy!

I'm making myself cry now. How mad am I? But you know me – Be Prepared as we were taught in Girl Guides.

Missing you already, brother dear! All my love Jessica Rabbit!

Xxxxxxxxx

Mo puffed and panted as she reached the door outside Rosie's classroom with minutes to spare. Joan greeted her with a smile, Cissy sound asleep in her cat basket.

'Good day?' Joan asked kindly.

'Actually, not bad at all. Surgery was busy but my supervisor was out all morning so Ffion and I had a good old catch-up.'

The classroom door opened just then, and the chattering of six year olds broke the peace of the afternoon. Mr Chambers did his usual scan of mothers present and mouthed, 'Can I have a word?' to Inga who was bringing up the rear after taking a good ten minutes to park against the kerb.

Joan loved Mr Chambers' eccentricity. His enthusiasm for learning and life was infectious to the children and she adored the fact that he wore a different brightly coloured tie every day. Today it was green with yellow spots. His matching yellow-framed square glasses were at a jaunty angle and his mousy hair was gelled up like a hedgehog's spikes.

'Hello darling,' Mo greeted Rosie. 'Have you got your lunchbox?'

The Brown clan found Joan, all three of them dragging their coats behind them on the floor.

'Skye, Clark, Kent – how many times do I need to tell you?' They all raised their eyebrows and coats at the same time.

Gordon held both arms out as Lily and Lola appeared hand-in-hand.

'Dad!' they both said in unison. 'Will you perleeese stop being so embarrassing,' Lily added.

'I don't know what on earth you mean,' he said in a perfect English accent.

'And why are you talking funny?' Lola asked.

Dana jogged up in her tracksuit and gave Tommy a beaming smile. 'Did you run here, Mum?'

'Yes, darleen. I thought it would do us good to get some fresh air and walk back through the park.'

'What – *all* the way back up the big hill?' Tommy said, handing over his school bag as Dana nodded. 'Carry this then.'

Emily Pritchard – Head of PTA, Netball Coach and Mother of Joshua P, seven, chief swot and playground kisser – overheard Dana.

'Good to hear you are thinking green,' she smarmed.

Gordon looked at Dana and whispered, 'Not even extreme Global Warming would thaw that uptight old cow.'

Dana laughed and with a newfound confidence, she looked meaningfully at Preachy Knickers' breast implants and just said, 'Naturally, Emily.'

Inga, wearing huge dark sunglasses and a minuscule skirt, held Eliska's hand and waited behind to talk to Mr Chambers as requested. It annoyed her that she had to take the rap on behalf of Alana. She assumed it was because of her charge's earlier bolt down the drive.

'Alana working today, is she?' Mr Chambers asked, knowing the answer full well. As free-spirited as he was, he sometimes found it hard to accept the excuse of the over-worked mother, when it was so obviously affecting the child.

Inga nodded while Eliska fidgeted.

'Young Eliska here appears to have been caught kissing Joshua full on the lips at lunchtime.'

'Oh dear,' Inga said, trying to look concerned.

Mr Chambers went on, 'It was made worse as Joshua tells me that she charged a pound for the pleasure.'

Eliska stamped her foot. 'He is a nasty liar!' she snapped. 'He made me give *him* a pound.'

'Oh dear,' Inga repeated. 'But I do have to say the reason she ran down the drive this morning was to collect a pound from me.'

'See? I told you.' Eliska sulked.

'Well, Eliska,' Mr Chambers said pleasantly, 'kissing is not for schooltime.'

'It wasn't schooltime, it was playtime,' the little girl retorted.

Mr Chambers managed to keep a straight face and looked to Inga. 'Now I bet Inga never kissed any boys she shouldn't have when it wasn't playtime.'

Inga suppressed a laugh by shaking her head. Surely Mr Chambers wasn't flirting with her? The teacher winked at her and went back inside the classroom.

Joan walked along with Mo, pushing her bike, whilst Clark and Kent shot ahead on the path, and Skye and Rosie held on to the handlebars. Joan stopped momentarily and pulled back Cissy's blanket to reveal the red carrier bag from the charity shop.

'Here, take these.' She handed Mo the bag. 'I found them in the bottom of my wardrobe this morning. Must have got them for Skye last year and forgotten all about them for some reason.'

Mo looked in the bag and saw a pair of shiny new school shoes of just the right size. Maybe she did have a guardian angel, after all.

'Oh Joan, are you sure? Can't you take them back?'

'Of course I'm sure. They won't change them this far on.'

'Well, I shall give you some money for them.'

'No, you won't. The state of my place, if I hadn't been having a clear-out they'd have been hidden there until the kids left home.'

'Thank you so much, Joan, you don't realise how much this means to me.'

The wise mum smiled, understanding exactly just how much it did.

Stephen McNair rolled over, lay back and looked up at the ceiling. His smooth chest bore just a few beads of sweat and his breathing was heavy. His auburn locks were all over the place.

'Do you think that now we've done it twice in seven years it counts as an affair?' he said with worry in his voice.

Alana rose up on to one elbow on the crisp white Egyptian cotton sheets in the minimalistic London hotel room, and looked into his eyes. 'It's what you want it to be, Mr McNair,' she slurred slightly, the effect of the two bottles of wine they had shared at lunchtime still with her.

He jumped up, went to the bathroom and gathered a robe. Coming back in, he sat on the edge of the bed and put his head in his hands.

'I haven't had sex for ages,' he blurted out.

'Glad I could serve a purpose,' Alana replied coldly. 'I can't leave my wife,' he reacted suddenly.

'I don't recall asking you to,' she said, her voice sharp.

He stood up and looked at his watch. 'Oh Christ, it's six o'clock – I really must get home.'

'Six!' Alana exclaimed. 'Inga wanted to leave at seven today – I'll never make it.' She shot up out of bed and began pulling her clothes on.

'Well, don't for one minute think you're driving, Alana Murray.'

'How else am I going to get home?'

In his calm and caring manner Stephen took charge.

'I will call Sandra, and she can book you a car. Just ask the driver to collect you in the morning then come back in to Chiswick to collect yours.'

'I feel fine to drive,' she whined.

'You're not driving,' Stephen reiterated. Catching Alana's eye, he gathered her to him, murmuring, 'What are we going to do? You know this isn't me.'

Alana pulled away quickly.

'Let's talk when we're sober, eh Stephen? At the moment it feels like an awful *déjà-vu*. Now, get me that bloody car, will you.'

Alana swore as she dropped her front door keys in her drive. The car that Stephen had ordered for her had been warm and comfortable and she had slept most of the way home. The stark reality of life hit her when Inga flew out of the front door, the whites of her pretty eyes showing.

'That is it, I quit!' The young au pair strode purposefully down the drive. 'I meet a boy at seven-thirty and it is now eight. He will not wait for me as the film start already. This is the fourth time you don't even let me know.'

'But Inga…' Alana tried to reason with her but Inga carried on down the drive, head held high.

'Wait!' she shouted after her. Inga turned around, her

face still like thunder.

'OK. I promise I will be more communicative in future and I will give you an extra twenty pounds this week if you don't leave me.'

Inga thought hard.

'No,' she said defiantly. 'I still quit.'

Alana was too weary to argue. She knew that it was too late in the day to get help for the morning and in a way she was relieved as she knew her delayed hangover would not be a good one. She would just have to cancel her meetings and work from home. Stephen could sort getting her car back sometime. She texted him quickly to tell him to cancel the car arranged for the morning. She chose not to end it with a kiss, just in case his wife was around. After all, it was just another one-off, wasn't it?

'*Mum*!' Eliska threw herself at Alana as soon as the front door shut behind her. 'Did you get my computer game?'

Alana closed her eyes, suddenly feeling an intense guilt that her daughter had not crossed her mind all day. She thought quickly.

'Darling, I've ordered you one as the shop had sold out. I can pick it up tomorrow.'

'But you promised it today,' Eliska sulked.

'Eliska, please. I'm very tired. It's been a busy day. How about I make you a nice hot chocolate, you get your pyjamas on and we snuggle up in front of the telly for an hour?'

Silence ensued as Eliska headed upstairs to her bedroom. Grateful she had managed to placate her daughter without too much trouble, Alana took off her smart jacket and put the kettle on. When silence still ensued, Alana began to worry. She slowly walked up the stairs to find her daughter lying on the top of her covers, curled in the foetal position with her thumb in her mouth. She was sound asleep.

Love rushed through Alana, and she carefully pulled the duvet up over the sleeping child. As she walked quietly to the bedroom door and turned the light off, she felt a piece of paper underfoot. On it were just four words written boldly in one of Alana's bright red lipsticks: I HATE MY MUM.

Alana gulped and blinked back tears. Surely she wasn't that bad a mother. Just as she was considering employing a child psychologist, there was a loud knock at the door. Thank goodness, Alana thought. Inga had come to her senses.

She ran down the stairs two at a time and threw the door open. A tall, smartly dressed woman with grey hair in a neat chignon pushed past her.

'Now, don't dither, Lani,' the woman slurred. 'I've a fierce thirst on me and I want you to go and fix me a large Scotch.'

Chapter Four

'Beans on toast tonight, kids, as you all had school dinners today,' Joan Brown told her brood.

'Can we have chips too?' Clark pleaded, scratching his head.

'No, but you can have chocolate ice cream for afters,' Joan said wearily, going over to do a quick search of his crown for any further nits.

'And chocolate sprinkles?' Kent added as Cissy bashed her plastic spoon up and down on her high-chair tray.

'Don't push it, Sonny Jim.' Joan pretended to clip his ear.

She suddenly felt very thirsty again and poured herself a pint of water. She looked at her mobile that was on the kitchen table. Strange that Colin hadn't texted to say he was going to be late. He was usually as reliable as clockwork. Just as she had that thought – beep – a text message appeared.

Going late-night shopping for invitations. See you later sweetness x

'Silly old sod,' she said under her breath. She was sure the precinct at Durton, where Colin's office was, didn't do a late night on a Tuesday. She called him to let him know and it went straight through to voicemail. She smiled as she heard his cheerful voice and began preparing the kids' tea.

They had been talking about having a joint fortieth birthday party for years and she couldn't believe that soon it would be a reality.

'Right, you lovely lot, television off while we eat.'

'Oh, Mum.'

'You know the rules,' Joan said sternly, suddenly feeling very unwell. Her vision became blurry again and she massaged her forehead.

'Mummy, what's wrong?'

'I need to ring your father.' Reaching for her mobile, Joan fell forward, crashing a plate off the table as she did so.

'Mummy?' Skye said again, then screamed loudly. Joan lay face down on the table, lifeless.

Kent leaped up from his seat, acting far older than his nine young years. 'It's OK. Quick – give me Mummy's phone.'

As Clark ran to hug his mother, Cissy screamed in herhigh chair. Squidge the dog ran round and around the kitchen table barking furiously.

Kent remembered what his daddy had shown him to do in case of an emergency and swiftly dialled 999.

'Hello. It's my mum, I think she's dead and I don't know where our daddy is.'

Mo Collins was rounding the corner to post a letter to Charlie, when she saw the ambulance. Grabbing Rosie's hand, she sped towards her friend's house. As she got nearer she could hear the children crying outside. Realising the ambulance was for Joan she shouted out: 'I'm a friend. What's happened?'

'Not sure yet, love. Looks like she just fainted, but she's still not right so we're taking her to Denbury General for a check over.'

Mo ran to Joan's side.

'The children,' Joan said weakly.

'Can't seem to get hold of her old man on his mobile,' the other ambulance- man offered.

'Can you look after them?' Joan managed.

Mo put her hand on her friend's forehead to soothe her.

'Of course. And as soon as Colin gets here I'll send

him to you. I can stay all night if I have to.'

'Mother?' Alana's mouth dropped to the floor as the tall woman barged past her into the kitchen.

'That's me, creator of you, my one and only child – but goodness knows why, for the torment it's brought me. The word offspring makes sense now,' the woman declared, her Scots accent almost incomprehensible with drink.

'You can't just walk in here after six whole years and start on me. Please go, Mum. I've got nothing to say to you.' Alana went to open the front door.

'I've left your stepfather!' Isobel Murray's voice grew more strident.

'Why this time?' Alana had grown up with her mother's transient affairs of the heart.

'He was having an affair with his secretary – been going on for years evidently. Makes a mockery of not only me but the whole bloody Bible, if you ask me.' She plonked herself down at the kitchen table. 'And I'm drunk, Alana. Drunk as a fucking skunk.'

Alana screwed her face up, finding everything almost impossible to take in.

Her hangover was kicking in from lunchtime and this was the last thing she needed. Since her father had died when she was just eleven, there had never been any love lost between herself and any of her mother's unsuitable suitors. Eric, whom she had only known for a year before her mother turned her back on her, was no exception.

Isobel Murray suddenly put her head down sideways on the kitchen table and began to sob uncontrollably. Alana handed her a tissue and filled the kettle. She had never once seen her mother cry and it unnerved her rather than upset her.

'It's OK, Mother, there'll be plenty more idiots lining up to whisk you off your pretty feet, I can assure you.'

'Oh, the humiliation!' Isobel lifted her head dramatically. 'Where did I go wrong?'

Alana thought she could fill a book the size of the New Testament in answering that one but she kept her mouth shut and put three heaped teaspoons of coffee into a mug.

'Here, drink this, you'll feel better in the morning.'

Isobel Murray sat up and blew her nose loudly. 'Thank you, Lani.' She looked at her daughter intently for a minute and then at a photo of Eliska in a wooden frame on a shelf.

'That's my granddaughter, I take it?' Pausing, she clumsily got up to stroke the glass. 'She's beautiful.'

All of a sudden she turned to Alana and grabbed her wrist.

'I'm so very fucking sorry for being such a bloody useless excuse of a mother.' Isobel exhaled deeply as if her whole soul had flowed out with the words. 'There, I've said it. Shit – I missed out the word "shallow".'

She let go of Alana and raised both her palms outwards, like a preacher. 'I am so very fucking sorry for being such a bloody useless shallow excuse of a mother.'

'It will take more than a blue apology to wipe away six years of you ignoring us,' Alana replied calmly.

'But you were having a child out of wedlock. You vowed never to tell me who the father was. I mean, what would they have thought at church? Tell me, Alana, what was I supposed to do?'

Alana felt herself welling up now. 'You were supposed to just love me, Mum.'

She tried to stop herself crying, but a real emotion can never be hidden and suddenly a strangled sob tore from her heart.

'I cannot believe you haven't even asked me her name,' she wept. She eventually got herself under control and then was engulfed by a wave of anger. 'Now, just piss off and leave us alone! We don't need you here, either of us.'

'Where shall I go?' Isobel said, selfish as ever and seemingly unperturbed by her only daughter's outburst.

'You can go to hell as far as I'm concerned.' Alana pushed her mother out, slammed the front door and put her back against it, then went and sat down and cried her eyes out.

When Alana had not one tear left inside of her, she poured herself a large glass of wine and downed it in one. The even larger whisky that followed caused her to crawl up the stairs. Reaching the landing, she kicked off her shoes, sneaked into her daughter's single bed and snuggled against her soft, warm neck.

The little girl, oblivious to the anguish of two generations before her, snored gently.

Chapter Five

'Diabetes apparently,' Mo said once, twice, three times over as various mums questioned why the ever-present Joan was not dropping her kids off. She overheard Emily Pritchard meanly comment that it was probably due to Joan over-eating the wrong type of foods, and Mo glared at her.

Alana held Eliska's hand and pushed her way through the gabbling throng of morning mothers. Despite her hangover, she still looked immaculate in her full make-up, designer jeans and heels.

'Where will I find Mr Chambers?' she asked Dana, who couldn't believe that after a year of her child attending Featherstone Primary, the other mother didn't know this. But the quiet Czech girl was not one to judge, and she kindly explained where he could be found.

'Ah, Mr Chambers, here you are. I'm Alana Murray,' she said and held out her hand, while Eliska waited outside on the drive.

He smiled, noting that her 'sugar baby' lipstick matched his bright pink tie. 'An agency nanny from Bebops will be collecting Eliska today and maybe tomorrow,' Alana told him. 'I don't have a name.'

'Wonderful, thanks for letting me know. Is Inga on holiday then?'

'Yes,' Alana lied. 'Everyone deserves a little break. Is Eliska getting on OK, by the way?'

'Um, well. I guess Inga told you about the kissing incident?'

'Oh yes, yes,' Alana lied again. 'Youngsters, eh?' She

managed a smile, thinking that she'd have to find out what on earth he was on about later.

Eliska hugged her as she came outside.

'Bye, Mum. I love it when you bring me to school,' the little girl said, and Alana ignored the pitying glances of those other mothers who were within earshot.

'Bye bye, darling. Be good for the Bebops person and I'll see you later.' She patted her daughter on the head.

'Oh, hi Alana. Long time no see,' Emily Pritchard shouted across to her. 'No Inga today then?'

Alana glanced down at her BlackBerry and then walked towards Emily. She had been the only mother on Eliska's first day at school who had made an effort to talk to her.

'The silly girl walked out on me last night, but she'll be back when she realises the grass isn't greener, I'm sure,' Alana explained.

'Oh dear. I do hope she hasn't gone far. She said she'd babysit for us next Saturday,' Emily boomed.

'Did she now?' Alana said, suddenly quite annoyed that her ex-employee had already been moonlighting. Her phone buzzed again. She looked down; it was Stephen McNair.

'Right, must get on, nice to see you again, Emily. Joshua really must come round and play soon.'

'It'll probably cost you,' Emily winked, leaving Alana none the wiser as to her daughter's antics.

Mo ran up the steps to the GP surgery. She nipped to the loo and hurriedly swept her hair up into its usual bun and powdered her shiny nose. She looked at her reflection and quickly looked away, disgusted at her bloated appearance and grey-flecked hair that was badly in need of a cut. She looked far older than her forty-one years.

She scrabbled in her bag and found an old cover-up stick. Whisking it over the small red mark on her cheek, a present from Ron for getting in late after looking after Joan's children, she sighed loudly.

If only she could just get enough money together to leave him. It was Wednesday – she must remember to get a Lottery Lucky Dip.

She was thankful that Joan was back home and on the mend. Colin had been completely distraught when he had returned home and found out what had happened to his wife. It was a relief for all that it was Type 2 diabetes, which wasn't so serious that it needed injections, just a change of diet and exercise habits.

The ever-effervescent Ffion immediately cheered Mo.

'Morning! Grim Lynn is on the war-path as Dr Delicious spilled a drop from a urine sample on her jumper. Heads down, here she comes.'

Mo got so close to her screen to avoid eye-contact that she actually hit her nose on it, sending Ffion into hysterics.

'This is a serious doctors' surgery, not a kindergarten, thank you, ladies,' the grim one expressed, her cropped grey hair and crinkly jowls making her resemble an old man's testicles.

'How many hours till lunch?' Ffion enquired at ten o'clock.

'Just the three,' Mo laughed.

'Shall we go to Rosco's?' Ffion wanted to know. 'I *so* need some lard. I got very drunk on tequila last night – like lighter fuel it was,' her Welsh accent tilting up an octave.

'I'll come with you, but just salad and water for me,' Mo replied. 'I have to lose this weight now; it's just getting too ridiculous. It's a vicious bloody circle though. The more fed up I get, the more I seem to eat.'

'Bless you, Mo, I promise to keep the biscuits away from you from now on.'

'Please do, and put both Nil by Mouth signs on my desk!'

A pretty Czech waitress took their order in Rosco's. Mo thought she recognised her from somewhere but couldn't think where. She had a Diet Coke to alleviate the guilt of the chips she'd just ordered with her salad – she couldn't resist them – whilst Ffion ordered a burger and gulped back lemonade by the pint.

'Now tell me about this son of yours,' Ffion said inquisitively.

Mo Collins' life path had never been an easy one. In and out of care homes as a youngster, she was determined that her own family life would be different. However, being a very promiscuous teen, she found herself pregnant at seventeen. Wanting more than anything in the world to love another human being and have them love her unconditionally in return, there was no question, despite several stern conversations with her carers, that she wouldn't have the baby.

Oh, how she loved Charlie's father, but he too was immature at seventeen – a free-spirited boy who lived in the same care home as her. His heart was big and in the right place, but his own issues from an abusive upbringing were significant. She couldn't or wouldn't want to rely on him for security, so she went for her best option – Ron Collins, ten years her senior.

Ron had always worked hard at a car plant, making his way up from tea-boy to production supervisor, and becoming a good provider. The guilt of taking advantage of Mo when she was seventeen had always stuck with him, and when she told him he was the father of her child, he questioned nothing and insisted they marry that month.

The relationship ticked along nicely but Mo wasn't in love with Ron. It was her son's happiness in a secure family environment that was paramount, and Mo's sacrifice to this end was all that mattered to her.

It was when her son, Charlie, had grown up and was away at university, that Mo had decided it was time to leave Ron. She didn't want a fuss. She would just say goodbye and up and go. However, the timing was not good as it happened to be the same day the car plant had decided to make her husband redundant.

Mo was just packing the final items into her case, when the bedroom door was flung open by her husband telling her his devastating news.

'It really knocked him hard, Ffion. Work was his life. Once the redundancy money had run out, he struggled to find a job. He felt a constant failure and didn't know where to turn. I couldn't leave him then.' Mo sighed. 'It was when he turned to the demon drink that our life became progressively worse.'

Ffion bit her lip as Mo gave a sigh and continued.

'I tried to help him but he wouldn't listen. I eventually plucked up the courage to go, but he caught me packing my case. He was drunk and angry and he raped me. I was pregnant with Rosie, so what could I do? I had to stay, and here I am now. Unhappy and fat, in a loveless relationship with an alcoholic layabout husband, and nowhere to go.'

When she finished, Ffion had tears rolling down her cheeks. 'You poor, poor cariad.'

Mo tried to return to her usual upbeat self.

'Listen to this moaning minnie, woe is bloody me. I just need to pull myself together. I've got my lovely lad Charlie, who's got a good job now, and that little darling Rosie to think about. She is the most loving and beautiful child and I intend the rest of her formative years to be happy.'

'And happy she will be,' Ffion said. 'I tell you what. How 'bout you take over my three afternoon shifts. I'm starting an evening hair and beauty course next month and I could do with the free time to prepare case studies.'

'You're not just saying that?' Mo frowned.

'I'm not that nice, Mo. I do need to think about my career path. It's just encouraged me to do something about it sooner, that's all.'

'You're such a lovely girl, Ffion.'

'Maybe, sometimes.' Ffion smiled and raised her glass of lemonade. 'Cheers to the Mo Collins' Freedom Fund.'

As Dana delivered the order to the corner table, she was sure that she recognised the plumper lady of the two from the school gates.

She loved the freedom that her new job brought, and by dealing with customers all of the time, her shyness had almost disappeared. She hadn't received any pay yet, but just knowing it was coming filled her with joy.

Her biggest problem when she had first got together with Mark was not having any of her own money. It felt alien to her to have to ask if she needed anything. From day one of their affair seven years ago, Mark had told Dana that once he left Carole, she was to have anything she wanted. He was adamant that he didn't want her to have to go to work. All she had to do was ask for money and she could have it. As an impressionable teenager, she was taken in by the glamour of this older man and all that a life with him offered. However, it was quite a transition going from a freedom-loving au pair to his partner, obviously not helped by one very disgruntled ex-wife and a very precocious ten-year-old stepson.

The divorce had come through quickly, which was lucky as Tommy was already on the way. Dana hadn't planned her life to be like this. She was sad that she had broken up a marriage, but despite the age gap, the love between her and Mark had been so strong that she couldn't let him pass her by.

Her plan had been to travel as an au pair for a while to improve her English, then to apply for a degree in Film Studies and find work in that field. After which she would settle down and have lots of children.

But life, as it so often does, had taken a different path and she had reached her end goal a lot earlier than she had thought she would. Even her wish for a large family seemed blighted, as despite trying for the past four years, she wasn't falling pregnant.

'Dana,' Tony called from behind the table. 'Two lattes ready for table eight.' Dana sped over to get them.

'Nice wiggle,' Tony joked, his long dark locks curling over his collar like those of a cool surf dude.

'I'm not a snake!' she smartly retorted.

'But oh, what you could do with that pert little asp,' Bruno, Tony's brother, added out of her earshot.

'She's a married woman,' Tony interjected.

'An unhappily married woman, I reckon.' Bruno's dark brown eyes glinted. 'The best sort.'

'What do you know, and what does that matter, eh?' Tony gesticulated wildly, his Italian accent becoming stronger.

'Calm down, *mio fratello*. I was just stating a fact.'

The café was so busy that time sped by and Dana couldn't believe it was the end of her first week already. She cleared the last lunchtime table and went out to the kitchen to hang up her apron and get her coat. Tony followed her and handed her a small envelope.

'Your first week's pay, signora.'

'I cannot tell you how excited I am.' Dana grinned.

'I'll split the tips later and give you those in cash next week,' Tony added.

'Oh, is my pay not in cash then?' Dana asked.

'It's a cheque; I have to put it through the books. An honest unit we are here, you know,' he smiled.

'Of course I realise that. I want it to be above board but it would make my life easier if I had cash.' She had no bank account of her own, so her intention was to squirrel the cash away, save up for a surprise weekend away for her and Mark and then come clean about her job.

Tony held out his hand and she gave the envelope back; he reached into his pocket, pulled out some notes and counted £120 into her hand.

'This is between you and me, Mrs Knight,' Tony

winked. 'And only 'cos I like you.'

Dana blushed to her roots.

Lily and Lola raced out of class and into Gordon's arms. He swept them both up, sending Lily's glasses flying.

'Daddy!' the little girls shouted in unison.

'TFI Friday, my lovely ladies!' he trilled loudly.

'What does that mean?' Lola asked, screwing up her pretty little face. Gordon realised what he'd just said and cringed inwardly.

'Thank Flora it's Friday,' a broad Mancunian male accent intervened.

Gordon looked up and smiled, as these timely words came from a guy who was quite a cutie.

'Who's Flora?' Lola asked. 'The Princess of Weekends,' the Mancunian butted in again and Gordon laughed out loud.

The twins, followed by Eliska, charged down the path towards the school gates and freedom.

'Sorry – I haven't seen you here before. But thanks for rescuing me!' Gordon acknowledged his saviour, taking in his fitted black T-shirt.

'I'm Robbie, Eliska Murray's temporary childminder, just helping out until her mother finds a full-time help.'

Gordon held out his hand. 'Gordon Summers. Nice to meet you, and I hope you have a good weekend. It's the twins' birthday party for us, so there's lots to get ready.'

'I'd get the wife on to that if I were you.' Robbie winked and set off to find Eliska.

Gordon had just got the children strapped in the car and was about to zoom off when there was a tap on the driver's window. It was Inga.

'Darling girl. Word at the gates is you've been fired and a right honey has got your job for now.'

'For your information, Meester Gay Gordon, word at the gates is wrong, I left the ungrateful bitch. And now I have no money, so can you spread the word please?' She handed him some leaflets outlining her babysitting services.

'I could use some help at the girls' party tomorrow if you're free. I'll pay your going rate; say from two till six,' Gordon said kindly.

'I think I may love you,' Inga crooned.

'From afar, sweetie, from afar.' Gordon flicked his wrist camply. Inga laughed out loud.

'Where you staying anyway?' he asked her.

'I am still sleeping on my friend's bedroom floor. I sneak in when the family she is au pairing for have gone to bed.'

'Oh, Inga darling, that's no good. Come to me tomorrow. I will feed you too.' He scribbled down his address and handed her a £5 note. Inga squished her face up. 'Pre-payment for your bus fare. See you.' Before she could object, the Mini whizzed off.

'See you – wouldn't wanna be you,' the girls shouted in unison and waved wildly out of the back window.

Joan rounded up her brood. She was feeling so much better now she knew what was actually wrong with her. She had had visions of being seriously ill and nightmares of dying and having to say goodbye to her family. Rosie ran out to greet her too. Joan had happily said yes to Mo, when she had asked if she minded taking her in on the extra afternoons she was at the surgery until five.

'Have a lovely weekend,' Mr Chambers shouted after her. He had a soft spot for Joan and her brood; they were such a delight to teach.

Tommy stood inside the class waiting for Dana. She was unusually late, and came running up the path at full pelt.

'So sorry I'm late!' She addressed both Tommy and Mr Chambers, who noticed a different spring in her step.

'By seconds, that's all,' he said kindly. 'Enjoy the weekend.'

Emily Pritchard reached the end of the road, then pulled up beside Inga, who was walking on the pavement, and opened her car window.

'Still OK to babysit tomorrow, dear?'

'Oh, yes of course Mrs Pritchard. I'm helping at the twins' birthday party first. So I can be with you for sevenish, if that's all right?'

'Birthday party, you say?' Emily said acerbically. 'Maybe Joshy forgot to give me the invite.'

'Oh...um, I am late,' Inga said hurriedly. 'I must go fast, see you tomorrow.'

Why did all these English mums have to be so bitchy, she thought as she headed back into town to place an advert in the newsagents' window. She hoped she never ended up like that!

Chapter Six

'Rosie's mum is coming up the path,' Skye shouted to Joan, who was just putting Cissy to bed.

Strange on a Friday evening, Joan thought. She kissed her younger daughter goodnight, relishing the scrumptious scent of baby, and made her way downstairs.

Mo almost fell through the front door. She was completely breathless.

'I am so sorry to bother you,' she managed to get out. 'It's just...' She did her best not to cry. Skye, Clark and Kent appeared at the kitchen door and Joan stood in front of Mo to shield the blood-sodden towel that was wrapped around her friend's wrist.

'Carry on watching telly you lot, we're just having a cup of tea.'

'Where's Daddy?' Skye whined.

'He's working late, sweetheart, he'll be back soon.' Joan too felt like whining. Colin in all the years she had known him had never worked late on a Friday – and by the look of Mo, she could really do with a man here.

Joan put the kettle on, got a bowl of warm water and gently removed the towel. Neither of them needed to speak; Joan knew that proud Mo must have been in a bad way to knock on her door. The two women had struck up a strong friendship since the night of the diabetes incident, and she was pleased that Mo felt she now had somewhere safe to escape to if things got really bad.

'Was it a fork?' Joan asked gently.

Mo nodded, thankful that the bleeding had subsided and by the look of it, no stitches were required. She sipped on the sweet tea that Joan had presented and took the two strong painkillers by her side.

'Rosie OK?'

'She's with Tommy at Dana's, thank goodness.'

'This can't go on, Mo. I'll be rounding the corner and seeing an ambulance at yours next.'

'I know,' Mo said weakly. 'I've started saving, you know with the extra shifts I do when you look after Rosie.'

'Well, that's a good start,' Joan encouraged.

'I threatened to leave him tonight and he said that I was too cowardly to ever do it and too fat and ugly for anyone to ever want me again, so why bother anyway.'

'Oh, duckie. He's ill – he needs help but he's got to realise it himself.' Joan put her arm round Mo's shoulder and squeezed her. 'There are hostels that you could go to as a last resort, you know.'

'Oh Joan, I couldn't subject Rosie to that and I would be so frightened that they might take her away that I don't want to even enquire. I am very well acquainted with the ways of Social Services, and I don't trust them an inch.'

'Do you want to both stay here tonight? We'll find room even if it's a made- up bed on the floor.'

'No, you're fine. Hopefully, he'll be crashed out asleep by the time I get back.I can just put Rosie to bed when Dana drops her back.'

'I tell you what, then. Why don't you come and spend the day with us tomorrow instead? We're going to the park to fly kites. The fresh air will do you good and Rosie would love it.'

'Joan, you're such a brick, and hark at me moaning on.'

'I actually don't think I've heard you moan once, so drink your tea and shut up.' Joan smiled.

'It's me who should be worrying about you anyway,' Mo said guiltily. 'How are you getting on with the new diabetes lifestyle?'

'It's fine actually – lots of fibre, less saturated fat, less meat, more fish and more exercise. And with regular visits to Dr Delicious, it can only do me good, I reckon. Plus it might even help me to shift a few pounds too.' Joan paused. 'Sorry, Mo, that came out wrong.'

Mo tutted. 'Sshh, you. I know I need to lose more than a few pounds.'

'Well, I've decided to start power-walking around the park from Monday, if you fancy coming with me? The kids and Squidge will enjoy it and it'll keep us fit.'

'I'm not sure,' Mo said. 'I can barely walk round the corner without puffing like an old woman.'

'Exactly!' Joan exclaimed. 'We need to get you running here without so much as a bead of sweat on your brow.'

Mo managed a smile. 'You're having a laugh, aren't you, but OK let's go on Monday and see how we get on.'

'That's the spirit, Mrs Collins.'

After seven years Carole still could not be civil when she dropped Sidney off every other weekend. Dana totally understood why the other woman would hate her. She had been just eighteen years old to Carole's thirty-five when she had met Mark. A pretty, naïve little girl who had not set out to steal a husband, but her infatuation for him was so strong, at the time she'd have moved a mountain for them to be together.

And now here they were, Mark and Dana, to the outsider the perfect couple, living in a huge house on Bramwell Hill with their own beautiful son, expensive car and all the other trimmings that go with a city boy's lifestyle.

Now, Sidney ran into the play room, where Tommy had a Scalextric track set up. It was a relief that the ten year old had not been tainted by his mother's poison: the half-brothers got along fine.

Mark made sure the boys were happy, then walked into

the kitchen to see Dana. She was peeling potatoes ready to make some homemade chips for lunch. 'Thanks for always being so understanding about all this,' he said, then draped his arms over her shoulders and kissed her cheek. 'And I meant to say earlier, it's so good to see you looking happier recently.'

When Dana put down her knife and turned around, she was crying. She wasn't used to her husband being so tender.

'Hey, what is it?' Mark asked lovingly.

'Hormones, I guess. No baby Knight again this month, I'm afraid.' She wiped her hands on a tea towel. 'I don't think I can bear it any more – every month thinking I'm pregnant. My boobs hurt, my tummy swells and then there's always the disappointment of the false alarm.'

'Oh love. I'm sorry.' He held her to his chest tightly. 'Actually, I meant to tell you that John Hoskins – you know, the new senior accountant I mentioned before.' Dana nodded. 'Well, his wife had IVF – and she's pregnant with twins now. If you wanted to go down that route, I'd be more than happy to support you.'

She was taken aback once more by Mark's thoughtfulness. Recently, they had seemed to be growing apart. She knew that his job was busy and he was under a lot of pressure, and yet, as much as it was annoying that he didn't want her to work and she had to keep Rosco's a secret, she did really love him and was happy that he had mentioned the IVF and not her.

She herself had been reading up about it in a magazine just last month and had intended to give it a little longer trying before suggesting it herself. They obviously could produce a healthy child; but for some reason now needed a little extra help. Evidently, this was not uncommon.

Mark continued: 'The Hoskins went to a clinic in Chelsea, said it was like a hotel, not a hospital. If you do want to go for it, that's where we shall head. Only the best for my little Czech angel.' Mark kissed her again and headed back towards the play room. 'Just say the word and I'll book us an appointment.'

Dana carried on peeling the potatoes as she looked out over the perfectly maintained garden and Tommy's trampoline. Old Malcolm the gardener noticed her and blew her a kiss as he cleared the recent leaves with his special garden vacuum cleaner. She laughed to herself, wishing that she could invite the LWL round for tea just to see their faces at all that was hers.

Minutes later, she walked into the play room – and smiled at the sight of Mark, Sidney and Tommy all shrieking in delight as their cars sped around the track at top speed.

Mark looked up at her and grinned widely. 'Let's do it,' Dana said loudly.

The children squealed their appreciation as their dad's car span wildly out of control and on to the floor.

Gordon waved to Inga from the flat window. She had been such a great help at the party. The girls loved her young energy, and she had left the place spotless. He flopped back on his comfy cream leather armchair and flicked on the television. The girls had decided to go back and stay with their real dad's sister for the night, so Gordon and Chris had the sofa, *X-Factor* and a whole evening to themselves. Bliss.

It had actually amused him that certain mums took offence if their dear little ones weren't invited to the various Year Two birthday parties. In fact, Gordon had not invited anyone from the school. It was just family and his friends. He found it easier that way. Nobody had ever discussed his situation, but he didn't want to have the girls trying to explain that they lived with their gay uncle and his boyfriend, hence the reason they called him Dad at school. He decided that when they were a bit older he would address the situation with them and they could choose what they wanted to do. Maybe he was being paranoid, but he knew how cruel kids could be.

Lily and Lola had been just three when their parents had died, and although they had missed them initially, especially their mum, with all the love and fun he threw at them, they soon took to their new life with their new daddies. Most of the mums thought that he was a straight single parent and he was happy to keep it that way for now. It was just Inga and Dana who knew otherwise. Old Preachy Knickers was the trickiest. Thank goodness she was married or he would no doubt be beating her off with a stick

Chris came in from the kitchen, two glasses of chilled white wine in hand. He looked suddenly older than his twenty-five years. Tall, clean-shaven and immaculate in jeans and a tailored black shirt, he struck a handsome figure.

He kissed Gordon on the forehead, handed him his wine and moved across the room to lounge on the huge squashy leather sofa.

'Smell or something, do I?' Gordon joked. Chris was silent.

'Tired, I bet,' Gordon said kindly. 'Thank you so much for cooking, Pooks. Those mini-burgers went down a treat, and as for jelly and home-made ice cream too, you excelled yourself, dear. You're a great dad, do you know that?'

A tear ran down Chris's face and Gordon ran over to him. 'Hey!' He lifted his partner's chin up lovingly.' What's up?'

'I don't know how to say it,' Chris said on a sob, and Gordon suddenly went cold.

'Go on. Whatever it is, we can deal with it together.'

'You know how much I love you and the girls?' Chris went on. Gordon nodded and bit his lip.

'But…' Chris looked at the ceiling and took a deep breath before stumbling on, 'I've realised I'm just not ready to play Happy Families. I never wanted children, Gordy, and from the day I met you, I always made that clear.'

Gordon cleared his throat to try to stop the tears.

'Fuck me, this is a bolt from the blue.' He stood up and began pacing.

'Not really,' Chris said quietly. 'It's taken me ages to find the right moment.'

'Oh, Pooks.' Gordon started to ramble. 'Who would have known that my sister would die? I love those girls, as much as I loved her, and it's where we are, and where I have got to stay.' He paused. 'And where I want to stay.'

'I know, but I can't do it anymore. I feel like I'm still so young and am missing out on life. I don't know who I am anymore. I feel trapped.'

Gordon felt a sob get stuck in his throat. 'What can I do to stop you? Maybe we could have separate houses? We could date again? You will get time to yourself then.'

'Don't be silly, Gordy. I've thought it through and through, but have decided that I need to get away. I've got myself a job with a Canadian airline – long haul this time. I can see a bit more of the world. Feel like I'm doing a bit more for just me.'

Gordon said hoarsely, 'When?' He could now feel anger licking at his lips.

'I leave for Montreal in the morning.'

'Well, fucking well done you! New job, new life. "I'll just walk out on my family", just like that!'

'But that's the whole point; they're not my family and never will be. I know it seems harsh, but I've got to be selfish on this one. Please don't be angry.'

'But we discussed everything before the girls came to us!'

'I know, but reality isn't quite like the fairy-tale, is it?'

Tears began to run down Chris's cheeks. 'I will miss you so much, but I have to do this. I don't want to resent you. I love you and really want you to understand.'

'What shall I tell the girls?' Gordon said abruptly.

'Just say that I'm working on some faraway flights. I will send you all postcards. It would be great if we could just leave us open. I just need to live a little.'

The *X- Factor* theme suddenly burst out of the surround sound.

'I'd rather we just ended it,' Gordon said flatly. 'At least then I can try and get over you. I don't want to be sitting here like some mad old Mrs Faversham with cobwebs on my wheelchair at ninety-five.'

'God, you're such a drama queen.' Chris had to laugh.

'But you're right, let's keep it sweet with the girls for a while. And what if I meet someone new?' Gordy challenged.

'Well, they've got to be better than me or the ghost of Jessica Summers will be haunting you, so it won't be easy.'

They both managed a smile.

Chris took his partner's hand. 'I cannot bear to think of you with anyone else, but if that's what it takes, because God knows you'll need the support, then I'll have to deal with it.'

Gordon took a slurp of wine. 'I can't believe you've sorted all this behind my back, without any discussion.'

'It was the only way. I didn't want to give you any time to persuade me otherwise.'

Gordon pulled Chris towards him. 'I know just how I can persuade you right now.'

Chris put his hands out to stop him.

The voice of Simon Cowell filled the room. 'I'm really sorry, it's four No's.' Gordon laughed, then promptly burst into tears.

Chapter Seven

'You work too hard, you know,' Stephen commented to Alana as they finished reviewing a new PR campaign for the first quarter of next year.

'I enjoy it,' Alana shrugged, gathering her papers up from the boardroom table in his office.

'Or are you hiding from the "now"?' Stephen commented wisely. 'I think you're frightened that if you stop, there'll be nothing for you.'

'Oh stop it, Stephen! You're always having a go at me.'

'I mean, when was the last time you had a relationship? And I mean a proper relationship, not just a drunken scuffle under the covers.'

'I haven't since Eliska was born,' Alana replied, feeling hurt that Stephen had completely dismissed what had happened that day as a 'drunken scuffle'.

'I thought as much – and that isn't healthy. You need someone to care for you as much as the next person.'

'I don't. I'm fine. I don't want to muck things up with what I have with Eliska,' Alana said.

'You work so hard you barely have time for her either.' Stephen wouldn't let up.

'Exactly. So how on earth would I fit in a man as well? And you've made it quite clear you are not leaving your wife, so what's your sudden concern anyway?'

'As hard as you may find it to believe, I really do care for you, Lani.'

Alana cringed. 'Please don't call me Lani – that's what my mother calls me. And even if you did leave your wife, we're not meant to be together.'

'One day you'll have to let down your shield, Alana, and I just hope it doesn't come crashing down hard, because that's my fear with you.'

'I'm fine, Stephen.' Alana softened, realising how wonderful it was for someone to care for her like he did. But she couldn't let him in, not now, not ever. 'Anyway, I must go,' she said. 'Inga has walked out on me and Eliska will be waiting at the gates.'

'So you're collecting her yourself – that's lovely for her.'

'Yes,' was all Alana could muster.

It was such a shame that Robbie the current agency help couldn't live in, not only because he was delicious eye candy, but also because Eliska really got on with him. But he had explained that his main responsibility lay with the Denbury Youth Centre. He was just doing the after-school child-minding for some extra cash.

Alana gathered her things and went into work mode.

'Right, if you can sort out a venue for the January press lunch and make sure you get your invoice in before the end of the month, then we're done.'

'Alana?'

'Stephen?' the feisty businesswoman replied flippantly.

'I love it when you go all corporate on me.'

Alana had to smile. She glanced at her phone as an email came in. 'Only three weeks to Christmas, can you believe it?' she said. Then: 'Right – see you at your work bash. Bye, Stephen.'

'Bye, Lani,' he said quietly, wishing she could just find it in her bruised heart to tell him the truth.

Dr Delicious was looking more delicious than usual when Mo arrived at the surgery.

'Mo, are you limping?' he enquired as she hobbled around to her desk.

'Not exactly, but my legs are aching. All I did was walk

around Denbury Park twice at speed.'

Noah Anderson tried not to laugh. 'Well good on you! Get through the pain barrier and it can only do you good.'

Thank God he can't see my chafed thighs, she thought, while having unchaste thoughts about him chasing her around Denbury Park naked.

Ffion skulked over to her desk.

'You're late!' The screech of Grim Lynn echoed around the surgery.

'I'm sure she's got eyes in the back of her bonce!' Ffion exclaimed as the grim one appeared from her office.

'What is it this time? The car wouldn't start?'

Ffion was too hungover to even think of an excuse. 'Actually, no, Lynn. I wouldn't start!'

Noah and Mo both burst out laughing and Lynn harrumphed back into her office.

'Why are you in such a jolly mood today anyway, Mo?' Ffion asked.

'Not sure really. I'm still married to a tosser and I've got no money to mention, but the Mo Collins Freedom Collection is underway, as is my weight-loss plan. I went twice round Denbury Park yesterday, I'll have you know.'

'Ooh, get you! Good girl. I don't suppose you'll want to come to Rosco's at lunchtime then?'

'There are two reasons why not, Ffion Jenkins. One: no money. Two: no willpower.'

At one o'clock, Dana approached the customer and her friend, whom Tony had nicknamed 'Lumpy & Pumpy from the surgery', at their usual table. The Rosco brothers had given the place a lick of paint and it was looking bright and cheery, with clean white walls and framed photographs of various models of red Ferrari.

'Chicken salad and chips for me, please,' Mo announced.

'Prawn and mayonnaise on brown for me, thanks,'

Ffion added. Without her friend noticing, she caught Dana's eye and mouthed, 'No chips.'

Dana winked and mouthed back, 'OK.'

'I could have sworn I ordered chips,' Mo announced when her tasty-looking salad arrived.

'No chips on my order pad,' Dana stated.

'You must have forgotten, Mo,' Ffion said, backing up the waitress.

'Oh, well don't worry now, love,' Mo directed at Dana. 'I'll be late back to work otherwise.' She tucked into her salad. 'How's the beauty course going anyway?'

'Loving it!' Ffion exclaimed. 'Really looking forward to getting my qualification and being able to work for myself. I'm learning some great make-up tips, too.'

'Good – you are wasted in that surgery. I haven't heard much mention of the love-life lately either?'

'I've been doing my research and have deduced that Denbury houses around ten good-looking men. I've already slept with eight of them, we work for one of them and the other one's my brother – and that wouldn't be right, now would it?'

Mo nearly choked on a bit of celery.

'You're so funny, Ffion. You deserve to meet somebody lovely. But you're right to be playing the field. At twenty, don't even think of settling down.'

'No, I'll just be lying down at the moment, I will.' At that moment, Ffion caught Bruno's eye behind the counter and realised that her count had immediately gone up to eleven.

'But I wanted GoGo pops, not toast!' Lily whined.

'And where's the chocolate spread?' Lola asked grumpily. Gordon ran his hands through his hair.

'Girls, please be nice to Daddy. I forgot to get milk yesterday. I'm sorry and I know I need to stock the cupboards.'

'Maybe Daddy Chris can help you today.' Lily picked up on Gordon's tiredness.

He tried not to show how upset he was.

'I told you, darling, Daddy Chris has gone on some long flights so he won't be back for a while.'

The girls carried on eating their breakfast. It had only been two weeks but Gordon literally ached with missing his partner. It wasn't just the fun and companionship he longed for. He also realised just how much Chris had helped him with the girls. It was so difficult to keep all the balls juggling, what with his airline shifts, after-school care and generally running the house. Some of the other parents had been great, helping out with school-runs and having the girls round for tea, but working shifts made it difficult to keep a consistency in the twins' lives and he knew he would have to reconsider his line of work.

He had to be realistic; face the fact that Chris wasn't coming back and just get on with it. He had had one quick email to say that his errant partner had arrived in Canada safely – and that was it. Gordon couldn't believe that after being so very close, Chris could just drop them all like hot potatoes, but maybe that was just his way of coping.

There was no way he was going to let his precious girls down, Gordon resolved. As hard as it was, he would manage and make sure their lives were full of love and laughter, just as his sister had asked him to do.

Thankfully, he now had three days off so he could get the house back in order and spend some quality time with his girls.

'Daddy?'

'Yes, Lily?' Gordon tried to keep the stress out of his voice.

'I need another cardigan,' the little girl said, lifting an arm to show the chocolate milk she'd just put her sleeve in.

'Oh, Jeez!' Gordon put his hand to his forehead. 'I

haven't got the other one clean. Come here, I'll wipe it with a damp cloth.'

'No!' Lily shouted. 'It will be all wet then!'

'Stop being so spoilt,' Lola piped up. 'Daddy told you he is doing the washing today. You can have another one tomorrow.'

'I miss Daddy Chris,' Lily screeched, running to her room and throwing herself face down on her bed.

'So do I,' Gordon whispered under his breath.

Lola got down off her chair, climbed on his lap and hugged him tightly.

'The rain in Spain stays mainly on the plain – repeat after me.' Mrs Burrows stood in front of Gordon, banging her walking stick to accentuate the vowels.

'The rain in...' Gordon faltered. 'I'm sorry, Mrs Burrows. I can't do this today.'

'Very well, dear,' the old lady said hurriedly. She went towards him and took his hand. He clenched his nostrils shut to avoid her coffee breath.

'How about we try talking? It is fine to ask for help sometimes if you need it.' She spoke very gently.

Gordon's bottom lip wobbled.

'What's the matter, love?' Mrs Burrows said kindly, in a much more natural voice.

Gordon burst into tears. Being held close to a saggy bosom had never felt so good, and for some reason it opened the floodgates of loss.

'I miss Chris, my partner, I miss Jessica, my sister, but most of all I miss my mum!'

'Oh, darling boy. They will all be looking down on you now.'

'It's only Jess who's dead,' wept Gordon. 'Chris has gone to "find himself",' he inputted bitterly, 'and my mum has Alzheimer's. She was only fifty when she got it, and what with that and Jess's death, Dad couldn't cope. He

70

headed off to Bangkok, of all places, took a Thai bride and now I get a Christmas card once a year if I'm lucky.'

'Oh, you poor love.' Mrs Burrows held Gordon's hand.

'I see Mum once a month but she never recognises me and I feel so guilty leaving her in that home, but I know I could never give her the care she needs.' He stopped and took a deep breath. 'And now I have those two precious angels to look after and I feel like I'm letting them down.'

'Fiddlesticks are you letting them down! The photos you show me, the way you talk about them – they seem very happy and well-balanced little girls to me.'

Gordon managed a weak smile. 'Thank you, Mrs Burrows.' He blew his nose. 'As you know, I work shifts as a flight attendant, and when Chris was around we managed the work/child balance – but now it's impossible. I vowed I would never get extra help. I would hate for Jessica to think that I couldn't cope.'

'Gordon – like I said, there's nothing wrong with asking for help. Get someone in to assist with the shopping and housework at least. Then, when you are at home with the girls you will have time for them solely. They will think no more or less of you for doing that. They're only six. Too young to judge. All they will know is that they love you. Yes, Chris leaving is unsettling, but kids adapt, Gordon. A lot of love and a bit of discipline go a long way, so don't you worry.'

Gordon was starting to feel slightly more positive, as Mrs Burrows went on, 'As for your mum, I am so sorry to hear that. Alzheimer's is a terrible disease, but she's still here in flesh and blood, so go and see her and give her a big cuddle soon. Whatever happens, you're still her little boy.'

Gordon began to sob again. Mrs Burrows cradled him in her arms, offering the comfort he had needed so badly since Chris had left.

'I'm always here too, as a voice coach or not. In fact,

stop wasting your time trying to speak the blooming Queen's English and get down to Tesco's now!'

Gordon sat up, wiped away his tears and blew his nose loudly. 'Thanks, Mrs Burrows.' He kissed her on the cheek.

'Esme,' she interrupted. 'And think nothing of it. You've got my phone number. My arthritis holds me up on physical chores, but if you ever need a listening ear, come and see me anytime – and I'd love to meet those beautiful girls of yours.'

Chapter Eight

Alana was used to the whispering when she pulled up at the school gates. She could imagine the small-minded chatter about losing her au pair. But she would show them that she could be a good mother, as well as have a career.

Inga smiled at her ex-boss as she got out of her car. She was feeling quite smug that Preachy Knickers had asked her to do a couple of school runs for her; and her evening babysitting had picked up. She was saving madly to try and get herself a deposit to rent a room somewhere.

Mr Chambers appeared at the classroom door, little human animals chattering behind him ready to be released into the wild. He saw Joan and gave her a big smile. Without making it obvious, he scratched his head and pointed to Skye. Joan raised her eyebrows and mouthed, 'Sorry'.

Mo power-walked up the school path.

'Well done you!' Joan exclaimed. 'Up for once round the park after tea?'

'I better had,' Mo smiled. 'I had three Hobnobs this afternoon.'

'Oh, Mo.'

'Oh, nothing,' Mo told her, 'I'm all up for getting fit and healthy, but I don't think I can bear all that pushing and prodding food around the plate like the joylessly thin do.'

Joan laughed out loud. 'Well, it's nice to see you smiling anyway. Right – here they all come, clear a space.' Skye, Kent and Clark came charging towards their mum.

'You'd better check Rosie's hair,' she added in a

whisper. 'Skye's got nits again!'

'OK, no worries; if she's caught them I'll make sure she cuddles up to her father's remaining strands before I shampoo her.'

'Mo, that's not very kind.'

'The words "taste, own, of, medicine" and "his" spring to mind,' Mo retorted. 'Right, here's little Miss Collins. Let's go.'

Gordon screeched up to the school gates in his Mini. He hated being late but at least he had managed to get three loads of washing done and had a boot full of groceries. He ran up the path and straight into Inga and Joshua P.

'Love, love, love,' he greeted his friend in a camp fashion. 'Inga, just the girl. I really need to talk to you.'

'Oh, Gordon, I'm in such a rush. I've got to get Joshua to his guitar lesson and as Emily doesn't trust me with the car we have to do the walking very fast.'

'Let me just get the girls. It'll be a squeeze but I'll give you a lift.'

Once Joshua P was safely at his guitar lesson, Gordon and Inga stood side by side pushing the twins on the park swings. The girls squealed with more delight the higher they went.

'So, what is it you want to talk to me about?' Inga asked innocently.

'How do you fancy living in a three-bedroom penthouse with one very handsome man?'

Inga laughed. 'And let me guess – two very pretty little girls?'

'You're a genius,' Gordon mocked.

'Can't believe it's taken you so long,' Inga quipped, then slowed down her pushing, much to Lily's displeasure. 'I could see you needed help,' she added. 'But I felt I had to wait for you to come to me first.'

The girls leaped off the swings and ran towards the climbing frame.

'So, what do you think?' Gordon asked her. 'The girls are happy in their bunk beds so you could make the spare room your own. I don't see you as a conventional au pair, so how about you treat it as renting a room from me, we liaise on my shifts and, as long as you are around for those, I'm flexible with what you do with any other spare time. Well, aside from helping out with a bit of shopping, cleaning and ironing and cooking the girls' meals when I am at work.'

'Gordon Summers, I think you were sent from heaven, that's what I think. It's perfect. It gives me time to have my own life too. To be honest I wanted a change, but if you can give me the freedom to do some different things then it's perfect. Thank you.'

'I haven't discussed it with the girls yet but I know they adore you. I'll talk to them over dinner. I just need to get a key cut and then, if you want to, you can move in tomorrow?'

'Sounds like a deal to me.' Inga put her arm loosely round him as they made their way to the climbing frame.

For the first time in weeks, sleep came easy for both the young Polish girl and Gordon Summers.

Eliska pushed her nose against the train window, noticing the scenery change from fields to skyscrapers. It was Saturday lunchtime and the train was packed with Christmas shoppers and revellers.

'Mummy, look at that big wheel!' the little girl shrieked, catching sight of the London Eye as they approached Waterloo station. 'Can we go on it?'

With her fear of heights Alana couldn't think of anything worse. 'We'll see, darling,' she prevaricated, and Eliska pouted. 'I thought we should go on an open-top bus first, see all the twinkly lights and then do some present shopping.'

'Awesome!' Eliska was easily appeased.

They bagged seats on the top deck, right at the front. It was a sunny winter's day but they were glad of their warm scarves and woolly tights as there was a cold nip in the air.

Eliska was kept amused spotting all the landmarks they had studied in a recent project at school.

The bus brakes squeaked as they pulled up outside the Tower of London. A young couple got on with their daughter. The bus set off again.

'Mummy?' Eliska looked up to Alana. 'Yes, darling?'

'When are you going to find me a new daddy?'

Alana cringed inwardly. 'When I'm not so busy.'

'But you're always busy, Mummy. I hate it that you have to work so much.'

'Oh, Lissy darling, it won't always be like that.'

Diversion tactics were required. 'Quick, look at that big boat on the river.'

The day flew by in a whirlwind of bus stops, food treats and clothes shops and in no time at all they were back at Waterloo station, laden with bags.

It was while they were queuing for a promised doughnut for Eliska to eat on the way home that Alana saw him, in fact saw them.

She could feel herself burning from her toes to her scalp, but it was too late to hide, as Stephen was waving. She was certain that if it wasn't for the fact that he wanted to get a proper look at Eliska, he too would have scurried in the opposite direction.

'Hi, Alana, and this must be little Eliska?'

Alana was mute. Stephen talked for both of them.

'This is my wife, Susan.' Susan smiled politely.

'This is Alana Murray and her daughter. Alana heads up PR at Langston and Smithdrake, a major client of mine.'

Alana pulled herself together, looked down at Susan in

her wheelchair, smiled, and shook her hand gently.

'What beautiful red hair.' Susan was looking intently at Eliska. Alana thought she was going to be sick and began to gabble.

'Right, good to meet you, Susan. See you at the Christmas party, Stephen. Must run, our train's about to leave.'

'But, Mum, my doughnut,' Eliska wailed as Alana dragged her as fast as she could across the concourse.

'I think Colin is having an affair.' Joan let out a plume of white breath into the freezing December air as she and Mo power-walked around the park, wearing matching bobble hats with miner-type headlamps attached.

Mo screwed up her face. 'There is more likelihood of me fitting into a size 10 dress by Christmas than Colin ever having an affair. He so obviously adores you. '

'Really?' Joan questioned.

'Really, really, really,' Mo emphasised. 'And anyway, why on earth do you think that?'

'Well, he always seems to be working late and even sometimes on a Friday, and he's never worked late on a Friday in his life. He always used to look at it as a family night.'

'Have you spoken to him about it?'

'He just brushes it off, saying he's busy catching up with work.'

'Are you still shagging?' Mo asked.

'Not much, but that's because he says he's too tired. Now I'm doing this exercise I've got so much extra energy. I want it all the time, so it's very frustrating.'

'Oh Joan, if he was dipping his wick elsewhere he wouldn't be bothered to do it with you at all, now, would he?'

'I suppose not. Or maybe he would so I don't suspect?'

'You've said it yourself; he's not exactly Colin Farrell,

is he?'

'More like Colin Barrell!' Joan chortled.

'Glad you said that and not me. I'd be a fine one to talk anyway,' Mo added as they upped the pace to warm their cold bones.

'I reckon you're looking better already, though, Mo.'

'Yeah, only three dress sizes to go. It doesn't quite sound so hard as saying three stone.'

'Well, I'm very proud of you.' Joan patted her friend's arm chummily and said, 'How's Ron behaving, by the way?'

'I've found that if I buy him six per cent lager, he's asleep after three of them so I just throw a blanket over him and leave him downstairs. I have moments of feeling sorry for him but they soon pass.'

'Oh Mo, that's no way to live.'

'I know, I know – but my escape fund is not large enough to make the break yet.'

Joan sensed her friend's anguish and changed the subject swiftly. 'Any word from Charlie?'

Mo smiled at the thought of her son.

'He called me last night actually. He's hoping he may come and see us at Christmas-time. The only thing is, if he sees how Ron behaves towards me, I'm not sure what will happen and I don't want to worry him – he's working so hard at the moment.'

'Bless you, Mo. Play it by ear. Ron might have stopped drinking by then.'

'And pigs may be pulling Santa's sleigh.' Mo smirked. 'Now come on, it's too bloody cold out here, let's go back to yours for a cuppa and a mince pie – minus the pastry, of course.'

'How's my *bellissima* blue-eyed waitress today?' Tony greeted Dana at the door of Rosco's.

'Tired actually. Tommy is having night terrors at the

moment – wakes me up at least twice a night.'

'Oh, *cara mia*, I shall make sure I fill you with plenty of espressos today then.'

'I'd fill her with more than espressos if I had my way,' Bruno commented in a low voice as Dana went to take her coat off in the back kitchen.

'You're filth, brother, you are.'

'Oh, come on, Tone. She's well fit. I know you would if you had the chance.'

'She's married, Bruno, and she has a kid – now just leave it, will you. Anyway, I thought you were shagging that pretty little Welshy from the doctors' surgery?'

'Yeah, but you know me, bruv, I'm a lurve machine. For some reason I want to fuck everything at the moment.'

Tony had to laugh. 'You're so wrong.'

'Why, what's he done now?' Dana appeared tying her apron.

'It would hurt your ears, Dana. I'm not even going there.'

As he spoke, the LWL brigade arrived. One of them clicked her fingers to get Dana's attention. Dana chose to ignore her and went over to two decorators in their white splattered overalls instead.

'I say!' the plummy voice called out. 'I do believe we were here first.'

'Terribly sorry, I'll be with you shortly.' Dana smiled sweetly over. 'Stuck-up cows,' she mouthed to the decorators, who laughed out loud while taking in Dana's pert breasts under her crisp black shirt.

'Where are you from?' asked the blonde leader of the LWL brigade, trying to make out Dana's accent.

'Lymington Avenue, up at the top of Bramwell Hill,' Dana said innocently, knowing that would shut her up.

'Oh, you live with a family up there, do you, dear?'

'Yes, my husband and my son.'

She took their order and laughed to herself as they all

tried to work out why on earth, if she owned a house in Lymington Avenue, she needed to be working in a café.

Between elevenses and lunch, there was a slight lull in service. Dana and Tony took their customary break in the back kitchen, whilst Bruno held the fort.

'So, how are you enjoying working with us?' Tony asked.

'I simply love it. Just having the independence and more importantly my own money. I can't tell you how happy that makes me.'

'So are you going to tell your husband you are working here now?'

'Not yet. It's actually quite a thrill having this little secret.'

'Do you have any other "little secrets" from him?' Tony flirted.

'No I don't, you cheeky one.' Dana took a mock swipe at his cheek. 'As much as I go on about independence, I do love Mark very much; in fact, we are going to try for another baby.'

'That's lovely,' Tony genuinely replied, although the thought of trying for a baby with Dana caused his loins to stir.

'I meant to ask you actually,' Dana added. 'I need to take the school holidays off. It will be too obvious to Mark and Tommy if I come in here.'

'That's fine. I expected that anyway,' Tony said kindly, still trying to control his amour. 'We may get a temp in, just so you know.'

The handsome Italian jumped up quickly, before he physically couldn't. 'Right, *cara mia*, let's down these espressos and get back to it.'

'Come on, Inga, let's send Daddy a video of it from your phone.' Lily pushed her red-framed glasses up her nose and ran round the flat excitedly.

Lola had already had to rush to the toilet as she had nearly wet herself laughing so hard.

'I'm not sure your daddy will be too happy,' the pretty Polish girl warned.

'Go on, Inga, do it again. He'll love it, I know he will,' Lily urged.

'Just one more time,' Lola pleaded.

'Oh all right then, you little monkeys.'

Inga lifted up her jumper, expertly placed the straw under her armpit, turned her head, put the other end in her mouth and blew hard. A gigantic fart noise blasted out from behind her shoulder. Minutes later, Gordon walked into the lounge to find both his daughters and Inga rolling around the floor of his flat laughing fit to burst.

'Pray do share.' Gordon put his rucksack down on to the armchair. It had been a tiring shift today as there had been a delay in Paris. It was such a relief for him to know that even if he was stuck somewhere, Inga would be at home and caring for the girls. His weariness waned with the elation of seeing his daughters so happy.

'Daddy, look!' Lily and Lola did an encore, and he too was reduced to hysterics.

'Let me have a go.' He grabbed a straw from the packet.

After an hour of perfecting the fart chorus of 'Jingle Bells' and with the girls tucked up in bed, Gordon crept down the hall into the lounge and handed Inga a glass of chilled white wine.

'Sleeping?' she asked quietly.

'Like babies, bless them.'

'They are such lovely kids, Gordon. Your sister would be so proud of you.'

'Heh, don't get me blubbing, you.' Gordon lifted his glass. 'Anyway, cheers, Inga.'

She lifted her glass. 'Cheers.'

'While we are being sentimental,' Gordon continued, 'I don't know what I would have done without you over the past few weeks. You really are a little star and the girls love you.'

'Oh, shush. You've made my life so bearable. It really doesn't feel like working, living here with you all.'

'What? You mean I'm more easy-going than Alana Murray?'

Inga laughed. 'Just a leetle bit. Mind you, now that I see her from a different perspective, I feel sorry for her in a funny sort of way. I think she works all the time as she is unhappy with her life.'

'That's the thing. People just don't know what goes on behind closed doors, do they?' Gordon chuckled. 'I mean, look at us two – the rumour-mongers are going to be in overdrive, I reckon.'

'Well let them talk, I say.' Inga took a slurp of wine. She cosied herself against one of the big fluffy cream cushions on the sofa and told him, 'I meant to ask you something, Gordon. Would you mind if I spent Christmas here? I haven't really got enough money to go home this year. Be honest if you'd rather I didn't.'

'Don't be silly. I'd love you to be here. It's the first time in six years that I won't be with Chris and it will help bridge the gap for the girls too.'

'Have you heard from him?' Inga asked gently.

'Only via postcards to the girls. He's certainly getting around a bit – he was in Sydney, last time we heard. I just hope it's not confusing them. It's definitely upsetting me.'

'Darling Gordy.' Inga went over and hugged him. 'It won't confuse the girls – they are used to you both being away. We shall make it the best Christmas ever for them anyway.'

'Yes, we shall!' Gordon said loudly draining his glass. 'Will the rest of your family be OK with me being here?'

'Mum is too sick to travel and the girls will head over

to their late dad's parents on Boxing Day anyway, so it'll be fine, honestly. We shall get a big turkey and all the trimmings and we can always get the straws out again after dinner,' Gordon grinned.

'I'm excited already.' Inga jumped up. 'Right. I'd better tidy the kitchen.'

'No, Inga. You'd better shut up and have another glass of wine.'

Chapter Nine

'Why didn't you tell me your wife was in a wheelchair?' Alana asked Stephen as they sat in the bar of the fashionable Central London hotel.

The SM Public Relations Christmas bash was in full swing and despite it only being two in the afternoon, the decibel level of revelling staff enjoying the free-flowing booze was already high.

'What difference does it make? I've still been unfaithful to her.'

'But it somehow seems worse.' Alana took a sip of her gin and tonic and began to question him further.

'What is...?'

'Multiple Sclerosis,' Stephen anticipated. 'Her condition has deteriorated a lot quicker than we thought.'

'Can you still – you know, do it?' Alana continued her interrogation.

Stating out loud that he could no longer make love to his wife cut him like a knife. 'No, it's impossible now,' he said quietly. 'But you can understand why there is no way I would ever leave her.'

'I'll say it again, Stephen. I've never asked you to. We've had sex twice – big deal.'

'Quite a big deal when a product of one of those encounters is a little human being,' Stephen shouted.

Alana drained her glass and immediately ordered another drink. 'Let's move over there.' She pointed to a table in the corner of the bar.

'So is she mine?' Stephen asked, once they were settled away from prying ears.

Alana shifted in her seat. 'I don't know.'

'What if I asked for a DNA test?'

'You wouldn't,' Alana replied cockily.

'I don't need to. It's glaringly obvious: she's got my chin, my eyes, my hair – shall I go on?'

The alcohol caused Alana to drop her defences. 'I don't want your money, Stephen.'

'You don't want anything, that's clear – but why didn't you just tell me? I could have helped you, emotionally if nothing else. It must have been very hard, especially with your mum deserting you.' Stephen was angry but did his best to retain his usual composure.

Alana softened slightly. 'Stephen, you are such a lovely man. I knew that you weren't a philanderer. I knew that you would want to help me – but I didn't want to break up your marriage, especially as I was the one who encouraged you to my room that night. I'm strong. I knew I could cope.'

'Nobody's that strong,' Stephen said quietly, a sudden rush of relief flowing over him now that he finally knew the truth. 'Sometimes, I wish you'd just take a break, take some proper time off,' he told her. 'I can't remember the last time you even took a week off.'

'That really is no business of yours, Stephen,' Alana slurred, but for once he wasn't deterred.

'Now that I know that her imaginary father doesn't exist, I realise that poor Eliska hasn't ever been on holiday, has she? '

'How dare you question whether my daughter has had a holiday or not,' Alana spat.

'Our daughter,' Stephen said far too loudly.

Alana felt sick. Just him saying those words hit home. Eliska was their daughter. That felt too weird. It had always been just the two of them, Alana and Eliska, living side by side, muddling through. Somehow a third party didn't seem right.

'You can't just waltz into Eliska's life now,' Alana stated.

'Look, I'm not stupid.' Stephen was exasperated now. 'And I would never leave Susan – in fact, could never ever tell Susan.' He cleared his throat. 'It would break her heart.'

'Anyway, we're doing fine just the two of us. And I don't need your input of any kind,' Alana said angrily.

Stephen was now completely rattled. 'Just take a look at yourself, Alana, will you? I adore you, but something's just got to give. If there is anything I can do to make your life easier, then you must tell me.'

'Do you know what?' Alana said aggressively. 'I wouldn't come to you if you were the last man on earth.' She threw her head back and downed her fifth gin and tonic in one.

'That's right.' Stephen raised his voice again. 'Get pissed. Go and hide. I've just found out you are the mother of my child and you're running off. Don't face the music, whatever happens: you're good at avoiding that. In fact, why don't you pick somebody here and go upstairs for a quickie? You're good at that too.'

And with that Stephen got up and went over to his colleagues, leaving an open-mouthed Alana sitting on her own.

The secret was finally out and she felt scared. Scared, and all of a sudden, very lonely.

The black London cab pulled up outside Rosco's. Alana paid the extortionate fare that over thirty miles in a taxi brings, and headed into the café. She had to try and sober herself up. Eliska would be back from Tommy's at around eight and she didn't want her daughter – or Dana for that matter – to see her in this state.

'Black coffee, please,' she said abruptly to Bruno behind the counter, throwing off her coat on to the seat behind her. 'Do They Know It's Christmas' was blaring out from the radio on the back counter.

'We're just about to close actually,' Bruno said politely, taking in the smart high-cut trousers and oozing cleavage of the attractive woman in front of him.

'Oh, just a double espresso then, please. I've had a hell of a day.'

'And a hell of a skinful,' Bruno whispered to Tony.

'I've got some wine out the back if you'd prefer,' Bruno offered, taking in the heady perfume that Alana had just sprayed on herself. She looked up at Bruno, and was quite taken aback by his dark brown eyes, stocky upper body and short dark crop of black hair. He gave her a cheeky grin.

'Coffee? Wine? Wine? Coffee? I mean, it is Christmas, isn't it?'

Tony shook his head in disbelief at the gall of this brother as he headed out into the freezing December evening.

'Oh, go on then, just the one glass,' Alana sighed, intoxication suddenly seeming the only answer.

Bruno locked the café's bright red door, put up the Closed sign and shut down the blinds. He poured two glasses of Chianti and joined Alana at the table.

'So why is a gorgeous woman like you having a hell of a day?'

'It's a long story and I don't want to talk about it. Let's drink.' Alana almost downed her glass in one.

A bottle of wine later, Alana learned that Bruno and Tony had taken on the café from their father Rosco Marino, who had now retired back to Italy. They had moved to Denbury ten years ago as children and loved the suburban way of life. The business was doing well, and for now, this was where they intended to stay.

The only thing that Bruno managed to glean was that sitting in front of him was a very desirable older woman, who didn't want to disclose anything about her private life.

The seven o'clock pips on the radio sobered Alana up.

'Shit, is that the time? I really must go.' She went to get up and staggered backwards. Bruno leaped up and grabbed her.

'Whoa there, lady.'

Alana was wasted. 'Look at you, my own Italian Stallion,' she hiccupped as Bruno kept his arm around her waist.

'Italian Stallion, eh? Then you can be my English Cougar anytime.'

'Fuck me,' Alana suddenly said gruffly.

Bruno pulled back her hair and kissed the wanton business woman full on the lips. Without any resistance Alana ripped off her shirt and before you could say Saint Nicholas they were having mad, bad, hot sex over the ice-cream freezer.

Back at the McNair household, Susan began writing a letter.

My darling Stephen

I read an article once – I think it was by that lovely American actress Cybill Shepherd. Anyway, she was talking about a former boyfriend and how she let him go with love, and how it was the hardest but most sensible thing she had ever done. The time has come for me to do the same.

She wiped the tears away with the back of her hand.

You are a kind, adorable man, I love you beyond infinity. When I was diagnosed, you didn't scream and shout and say, 'Why us?' You dealt with everything in your practical and loyal way, making sure I was always comfortable and adapting the house to suit my needs, without any thought of yourself or your own wants.

It's time now for you to have your own life. We have travelled the world and been everywhere I've ever wanted to go. I can't produce children for us, and I know even though you said you didn't mind, a family is something you always craved.

I certainly don't want to be a burden to you as my condition deteriorates. You deserve the best, Stephen, you deserve to be happy. You deserve your conjugal rights! I want you to know that you must feel no guilt for anything you have done whilst being in this relationship.

I love you unconditionally, and there is no man in this world who could have made me happier than you have.

So – that is why I am sitting here waiting for Cheri to come and collect me and take me to the airport. The sun on my face in Cyprus will make me smile, and do me nothing but good – and although my sister's love and care will not be quite up to your standard, you know I'll be in safe hands. I dithered whether to wait until after Christmas, but like giving up anything you love, there would be no easy time to do it, so why not now.

I love you, Stephen. You have given me the best years of my life. Please do not contact me. I want you to start a new life without the burden of me and my illness.

Yours forever, Susan xx

Mo flew up the stairs of the doctor's surgery; she had seen Grim Lynn pulling into the car park and wanted to be sat at her desk when she arrived. It was a crisp, sunny December day and she had actually enjoyed her power-walk from the school to work. She noticed that it was taking her less time than at the beginning of the term, and she had to admit that she did feel better in herself. She knew that she had Joan to thank for pushing her to do the exercise, but as they were doing it together it had ceased to be a chore and she really enjoyed their regular catch-ups, as they marched around the park with their torches on their hats.

She was also in an especially good mood today as Charlie had called her last night to say he was coming to visit on Christmas Eve.

'Nice to see you in on time for once.' Lynn breezed in, acknowledging Mo. She stopped and started rooting in her handbag. 'Thought you and Ffion could get the tree out and decorate it today.' She handed three pieces of threadbare silver tinsel to Mo and carried on through to her office.

Dr Delicious walked out of his treatment room in time to see what was happening.

'Nothing like cheering the sick patients with a sparkling Christmas tree,' he laughed, then got a crisp twenty-pound note out of his wallet and handed it to Mo. 'When you get a minute, why don't you whizz down to the charity shop and buy some decent decorations. I noticed in the window that they're stocking a range with proceeds to various charities. Get a set for yourself, too, if there's any spare cash.'

'That's a lovely idea,' Mo smiled. 'And thank you very much.'

'By the way, that colour really suits you,' the doctor added, leaving Mo slightly flushed and silently thanking the Nil by Mouth sign hanging on her desk.

Ffion ran to her desk. Her eyes looked red and swollen. She drained the coffee carton she was holding, pulled off her green bobble hat and scarf and sat at her desk in her coat.

Mo approached her gently. 'You all right, darling?'
'Not really, Mo.'

'Come on, what is it?'

Ffion sniffed. 'You know the Italian one from Rosco's?'

'Tony, isn't it?'

'No, the shorter one, Bruno. Well…'

Just then, the first patient of the day appeared. 'I've g-got an appointment with D-Dr Anderson at nine-fifteen,' the nervous young male patient stuttered.

'OK, fine,' Mo said kindly. 'If you can just register on the screen over there... Go on,' she urged Ffion in an undertone.

'Well, instead of letting him stand me up, I decided to walk down to Rosco's – and I caught him red-handed, I did!' Her Welsh accent was made stronger by her emotion.

Dr Delicious rang his buzzer to say he was ready for his first patient. Mo waved the young lad in as Ffion continued.

'There was some blonde woman coming out of the café, no disrespect to you, Mo, but she looked about forty! I just knew she'd been at it with him. She looked drunk and totally dishevelled. He waved her off in a taxi and his shirt was hanging out.'

'Oh, Ffion, that's no proof.'

'Mo, it gets worse. He just brushed me off saying that he had been interviewing the blonde bitch for a job and had totally lost track of time. And that he was tired and he'd see me another day. He stank of drink and I just knew he was lying.'

'But I didn't think you really cared about him anyway?' Mo tried to see reason.

'I actually like Bruno, he's funny and always up for the ride.'

'Let's go out for lunch and we can talk about it,' Mo said in motherly fashion as the waiting room started to fill up.

'I'm not going anywhere near Rosco's. Let him bloody miss me!' Ffion said adamantly.

'No, we can go to Fishers and get a posh sandwich. Dr Delish has also asked me to go and buy some decent Christmas decorations, so we can do that too.'

'Ladies, this is a workplace, not a social club,' Lynn's

voice barked from her office.

'Bitch,' Ffion breathed to Mo, adding in a murmur while looking at the office: 'And a very Happy Christmas to you, too, you miserable old cow!'

Chapter Ten

The Featherstone Primary School Christmas production was the highlight of the autumn term.

Joan ran madly around the dedicated dressing-up classroom with pins hanging out of her mouth. She sewed and clipped, fussed and soothed as she did so. When Mr Chambers popped in to see how she was getting on, he grinned secretly to himself, noticing that the children were drawn to Joan like The Pied Piper of Denbury – which they were going to be acting out later.

Within an hour, and with the help of Preachy Knickers – little villagers, pipers, farmers, animals and angels emerged beautifully made up and dressed, all ready for their moment.

Alana had dropped Eliska off an hour before. She awoke with a start to realise that she was still sitting in the car outside the school gates. Despite it now being dark, she was still wearing her sunglasses, and a smidge of dry white dribble sat on her chin. She was mortified that anyone might have seen her in this state. She still felt absolutely terrible. Not only physically because of all the alcohol she had consumed the night before, but she was also in great distress that Stephen now knew for sure that Eliska was his daughter.

He had made no effort to contact her, which hurt her greatly – and when she had tried to call him that morning to arrange to meet to talk things through logically, his phone had been switched off.

To top all of this she could barely remember what had been said at Rosco's with the young Italian, let alone what she had done. But every so often she got a flashback of pictures of choc ices and writhing nakedness – and groaned to herself.

She was a forty-two-year-old woman who was acting like a twenty-year-old slut! She cringed again, thinking of kind Dana, who on seeing what a drunken mess she was in, had whisked Eliska straight back to stay at her house. What on earth would she think of her?

Shivering, Alana removed her sunglasses to reveal bloodshot eyes. Reaching into her make-up bag, she did the best touch-up job she could muster.

That was it: she had to stop drinking, it was the root of all evil!

She combed her hair and opened her car door, nearly knocking Inga off of the path as she did so.

'Alana,' the pretty Pole said civilly. 'Hi, Inga. All OK with you?'

Inga was shocked, firstly at how friendly her ex-boss was and secondly, how rough she looked.

'Yes, thank you. I work for Gordon full-time now.' Gordon was scurrying up behind her, tweaking and preening his brown locks as he did so.

'She's a treasure,' Gordon uttered, then clocking Alana's haggard face under the streetlamp: 'Good night, was it?' And without waiting for an answer he grabbed Inga's hand and scampered up the school path.

Alana wearily made her way through the gates and up to the school, where she spotted Dana, who was buying raffle tickets in the entrance to the main hall.

'I am so very sorry,' she began, but Dana put her hand up to stop her and looked Alana straight in her bloodshot eyes.

'We all make mistakes, Alana,' she said kindly. 'And I don't think you'll be making the same one again, will you?'

Alana shook her still-pounding head and shuffled to

find a seat towards the back of the hall. She looked around her at the chattering mums, dads, grannies and grandads and suddenly felt very lonely. How nice it would be to have somebody who cared to sit next to her right now. It dawned on her that since she had moved to Denbury, she hadn't made a single friend. Her work had become her life, and apart from the very few times she took her daughter out, she more often than not ended up on her computer late at night, drinking too much wine and going to bed far too late.

What sort of life was that for her or Eliska? Feeling an overwhelming urge to speak to Stephen, she pressed redial. There was no answer, so she sent off a quick text instead: Call me! We can work this out. I'm truly sorry.

Joan made her final tweaks backstage, then ran out front to join Colin and Mo, who were poised ready in the front row. Cissy was sleeping soundly in Colin's arms.

Inga and Gordon sat behind them, laughing as Preachy Knickers' husband, Kenneth, lined up his tripod perfectly, then had an obvious strop when Mr Chambers said he wasn't allowed to film the event.

Inga smiled politely as a seething Kenneth Pritchard reluctantly sat down next to her.

Gordon dug his hand into her thigh and whispered: 'You could've told me Preachy's husband was so hot.'

'Stop it!' Inga whispered back, raising her eyebrows, suddenly seeing him in a different light herself.

The music started and a hush went around the hall. Right on cue, Cissy woke up and started to scream. On came the narrator, who was one of the Year 6 girls, swiftly followed by the animals.

Preachy Knickers began to huff and puff as her darling eldest daughter's voice was overshadowed by the lungs of a one-year-old.

'You'd think they'd take her outside,' she said far too

loudly, and a compliant Colin got up and began to rock his beloved daughter out in the entrance hall. Gordon couldn't contain himself when Lily, wearing a fluffy white lamb headdress and with glitter stuck to her glasses, started her solo. The proud father stood up and began clapping like an excited seal, pointing just to make sure everyone knew that was his daughter up on the stage giving it her all. Just as Inga was pulling the bottom of his jumper to make him sit down, Lola appeared as an angel. That was just too much for Gordy, who had to sit down and wipe his gushing eyes with the tissues Inga had thoughtfully got out ready for him.

Eliska sat cross-legged with the other villagers and sucked her thumb. Alana kept trying to get her attention to take it out, but after all the goings-on of the night before, the little girl was exhausted. Before the second song had even started she leaned to her left and fell fast asleep against Tommy, who was gabbling his way through the verses, not knowing any of the right words.

Alana, already bored and still feeling decidedly the worse for wear, checked her phone again and felt a tear prick her eye. Where was he?

Rosie literally shone as a little star and Mo thought she was going to burst with pride. She couldn't believe what a lovely well-adjusted little girl she was, considering everything she had to put up with from her father.

Joan looked to Colin and grimaced as Clark and Kent started to fight, using their recorders as weapons in the back row. The fighting stopped and a feeling of relief swept over the Brown parents, until Skye started to scratch her head the whole way through the final number.

Chairs scraped back as the applause subsided, raffle prizes were given and the usual thanks by a flashing-bow-tied Mr Chambers came to an end.

'I believe there is a new nit gel on the market now which is failsafe,' Preachy Knickers said loudly to Joan on her way out.

Colin swore under his breath. 'Shame there's not a new f'ing bitch-eradicator gel on the market too.'

Joan laughed, suddenly feeling closer to her husband than she had in a while. 'Take her with a pinch of salt, my love – we all do.'

Alana carried Eliska, who was tired and now very emotional. She half-smiled at Dana as she passed her, dreading to imagine what the pretty Czech would be thinking now.

Mark and Dana swung arms with Tommy in the middle of them and headed off into town for a pizza. Inga went down the path to warm the car up as Gordon made his way to the back classroom to collect the twins. He suddenly heard a familiar Mancunian accent behind him.

'No wife again tonight then?'

Gordon turned around and recognised Robbie, Alana's temp childminder.

'No, not tonight.' He couldn't face a long explanation.

'Shit, do you know what? I'm a nosy bastard – sorry,' Robbie added, picking up on Gordon's sadness.

'What are you doing here tonight anyway?' Gordon was pleased to change the subject.

'Helping out with the set and lighting. Will…' Robbie paused. 'Mr Chambers to you, is a mate of mine. He helps me out with the Youth Centre Christmas gig and I return the favour.'

'Oh right.' Gordon noticed Robbie's deep-set dark eyes. He was ten years younger than him, and a good foot shorter in fact, just his type.

'Actually, it's the Youth Centre do tomorrow night if you fancy coming?'

'Will it suit the kids?' Gordon enquired, beaming as a now bare-faced Lily and Lola came charging over to him.

'No, it's for the sixteen to eighteens; we've got a really good live band coming and will provide refreshments. I could use some help and it's a laugh normally.'

'If Inga can babysit then I'd love to help out, thanks.' Gordon looked down at his beloved charges. 'Right then, you gorgeous girls, let's get you home.'

'Starts at eight, we're next to the MOT place in town,' Robbie shouted after them.

'Great, hopefully see you there,' Gordon replied back as Lily and Lola started to fight about who had been wearing the best outfit.

Dana put some gold tinsel around her blonde crop and applied a silvery glitter eye-shadow. Tying her apron, she looked at herself in the mirror. She felt a sudden guilt that she might be trying to make herself look just a little bit too sexy, so wiped off her bronze lipstick and replaced it with a clear gloss.

Bruno wolf-whistled as she came out into the café. Lights were flashing on the little Christmas tree on the counter.

'Look at you, Signorina Christmas Cracker!'

'Well I thought I'd better make the effort to get festive.'

'You look gorgeous,' Tony said quietly, and then on seeing who was coming through the door, quickly gestured for Bruno to go out the back.

Ffion's eyes darted around the café. 'A medium skinny latte and a large fat mocha, please,' the Welsh girl requested politely.

'No problemo, signora. Take-away?' Tony asked with his usual flirtatious banter.

'Yes, please.' This was Ffion's chance. 'So, did you take on a new waitress then?'

Dana frowned; she didn't realise they had already started recruiting her temp replacement.

'Why? Were you thinking of applying?' A fully briefed Tony turned it around.

'Oh, erm no.' Ffion wasn't sure what to say next.

Tony helped her out. 'Bruno is on constant look-out for good staff. He tries out anyone who shows an interest in the post.'

Ffion grabbed her coffees and marched furiously out of the café.

'Tony!' Dana said. 'That poor girl!'

'What do you mean? I thought that would make her feel better.'

'Men!' was all Dana could say as she headed off to serve the four builders who had sat themselves down in the window seat.

While they were having their customary 'lull', Dana questioned Tony.

'So, now you have to give me the gossip. It's obvious that the pretty young Welsh girl has been seeing Bruno, right?'

'Right so far. But Bruno translates the word "seeing" into "shagging" – you know that?'

Dana shook her head and smiled. 'Like brother, like brother, is it?'

'Now, now Mrs Knight, I would hate you to tar me with the same broom.'

'Brush, you mean.' Dana laughed out loud. She herself was only just getting used to the funny British expressions herself.

'Whatever,' Tony went on. 'Anyway, I shouldn't really divulge my brother's antics, but as it's you...' The young Italian drained his espresso. 'We were just closing up last Thursday and this blonde woman came in, very attractive, must have been at least forty. In fact, old enough to be my mother! Shit, that's funny.' Tony laughed at his sudden realisation of this. 'Anyway, Bruno fancied her. She was very drunk, he got her drunker and then...' He stopped.

'Go on,' Dana urged.

'Well, he you-know-what-ed her,'

'In here!' Dana's eyes widened.

'Well, yes. Over the ice-cream counter, apparently.'
'Thursday night, you say?'

'Yes,' Tony said, suddenly feeling worried that he might have dropped his brother into something he shouldn't have.

'What was she wearing, this woman?'

'Erm.' Tony now felt as if he was standing in the dock. 'I only saw her briefly.'

'Go on – try and remember,' Dana urged.

'Black and white – yes, a crisp white shirt. I remember thinking we should get similar waitress uniforms for our staff.'

'Oh my God, I think it might have been the mum of one of Tommy's friends.'

'Oh no! And now you are going to tell me she has a big burly husband and we are going to have to hide Bruno out the back for ever.'

Dana laughed. 'I've never known her to have a man actually. Rumour at the school gates is that she got pregnant from a one-night stand. The lesbian theory can be dropped now though.'

'Well, the good news is she won't be pregnant this time round. What is it that Bruno says? Ah – I remember. That he will never ride bareback with a stranger. Not after a bad experience he had in Crete anyway.'

'What is your brother like!' Dana tutted disapprovingly.

'Well, at least she wasn't a married woman. Mind you, that never usually stops him either.'

At that moment, Dana's tinsel fell from her hair and they both reached to get it. Tony kept hold of her arm as they stood up.

'It usually stops me…' He paused. 'Until I met you, that is.' As he leaned forward to kiss Dana on the lips, she quickly turned her head so that he planted it on her ear.

'Tony!'

'Oh, I am so sorry. I… it just…I just. You are…I am.' Dana swiftly kissed him on the cheek.

'It's OK. You are a very beautiful person, Tony, but I am married and I intend to stay that way with a clear conscience.' She disappeared out through the staffroom door to regain her composure.

Locking the toilet door behind her, Dana took a deep breath and put her hand to her ear. She could never ever admit it to anyone, but at that precise moment she had wanted nothing more than to kiss the handsome Italian back. Properly.

Chapter Eleven

'He's taking a whole month off you say, just like that?' Alana demanded.

'Yes, that's what I said. He'll be back at work in February.'

'But he must be online surely, Sandra?'

'No. He will be back working next year. Now, if there is anything I can help you with directly?'

'No – no, thank you.' Alana's voice trailed off. Knowing how private Stephen was, she doubted that even his PA knew where he was.

Surely, the fact that he had found out Eliska was his, would make him happy?

Where was he? He was like her – he always worked!

She tried his mobile again. It was switched off. She logged on and sent him an email. His out-of-office message came back, confirming that he would not be checking voicemails or emails until 4 February, and instructing her to contact Sandra, who would re-direct any queries appropriately.

Alana experienced that empty feeling again. Stephen was always at the end of a computer or phone and his absence suddenly overwhelmed her.

'Mummy?' Eliska pushed the door open to her mother's home office.

'Yes, darling?' Alana took in her daughter's curly red hair and shiny green eyes and saw Stephen so clearly that it made her want to cry.

'Can you help me write a list to Father Christmas today, please?' Alana swept her up in her arms.

'Do you know what, pumpkin? Mummy can do better than that. Me,' she brushed the tip of her daughter's nose with her index finger, 'and you, are going on a little holiday.'

Gordon suddenly felt old. His ears were ringing from the thumping music that had been blaring in the Youth Centre and he was glad to get outside, to the peace of the freezing cold night. Robbie had tasked him to stand behind the makeshift bar and serve Coke, crisps and chocolate to the mêlée of teenagers who were jumping around to the live music. And apart from Robbie coming over once to check if he was OK, he hadn't even really spoken to him. Although being a martyr for the great and good of the Youth Centre was obviously satisfying, and seeing eighteen-year-old cute boys ducking and diving in front of him was quite arousing, Gordon was actually quite peeved that he had wasted his evening in this way.

In fact, he was relieved when ten o'clock came so that he could escape the noise and go back to all of his girls. He had tried to find Robbie but in the mass of bodies couldn't see him.

A couple of lads having a cigarette out the front moved aside as he pushed the big black church hall door open, their dragon-like plumes of smoke enveloping him as he walked through. As he was about to get into his car, Robbie came running up to him.

'Sorry – I didn't realise it would be quite so hectic. You're not going home yet, are you?'

'Well yes, I thought my work was done for the night,' Gordon replied.

'Your work may be done, Gordon Summers, but definitely not your play.' Robbie grinned. 'Let me grab my coat. Will Chambers can lock up.'

The Featherstone Arms was heaving with Christmas

revellers, creating even more of a racket than in the Youth Centre.

''Tis the season to be jolly – well, it would be if I had a bloody drink in tow,' Robbie stated as they stood three-deep at the bar just as the Last Orders bell was rung.

Gordon felt a little odd being in such close proximity to someone other than Chris. He still missed him terribly but he knew he had to move on for his own sanity – and Robbie was really hot.

They managed to get a drink and within what seemed like minutes they were being asked to leave.

Robbie lit a cigarette as soon as they got outside and put his other hand deep into his coat pocket. He began jogging from one leg to the other to try and keep warm.

'It'll stunt your growth,' Gordon joked, and they both laughed.

'Got to die of something,' Robbie shrugged, but he dropped the cigarette, put his foot on the butt and stubbed it out. 'Right, where to now? I'm guessing not to yours. I mean, your wife might not take too kindly to a raving homo appearing in the midnight hour.'

Gordon laughed. 'No wife – just beautiful children who are used to following the Yellow Brick Road with me. But I wouldn't want them to wake and see you, not until I've properly introduced you anyway,' he carried on cautiously.

'That's understandable,' Robbie replied. 'My flatmate's having a quiet one with a new girlfriend so I said I'd stay out as late as I could, so mine's out of bounds too.'

'Well, I guess that's it then. Do you want a lift?' Gordon clicked his key fob and the orange lights of the Mini glowed almost eerily in the thick cold air.

'No, no. I'm happy to walk. I can have another ciggie en route. I'm not far from here.'

'OK, well erm, here's my number,' Gordon said, nervously handing over a scruffy piece of paper.

'Cool, ta. Will buzz you.' Robbie lit another cigarette

and started walking away.

Robbie could hear the TV blaring when he pushed open his front door. His flatmate was lying asleep on the sofa, a couple of crushed beer cans by his feet. Robbie kissed his lips and woke him.

'Hey you?' John slurred sleepily. 'Good night?'

'Yep, and it's made me feel hungry,' Robbie said huskily, undoing his skinny jeans. 'Hungry, for a hard cock.'

'No chance of some three-way fun then?'

'More chance of the Pope giving out free condoms from his buggy, I reckon. Cute though. One for the wank bank at least. Now come here, you.'

The charity-shop whippet recognised Mo and Ffion from the doctors' surgery as they walked past the counter. She prayed they hadn't looked at her notes recently. It wasn't big or clever to have contracted an STD at her age, but she felt quite comforted by the recent article in *Woman's World* that said it was now common for post-menopausal divorcees to get caught out. The fact that it was the local vicar who had given it to her was more of a distressing factor.

Mrs Glancy, the vicar in question's wife, was at the back of the shop loudly singing along to 'Onward Christian Soldiers'.

'Can I help you, dears?' she asked in her plummy deep voice when she noticed her new customers.

'Yes, we're just stocking up on Christmas decorations for the surgery. Dr Anderson seemed to think you had some new ones in.'

'Oh Dr Anderson,' Veronica Glancy put her hand on her heart dramatically. 'Shame he didn't come in himself. Just the thought of him touching me with his stethoscope makes me the right side of moist, I can tell you.'

Ffion couldn't contain her laughter as the irreverent vicar's wife bellowed: 'Right, decorations! For the surgery, you say. Here, follow me.' She piled up baubles and tinsel and stuffed them into a bag.

'We must surely give you some money for the charity?' Mo asked, now completely bemused.

'No, just go.' Veronica Glancy shooed them with her hands. 'The Sally Army's outside later, they'll boost us no end. But please do make sure Dr Anderson is aware of the gift. Who knows, he may pay me in kind.' Her large bosom rocked as she let out an unsavoury guffaw.

The whippet raised her eyebrows and thanked Mo, as she put a crisp ten-pound note in the charity box on the counter.

'By the way, how's the Mo Collins' Freedom Fund going?' Ffion enquired as they walked down the High Street, side-stepping the Salvation Army band that was currently singing 'Away in a Manger' outside the chemist.

'Very well actually. I'm hoping that by Easter, Rosie and I will be going it alone.'

'I'm really chuffed for you, matey. Right, let's get some lunch. Dr Delish will never know we've spent his change on it.'

Fishers had a queue snaking out of the door.

'Must be Christmas order collections,' Mo noted. 'Now, how about we go in to Rosco's, you sit down with your back to the counter, and I'll do the talking?'

'Oh, all right then,' Ffion said huffily, her hangover taking charge of her hunger. 'And no, we are not using Dr Anderson's money to pay. The vicar's wife may be bent, but I'm certainly not.'

Bruno saw Ffion as soon as the two women sat down, and he rushed over to their table, a red rose in his hands.

'*Signore*, you are both looking as beautiful as this rose – now how can I pleasure you? I mean, what can I get for you lovely ladies?' His handsome face lit up and melted

Ffion's stubborn heart.

'A ham and cheese toastie, please,' she replied, pushing the rose to the side of the table.

'Make that two, as it's Christmas,' Mo piped up, feeling the momentary guilt that ordering cheese brought her.

Bruno continued his patter. 'And ladies, for drinks, can I interest you in my most recent love potion? A Ravishing Rosco's spicy Christmas milkshake.'

Ffion laughed. 'You're not funny.'

'And I'm not giving in.' Bruno ripped a page from his order pad, put it down next to his Welsh lover and sauntered back to the bar, eyeing up a tall brunette who walked in as he did so.

Ffion pushed the piece of paper over to Mo.

DINNER AT 7, meet me here. Love B xx

'You're not going to go, are you?' Mo asked with concern.

'Oh, Mo, I know full well that I shouldn't, but as much as I say I don't want to settle down, I really do like Bruno.'

'But what if he was in here doing things with that blonde you saw the other night?'

'I've got no proof and as long as I'm careful, what's the harm?'

'The harm is, young lady, that he is using you and you may get hurt. A little bit of self-respect goes a long way, you know and...'

Mo stopped mid-sentence, took a sharp intake of breath and jumped up out of her seat. She ran towards the door, arms outstretched.

'Charlie! My darling! You're early!'

Ffion whipped a mirror out of her bag and applied some lipstick, as in the blink of an eye, the Denbury Dish Total had most definitely just gone up to twelve.

When Charlie Collins sat down at the corner table, Ffion for the first time in her life was speechless. The twenty-four-year-old in front of her had high cheekbones and full lips of which a trout would be proud. He had a trace of stubble and his floppy fringe just covered one of his puppy-dog hazel eyes. The young Welsh girl screwed up her dinner invite and threw it in her bag.

'I'm Charlie,' Number 12 said, as Mo went off to the counter, making Ffion blush for no other reason than that she noticed his flat stomach and slim hips.

'Are you stoned?' Ffion blurted out, seeing that his puppy-dog eyes had enlarged pupils.

'How presumptuous,' Charlie laughed, and then put his fingers to those beautiful lips to shush her as his mum approached with a tray laden with goodies.

'So,' Mo started. 'You're a week early – and how on earth did you know I'd be here?'

'Questions, questions already, Mother,' Charlie teased, squeezing her hand. 'I tried the house and there was no answer, so I thought I'd grab a sandwich and then try the surgery and here you both are.'

Ffion giggled and fiddled with her hair.

'So have you finished work for Christmas then?' Mo wondered.

'I've been made redundant. Recession and all that,' Charlie lied, knowing he couldn't possibly tell his mum that the design company he had worked for had got sick of his lateness due to his constant partying.

'Oh, darling, what are you going to do? You loved that job.'

'Well, sorry to spring this on you before Christmas and all that, but I was hoping maybe I could stay with you until I get myself sorted out again.'

Ffion wished at that moment she could eradicate her flatmate. Mo, thinking the same about her husband, tried not to panic.

'Phew, that's a surprise. I'm not quite sure where we'll squeeze you in, but we will.' She felt a surge of love for her firstborn. 'In fact, I've just had a really good idea.'

'Take it easy, take it easy, take it nice and slow.' Gordon danced around the kitchen singing as the girls blasted out their *Mamma Mia* CD.

'Breakfast,' he shouted loudly, adjusting his felt Santa's hat. He had taken two whole weeks off over the Christmas holidays so that he could give his girls his full attention. Inga was staying with a friend in London for a couple of days.

'You sound so posh,' Lily commented as she sat down at the kitchen table. 'Well, your mummy didn't want you picking up my Canadian accent.'

'Oh. I thought it was American like on *School's Out* and that's cool,' Lola said, screwing her face up in confusion.

'Yes, talk American, that's awesome.' Lily pushed up her glasses and tucked into her cereal and fruit. 'Mummy would be pleased we've got one of our five a day,' she added, pushing around the strawberries on her cereal.

Tears pricked Gordon's eyes. It was so sweet that they had taken in all of her wishes.

'But she wouldn't want you to be lonely without Chris. He's been gone ages, Daddy Gordy – when is he coming home?' Lola asked.

Gordon had been dreading this question. He had been hiding the now-dwindling postcards, hoping that he could wean the girls off Chris's memory slowly. It also hurt him greatly to wonder what his beloved ex was up to, and he really hoped that he hadn't met anyone else yet. In a way, he was also glad that contact was getting less so at least then he could start to properly get over him too.

'Now, girls, I know this is very sad, but I think Chris will be gone for a long time. He's having lots of fun around the world.'

'So he won't be here for Christmas then?' Lola asked

innocently.

'No, darling, but Inga will. We shall have a really good party.'

'Yeah!' Lily shouted. 'We can play the trumpet straw game.'

'Yeah!' Lola joined in.

'I've got a new friend I want you to meet soon,' Gordon said tentatively. 'What's their name?' Lola asked, spilling milk down her front as she tipped

her cereal bowl up. 'Robbie.'

'Oh, a gay boyfriend, you mean,' Lily said, far too

knowing for her six years, then, without waiting for an answer: 'Come on, Loles, let's go and practise our dance routine.'

Gordon shook his head and smiled. Since seeing Robbie the other night he had found himself checking his phone for messages far more often than usual. Chris was obviously not coming back and it was about time he had some fun. He only wished that he had taken Robbie's number, and then he wouldn't have to play the waiting game.

Ron Collins scrabbled pathetically on the kitchen floor, trying to get up from the punch his stepson had just thrown at his left cheek. When he did manage to heave himself to his feet, Charlie punched him again. Blood was pouring from the drunk's mouth.

'That one was for Rosie!' Charlie was shaking with anger.

'My God, Charlie, what are you doing?' Mo arrived home and rushed to her husband's side. He was now slumped face down over the kitchen table, blood forming a pool on the surface. 'Ron, Ron, talk to me.'

Ron groaned in pain and fell to the floor. Sick was pouring from his mouth. The Christmas tree had fallen on to the carpet in the lounge.

Mo was hysterical. 'Call an ambulance, Charlie! Call an ambulance now.'

Charlie was calm. 'No, Mum, he's far too wicked to die. Let him suffer down there for a bit.'

'He's ill,' Mo wailed.

'He's an abusive alcoholic shit, and I will not have him treat you or Rosie badly anymore.'

'We've got to help him,' Mo pleaded. 'You're no better than him for doing this.'

'He's got to help himself first,' Charlie said coldly and walked out of the house.

The stench of beer-laden vomit was revolting. Thanking God that she had just dropped Rosie at Joan's for her customary Friday-night sleepover, Mo rang the emergency surgery number.

'Oh Mo, I wish you'd have told me things were this bad,' Noah Anderson said as he sat at the kitchen table with her. Ron was now in bed, cleaned up and sleeping soundly after his strong dose of pain relief.

'"Hello, my name's Mo and my husband's an alcoholic", that's just not me,' Mo said. 'I've always managed.'

'There's a lot of help out there to be had for both you and Ron, you know. ' The doctor gently wiped a tear from Mo's cheek with his finger, his tenderness causing her to sob loudly. He held her hand and patiently waited until she was ready to speak.

'Right, on Monday morning we sit down and I get some numbers for you. You're not alone in this now.' Mo bit her lip and nodded.

After she had closed the front door behind her very own Christmas angel, she plonked herself down at the kitchen table. The heating had gone off and she shivered.

In his raw state Charlie looked so like his real father. Very dark and brooding, in contrast to the red hair and fair skin Rosie had inherited from Ron. Maybe now she owed it to her son to tell him that this excuse for a father was not really his, after all.

She put her hands to her head. No, she couldn't do it, not now, probably not ever. It wouldn't be fair to open such a can of worms – and what if her precious son never talked to her again?

She began to cry again for the mess that was her life. She was mortified that Dr Delicious had helped clean up her bloody and sick husband on her kitchen floor. She was sad that her son had had to hit his own father, who wasn't his father at all. The only saving grace was that she could now see the light at the end of a long dark alcohol-induced tunnel. She didn't need to cry for help; in his own way Charlie had done that for her – and for that she would be eternally grateful.

Alana gently pulled a blanket up over Eliska as she slept soundly against the aeroplane window. Their trip to Lapland had been even more magical than she had expected. Just to see the look on her daughter's face when they arrived was worth the extortionate amount of money the last-minute trip had cost her.

Work had quietened down as it always did the week before Christmas, which was bittersweet. It was undoubtedly great to be able to focus on Eliska for once, but it gave her even more time to wonder what Stephen was up to.

Before they had gone away, she had waited three whole days for a reply to her many messages. Rather than be her usual stubborn self, she decided to swallow her pride and pick up the phone. She made sure her number wouldn't appear on his screen and was delighted to hear a ringing tone. But it was an overseas ringing tone, which was quickly cut off as soon as she said 'hello.'

Where was he? Why wouldn't he take her calls? He

had obviously been angry with her about her reaction to him knowing he was Eliska's father, but Stephen was a kind man.

Overtaken by a sudden rush of tiredness, Alana fell asleep, then awoke to the stewardess telling both her and Eliska to put on their seat belts for landing. Eliska opened her eyes sleepily and put her favourite teddy's ear in her mouth. 'Have a safe onward journey and Happy New Year,' the Captain crooned over the tannoy as the plane approached its landing station.

How could it possibly be a happy new year, Alana thought – if Stephen McNair wasn't going to be in it?

– Spring Term –

'Being a full-time mother is one of the highest paid jobs,
since the payment is pure love.'
Mildred B. Vermont

Chapter Twelve –

'Oh yes. Harder, harder – just there.'

A baby began to cry in the next room. 'Damn. Don't stop. Yesssss!!'

Cissy was standing up in her cot, arms outstretched as her mum ran in, curly blonde hair in complete disarray, black silk nightdress around the wrong way.

'Dad, dad, dad, dad,' the little one shouted as Joan turned off the baby monitor.

'Sshh now, darling. He's at work. We'll see him tonight,' Joan soothed, feeling completed sated for the first time in ages as the back door banged shut below.

Emily Pritchard – Head of PTA, Netball Coach and Mother of Joshua P, seven, chief swot and playground kisser – marched up the school path wiggling her bottom in her new bright red-belted mac.

'Didn't realise you were expecting again?' she greeted Mo who, flabbergasted by the comment, stood mute until Joan spoke for her.

'For your information, Mo has recently lost a stone, and at least all of her is real woman.' She ushered her friend away, telling her to take deep breaths to stave away the tears.

Gordon had overheard Preachy Knickers' vicious comment and said to himself, 'Never ask a woman if she's pregnant unless you can see the head, I say.'

Luckily Mo didn't hear this either. Joan, who did, stifled a guffaw.

'I've eaten so much over Christmas – it's the stress of

119

everything,' Mo grumbled.

'I know, I know. She's just a bitch, Mo. We'll get back on track now the kids are back at school,' Joan sympathised.

'Yes, we must.' Mo tried to regain positivity. 'I feel awful as well, as with everything going on I haven't even asked you how Charlie's been behaving, living in your caravan. I hope he's not too much trouble.'

'Trubble, shrubble. Mo, it's a pleasure having him. I just have to make sure he's kept warm in this weather, that's all.' Joan smiled and blushed. 'Now come on, let's say goodbye to those little darlings of ours.'

'Oh Gawd, yes, look at the time. Ron is actually venturing out to the surgery for a check-up and I'd better be there when he arrives.'

Feeling as grey and dull as the January day upon them, Alana pulled up at the school gates. She was due to go back to work today, but had awoken feeling really sick, so thought it might be safer to work from home. This obviously delighted Eliska, as she knew that 'a silly old tummy bug' wouldn't stop her mummy taking her to school.

The little redhead loved the clicking sound her new school shoes made on the concrete and she ran straight up to the twins to show them. Alana smiled as she waved goodbye, then turned to her phone. Robbie had said that he might be free for the spring term, so she must get in and book him early.

Wishing Gordon a Happy New Year as he walked back to his Mini, she likened him to Stephen – smart, upright and debonair. Kind as well, she thought. It had taken her years to realise it, but she'd swap kind for flash any day.

Dana and Mark pulled up in their silver 4 x 4, and an excited Tommy shot out of the back door and up the drive. Mark swiftly followed.

'Run! He's going to be late,' Dana shouted after her husband, noticing Alana as she got into her car.

Dana thought that she looked even sadder than usual and made a New Year's resolution that she must try and make more of an effort to befriend some of the mums at the school gates. You didn't always know what went on behind closed doors and it must be tough for Alana without a man around.

Also, with the chance of a new addition on the horizon, she too would need all the help she could get. She smiled to herself at the thought of a lovely new little bundle of joy in her arms.

Dana looked around her in the waiting room of the expensive London clinic. She found it hard to believe that so many other women were thinking of going through IVF. There were ladies of all ages, all nationalities, all with the slight sadness that childlessness brings.

What Mark found hard to believe was that with the money it was costing him, they actually had to wait to be seen. The view of the Thames and comfy seats did nothing to compensate for his brewing anger and Dana had to shush him as he started his own private rant.

Today was the day to pick up the all-important drugs that would stimulate her ovaries to produce the eggs that were to be eventually fertilised by Mark's sperm.

'I hope they give me some decent porn to wank off to,' Mark said far too loudly in to his wife's ear. 'In fact, for this bloody price I expect a live lap-dance.'

'Mark!' Dana couldn't believe her husband was making such a show in public. 'They actually give you a blow-up doll, I think,' Dana jested, knowing that underneath all the bravado Mark was actually really quite nervous about his whole performance bit.

'That's not for a couple of weeks anyway,' Dana encouraged. 'Once the eggs are ready and removed.'

'It's all so bloody clinical! Are you sure this is what you want?'

Dana's face fell and Mark grabbed her hand. 'I'm sorry, darling; it just seems a weird way of creating a little life, that's all.'

'Mr and Mrs Knight?' A chic young nurse came into the waiting room.

'Well, maybe things aren't so bad,' Mark whispered to Dana, who pinched his hand as they made their way to the consultant's room.

'Happy New Year, *bellamissima signorella*,' Tony sang as Dana walked into Rosco's.

She giggled. 'What on earth have you been putting in that espresso, eh?'

'Just pleased to see my favourite waitress, that's all. We both missed you, didn't we, bruv?'

Bruno blew her a kiss, and then turned back to the coffee machine. The LWL were back in full force, gabbling like a flock of parakeets as they compared the gifts of jewellery they had received for Christmas. Fur coats and cashmere scarves were piled high on the hat-stand as it was a bitterly cold morning.

Dana was pleased that the Christmas break had come when it had. She hoped that it had dampened Tony's ardour and also her own feelings that she had found oh so difficult to keep under control.

She realised that it would be impossible to go through her whole life not fancying other people, but she did love Mark, and her urge to have another baby was so strong that she would never allow anything to get in the way.

Two hours passed before Tony and Dana had time for one of their customary short breaks. Dana sighed and lay back in the chair in the kitchen, kicked off her shoes and rubbed her throbbing feet.

'You OK?' Tony brushed her cheek with his hand.

'Phew, yes.' She put her hand to her face. 'I've just started IVF treatment and the drugs are making me a little more tired than usual.' Deep down she knew this was something she shouldn't really be telling an employer, but it was Tony, so it somehow felt right.

'Would you prefer to work fewer hours?' he said immediately, her welfare uppermost in his mind. 'It's a long time to be on your feet with all that going on in that lovely little body of yours.'

'No, don't be silly. I'm only here three days anyway. I'll be fine.'

'Well, you must promise that if you want to take some time out, you will tell me.'

'Thanks, Dad,' Dana laughed. 'But joking aside, I may have to take you up on that when I'm pregnant.'

'When will you know?'

'In around five to six weeks. I will have to take a day or two off when the eggs are collected at the hospital, but hopefully it will fall on my days off anyway, but that's it.'

'It's quite weird knowing exactly when you will fall pregnant, don't you think?' Tony asked, not in the least bit phased by talking about such a personal issue.

'I hadn't really thought about it, to be honest. I just feel *so* excited to think that this time next year, I will hopefully have another little person to call me Mama.'

Dana finished off her herbal tea. She had decided to avoid all caffeine or alcohol during the treatment – anything to help it on its way. She bent to put her shoes on and straightened her skirt. Tony watched her as she did this.

'Dana?'

'Yes?'

'I'm sorry about the – you know – the kiss thing.'

Standing up, she faced him and put her hands to his cheeks.

'Tony Rosco, the kiss thing, as you put it – was actually

123

very flattering, and if I was in a different place then I would most definitely have not moved my face away.'

The young Italian smiled widely. 'Really?'

'Really. Now, we'd better get out there and help that brother of yours before he starts throwing plates around.'

Inga looked grey as she took a cup of tea in to Gordon.

'What is it, chick? You look like someone has died.'

'They have. It's Mr Brown Nose. I just went to feed him and there he is, all legs in the air and stiff.'

'Damn, they loved that bloody hamster; we'll have to get them another one. Although, the stench of it,' Gordon went on, camply. 'Can't say I'm not a tinsey wincey bit relieved.'

He jumped up out of bed, causing Inga to check out his buff body, covered only by a small pair of designer boxers. He had been working out a lot more since Chris had left.

'Nice arse,' she commented. Gordon immediately thought of the elusive Robbie.

Parking that thought, he sprang immediately in to Superdad mode.

'Right, quick, get the dearly departed Mr Brown Nose into a cardboard box and we'll sneak out and get a looky-likey straight after I've dropped the kids at school.'

'The girls, they are not stupid, they always feed him before breakfast,' Inga relayed sensibly.

'Right. Take the whole cage out of the study and say you are cleaning him out in your room and they mustn't open the door or he'll escape. Shit – is that the time, I have to jump in the shower.' He disappeared into his en-suite.

As Inga juggled open her bedroom door with one hand, while holding the cage with the other, the girls came charging down the corridor. In her hurry, Lola knocked the base of the cage, opening the cage door and sending the wheel, the water bottle, the sawdust and poor old stiff Mr Brown Nose onto the carpet.

On hearing the commotion, Gordon appeared with a towel around his waist. Lola ran to him, screaming, 'Daddy! Inga has killed Mr Brown Nose!'

He couldn't stop himself from smirking at the whole scenario. 'Daddy, it's really not funny.' Lily started to cry.

He knelt down and gathered his beautiful girls to him; one on each knee. He lifted Lily's red spectacles and wiped away her tears with his index finger.

'Inga didn't kill Mr Brown Nose. He died in his sleep and she was just moving him, so as not to upset you before school.'

'Oh,' the twins said together.

'Now you know where he's gone, don't you?' Gordon went on gently. Lily put her hand up as if she was at school.

'Is it Hamsterdam? Mr Chambers told us about his holiday there.' Inga had to leave the room for fear of laughing out loud.

'Well, he might have gone there, but I think he's more likely to be in heaven with Mummy now.'

Lola took her thumb out of her mouth. 'Did Mummy like hamsters?' 'Yes, she loved animals, darling, so he'll be just fine.'

'Did she love animals more than she loved us?' Lily asked, her voice a bit wobbly.

'No way!' Gordon said firmly and cuddled his girls tightly. 'Now.' He helped them to their feet and stood up. 'Daddy Gordy has got to go to work. Inga will take you to school and then when she picks you up, she can take you to the pet shop to choose another hamster.'

The girls looked at each other and both turned their noses up. 'Can we have a kitten instead?' they said in unison.

These days there wasn't even the uncertainty of a faint blue line. No need to hold the white plastic wand of fate up to the light, no need to wait just a minute more to see if the line got darker the longer you left it. No, these days the word – PREGNANT – screamed out from the test.

Amazing if that was the desired state. Horrifying, if it wasn't.

Alana sat on the side of the bath. She felt numb. She felt sick. She felt desperate. One could almost be allowed to make the stupid mistake of becoming pregnant once – but twice? Now that really was pathetic.

'You stupid cow,' she said aloud. 'You stupid, stupid cow.'

'Chicken madras for me, and a chicken korma, sag aloo, plain rice and a keema nan for the lady, please,' Colin addressed the smartly dressed waiter in their local Indian.

'How did you know that's what I wanted?' Joan asked.

'Because it's what we've ordered for the past ten years, my darling wife.' 'Well, maybe I'm bored of having korma.'

'Or maybe you're just bored of me,' Colin said nervously.

Joan said nothing and took a slurp of her beer. It had seemed like such a treat when Mo agreed to babysit, allowing her and Colin to have a long- awaited night out. However, she could now feel a rising guilt inside of her and wished they were home watching the Friday-night soaps instead.

'Is everything all right, Joanie? I know that the diabetes thing knocked you for six, but you just don't seem yourself at the moment.'

'I'm fine, pet. Just a bit tired, that's all.'

Joan looked at her husband's soft kind features, encased in his big round face. The crinkles around his eyes told the story of a life full of love and laughter, and she felt as if she was going to cry.

'We don't even have our Friday nights anymore,' Colin

went on. 'In fact, I can't even remember the last time we did have a shag. Is it because I've put on weight?'

'Don't be such a silly old fool. It's nothing, honestly.' The waiter placed the hot plates on the table.

'Actually, it isn't nothing, Col,' she suddenly blurted out. 'Look – just tell me straight: are you having an affair?'

If somebody had hit Colin in the face with an iron bar it would have hurt less.

'An affair?' He could barely get the words out. 'Joan, have you gone completely mad?'

'Well,' she spluttered. 'You are always working late, and sometimes you don't pick up your phone. In fact, I thought it was you who didn't want to have sex with me anymore. What's happening to us, Colin? We barely talk these days.'

Colin then started to laugh. In fact, he tipped his head back and guffawed so loudly that his big belly danced around and banged the table so hard it made the glasses clink. Other people in the restaurant were staring.

'Stand up, Joanie,' he commanded.

'No, I shan't.' She looked around her and felt embarrassed that he was causing a scene.

'Come on, you silly old mare.' He helped her up. Joan Brown made a quizzical face as her husband of ten years came to her side and led her from the table. She adjusted her bosom in the new red dress she had got from the charity shop that afternoon.

The maitre d' opened a door at the rear of the restaurant and Colin ushered his wife through to the back room of the curry house.

'SURPRISE!' shouted thirty grown-up and children's voices.

Clark, Kent and Skye covered her in party-popper ribbon, while Cissy slept face-down in her high chair in the corner. The DJ played 'Happy Birthday' by Altered

Images.

'Happy fortieth, my beautiful wife.' Colin grabbed her and gave her a big kiss.

Joan was dumbstruck.

'But it's not until next week,' she gasped.

'It was the only day I could get everyone together.'

Joan laughed and kissed him back. Then, she ran around joyfully greeting relatives and friends she hadn't seen for ages.

'Mo, I cannot believe you kept this quiet!' Joan squealed to her friend.

'It was bloody hard work. I nearly had to tell you. I mean, as if Colin would *ever* have an affair.'

'I know. It all makes sense now,' the birthday girl grinned.

'Of course it makes bloody sense,' Colin interrupted. 'Not only have I been working overtime to afford this extravaganza – I've had to be out of range of your flappy ears to allow me to talk to everyone.'

He picked her up and swung her around, his moon face growing redder as he did so.

'I love you, Mrs Brown.'

'And I love you, Mr Brown,' Joan squealed, nearly falling as Colin placed her down clumsily.

'Whoa there, birthday girl.' Charlie steadied her. 'You don't want to be doing gymnastics at your age, you know.'

Joan went as red as her husband. Ffion giggled. 'Don't be so rude, you.'

'I actually used to be good on the floor at primary school,' Joan blurted out.

'I bet you did,' Charlie winked. 'Now come on, Ffi, let's get a drink.'

'It'll take more than a Pinot Grigio to get me in that caravan with you,' the Welsh girl trilled, as Mo's eldest led her to the bar with a swagger.

'Somehow I doubt that,' Joan said under her breath.

'Your hair looks nice today,' Ron commented from his armchair as Mo buttoned up Rosie's coat ready for school.

Ffion had cut and coloured her hair for free as part of her beauty course and Mo had to admit to herself that it did take years off her. She also felt better in herself as she had still managed to keep the stone off she had lost before Christmas. However, it had been just too cold and dark to go walking in January and she was becoming concerned that she would be back at square one if she didn't get focused again soon.

'Thanks,' Mo said dismissively, although feeling slightly warmed by this first show of affection from her husband since he'd stopped drinking.

'I was thinking that I might walk down to the Job Centre today, you know. Just see what's about.'

'Good idea, love. Although you'd better get going quickly, by the look of this weather.'

'Snow!' Rosie shrieked. 'I'm so excited. Mummy, can I go outside and play?'

'No, I've got to get you to school, then get on to work. Come on, it's already settling on the pavements. You'd best wear your wellies.'

'They don't fit any more.'

Mo grimaced and made a mental note to delve into the Escape Fund at work and go shopping in her lunch break.

'See you later then, love.' Ron kissed his wife on the cheek and headed out into the white flakes that were now coming down hard and fast.

Biting her lip, Mo reached to touch her face. She felt awful thinking it, but she actually wished that Ron wasn't on his road to recovery. Yes, Charlie was right to bring things to a head, as she had been too weak to take control. But, she had got everything in place to leave the abusive alcoholic and now as each day passed and the drink left his system, Ron started to become his old reliable self. Which, in her eyes, left no justifiable reason to walk out of the door.

Yes, he had done and said some terrible things to her but Rosie seemed so much happier – and who gave her the right to take a daughter away from the father she so dearly loved?

'Mummeee!' Rosie was now chomping at the bit to get out in the snow. 'Come on. Shall I just wear my school shoes?'

'I tell you what, put your old trainers on for now and I'll see if I can get you some wellies later.'

'The forecast says we are to expect six inches today and they can't see it thawing before the weekend,' Ffion announced loudly as she strolled into the surgery half an hour late. 'Had to dig me bloody car out of the drive this morning, I did.' Then she whispered to Mo, 'Is the grim one in?'

'No, it's just me, you and Doctor D. She lives up the top of a hill evidently and felt it too risky to come in, in case she couldn't get back up it.'

'Whoopee, it's party-time then. In fact, we should be quiet all morning, as I bet loads of people will cancel,' the young Welsh girl trilled.

'Well, unless they get brought in with snow-related injuries,' Mo replied. Noah Anderson walked out of his room into the office area.

'They should go straight to A&E, in that case,' he commented.

'Yeah maybe,' Ffion replied, getting up to go to the kitchen and put the kettle on.

Once alone, the doctor put his hand on Mo's shoulder. 'How's it all going at home?'

'Fine,' Mo said in a non-committal fashion.

Since that dreadful night, once the initial mortification had worn off, she felt so much closer to him.

'Ron still going to the meetings?'

'Oh, yes. In fact, he was heading off to the Job Centre this morning.'

'Wow. That's great, Mo, isn't it?'

Mo faltered. 'There's so much water under the bridge, it's going to take time. I'm not quite ready to trust him.'

The doctor felt he couldn't pry any more. 'Well, if you need any advice or just a plain and simple chat, then I'm always here for you.'

'Thank you. I really do appreciate all you've done for us.'

'Your hair looks stunning, by the way,' he offered as he went back to his treatment room.

'He fancies you,' Ffion murmured, placing a tray of hot drinks on her desk. 'Don't be so bloody daft,' Mo scoffed. 'Next, you'll be telling me there's a knight on a white charger knocking down the door to whisk us both away.'

Ffion and Mo dealt with the many cancellations that came flooding in. The snow was coming down thicker than ever – a mesmerising white-out of slow motion flakes that settled neatly on everything that would let it.

'More tea, matey.' Ffion plonked a mug on Mo's desk, then scrabbled around in her drawer to reveal a packet of digestives. 'Biscuit?'

'No, ta. I'm on a mission to lose more weight before the summer comes,' Mo replied, without looking up from her game of Solitaire.

'Talking of losing, I feel *so* lost now Charlie has gone.' Ffion stuck out her bottom lip.

'Me too,' Mo concurred. 'But with the job market as it is, he couldn't refuse it when his boss realised he'd made a mistake. And anyway, in this weather he would have frozen to death in the Browns' caravan.'

'Yeah, I realise all of that.' Ffion sighed and sat down.

'Anyway, he's only in London. You'll still see him, won't you? And he's promised to come and see us a lot more regularly.'

'Yes, but probably only some weekends,' Ffion replied quietly.

'And Bruno?'

'Bruno who?' The youngster smirked.

'Well, that's good. As although I know my son is far from perfect where the ladies are concerned, I couldn't openly condone you two-timing him!'

A middle-aged man came to the hatch, wearing bright red wellies. Mo ushered him through to the doctor.

'That reminds me – I need to get some money out of my Escape Fund.' Mo started rooting around in her in-tray for the key to the cash-tin that was hidden in her bottom drawer. 'Have you seen it, Ffi, the little gold key that opens my cash tin?'

Ffion went a deep shape of pink.

Mo opened her bottom drawer to see if she had maybe left the key in the lock.

Ffion put her hand to her head.

'Mo, I'm so sorry – I think I may have made an unforgivable mistake.'

'Charlie?' Mo closed her eyes momentarily.

Ffion nodded. 'During all the commotion, he told me that you had asked him to come and collect the money.'

'All of it?'

Ffion nodded again.

'There was nine hundred pounds in there.'

'Oh Mo, I'm so sorry. Shall I call him? He may not pick up for you, if he thinks you've found out.'

The number you are calling is no longer registered, greeted Ffion's naïve young ears.

'I could try his workplace. Do you have the number, Mo?'

Mo stood up and put her arms around Ffi. 'I think the Denbury Dish total has just dropped a peg, love.'

Her son had just duped her again and she wasn't even angry. Nature – nurture? Nurture – nature? You can take the boy from his dad, she thought – but you can't always take the dad out of his boy.

Chapter Thirteen

Robbie clocked Gordon before he clocked him. He walked up behind him at the classroom door and whispered, 'Don't scream or you're outed,' whilst slyly pinching his bum.

Gordon felt a shiver run through him, and then composing himself, he said coolly, 'Hi, Robbie, how you doing ? Happy New Year and all that.'

'Yeah, good, thanks. Sorry I've not been in touch. I had a couple of weeks off after Christmas and you know what mums are like. Mine insisted on feeding me up like next year's turkey before I left.' The blank face of his mother flashed through his mind, as Gordon laughed.

'Yeah, mums eh.'

'Well, I'm glad you're here today as it saves me a phone call. Fancy a drink sometime this week?'

'Yeah, OK. I'm on standby for the next three days, but if this weather holds out I don't think anything will be going from Heathrow.' So much for him being strong and telling Robbie to pee off when he eventually made contact, Gordon thought.

Robbie scribbled on the back of a receipt. 'Here, take my number. Just let me know when's good for you.'

Mo in her lateness tried to run up to Rosie's class slipped in the wet snow and fell flat on her back. The tread on her shoes was so worn that she struggled to get up.

'Like a bloody stag beetle,' Emily Pritchard announced to no one in particular.

'At least they have a backbone,' Joan sniped back,

rushing to her friend's side. 'Are you OK, love?'

'Just my pride a little bruised, I think. Thanks God Rosie didn't see me – she'd have died of embarrassment.' Both women laughed.

Dana appeared in her snow boots and fur-lined silver hooded anorak. She felt unusually tired and put it down to the IVF drugs. She was thankful of the 4x4 today, as there was no way they could easily get up the hill to their house otherwise.

The little people rushed around grabbing coats and food boxes, chattering with excitement at their impending journeys home in the snow. Mr Chambers came to the door and checked out whose parents had arrived.

'It's highly likely we may not open tomorrow if the forecast is to be believed,' he announced, the loud cheering of his charges behind him drowning out the groans of several parents.

'Please keep checking the school website. Hopefully we'll get an early decision and a text out to all so nobody has a wasted journey.'

'Thanks, Mr Chambers,' Emily Pritchard said obsequiously, just as Joan imagined the stuck-up old bag would have slimed up to her own teachers at school.

'Right – Lily, Lola, Josh, Rosie – come on. You've all got homes to go to,' the teacher continued.

Dana noticed Mo rubbing her back.

'If anyone who's walked here would like a lift, I've got room for three more,' the pretty Czech announced.

Mo recognised Dana from the café and said gratefully, 'Ooh, yes, please.'

'Oh, you saviour,' Emily Pritchard announced loudly. 'Joshy, Petula and I would just love a lift. This snow is just so ghastly.'

'Too late – I'm full. Sorry, Emily,' Dana said with complete joy.

'Now who was it sang "The Long and Winding Road",

Mo?' Joan joked, gathering her brood for the chilly walk home.

Alana finished off her conference call with the German venue, sat back on her study chair and let out a big sigh. Thank heavens for technology, she thought. At least she could be ill in the comfort of her own home and still not fall behind with work – especially as there was a big launch coming up in Berlin. Sadie from SM Public Relations was doing a fine job but without Stephen at the helm, Alana lacked confidence in the whole event.

She crossed another day off her calendar and tears pricked her eyes. Not long now and he would be back from wherever he was. She had imagined all sorts of scenarios. Stephen being ill. His wife being ill. Maybe a breakdown at the fact that he hadn't been involved with bringing up his own child. She couldn't bear to think that he had turned his back on her and Eliska, even though after the way she had behaved he had every right to. But, no – he was too strong for that, wasn't he?

She put her hand on her abdomen. And now there was another little baby on the way. A little baby, and even she couldn't be sure who the daddy was. She ruffled her hair as if to clear her thoughts. Right now, the baby was just a little bundle of cells inside of her and it would be far too complicated and selfish to even consider going ahead with this pregnancy.

She turned to her computer and did a search for private clinics. Just as she was about to pick up the phone to make an appointment, the front door bell rang.

'Mummeee!' Eliska belted through the front door. 'Can Tommy come for tea and make a snowman?'

'What – now, sweetheart?'

'He's in the car.' She opened the front door more widely and waved vigorously at Dana's silver 4x4. Alana thought of all the times that Dana had been her saviour, so

137

she gave in.

'All right then, but we'll have to get a take-away. I've got no food in.' Dana walked carefully up the icy path and stopped in the porch.

'Sorry it's such short notice, but Eliska was insistent it was Tommy's turn to come to you.'

'It's fine. I'm just a bit confused to see you as Robbie was supposed to be getting her.'

'He did. I just dropped Mo and Rosie off, saw Robbie and Eliska walking – or should I say skidding in the snow – so dropped him at the Youth Centre and came straight here. He said he was going to text you.'

'He probably did. I've been on a call.'

Dana suddenly went very pale and very quiet. She put her hand to her forehead.

'Sorry Alana, can I come in? Suddenly feel a bit dizzy,' she said quietly.

Alana ushered her to the kitchen table and put a glass of water down next to her. She caught a glimpse of Tommy and Eliska through the window, running around like mad things throwing snowballs at each other.

Dana took a sip of water and sat upright. 'That's better. Thanks. How embarrassing.'

'Not pregnant, are you?' Alana said instinctively.

'I wish, I wish,' Dana replied. 'I've been trying for a long time now, after Tommy. I think I'm just a bit tired, that's all. Always in three places at one time, me.'

'Oh, right,' was all Alana could muster, feeling already that too much had been said. 'Well, if you're OK now, sorry to rush you off but I have another quick call to make and then I shall order the children some tea. I'll ring for a taxi for Tommy later – it's too damn snowy to drive.'

Dana was horrified at the other woman's uncaring attitude but didn't show it. 'It's fine. I've got to pick Mark up from the station at seven, so I'll drop by then and get him.'

Dana got into her car, thinking how glad she was that she hadn't confided in Alana about the dizziness being caused by the IVF. She was more than happy to give anyone a chance and yes, she wanted to make new friends. But Alana Murray was a hard icicle to melt and Dana didn't have the energy at the moment to even want to try.

Alana went straight to her study and picked up the house phone.

'Good afternoon, the Salisbury Clinic, Rene speaking, how can I help?' the posh voice at the end relayed.

The elated screams of Eliska and Tommy playing caught Alana's ear. 'Oh, er, sorry – wrong number.'

Alana put her hand to her stomach, tears rolling down her face. She keyed in Stephen's number. The mobile you are calling is switched off.

'Where are you?' she shouted to the air. 'Where the bloody hell are you?'

'Kat and Alfie won't stop fighting, Daddy,' Lily screeched from the bedroom. 'And Lola won't let me play with them.'

Gordon raised his eyebrows at Inga and put down the newspaper he was reading. Lola came tearing into the lounge showing off a small scratch on her hand.

'Lily made Kat scratch me,' Lola whined.

'Right, that's it.' Gordon got up. 'Lily, in here now.'

Inga gathered both girls on her lap as Gordon headed to the bedroom.

As he pushed open the door, the black tom shimmied up the pink curtains and the smaller prettier tortoiseshell just looked at him as if to say, 'Wasn't me.'

Gordon retrieved them both and shut them in the kitchen and walked back into the lounge to address his girls. 'Right, you two. You are very lucky to have Kat and Alfie. You know that I didn't really want any more pets, so you must play nicely with them, do you hear?'

'Yes, Daddy,' they said in unison.

'No wonder they fight if all they've got to go on is you two monkeys shouting at each other. You must set them a better example. The kittens are in the kitchen for now having their tea, so leave them be for a bit, OK?'

'OK,' they chorused.

'I'm hungry,' Lily piped up.

'Dinner eez in half an hour,' Inga told her.

Gordon started to laugh when the twins were out of sight.

'I can see why Chris hot-footed it now. It isn't easy, this parenting lark, now is it?'

Inga laughed back. 'Gordon, kittens eez nothing. Wait until it's boys they are fighting over.'

Her voice softened. 'Any news from Chris?'

'Yes, actually. The Christmas card that I showed you, and an email last week. He's moved back in with his brother in Toronto as a base for now.'

'Do you still miss him?'

'Of course, but it's getting easier. Time is a healer, that's for sure. The girls rarely mention him now.'

'You gotta fight, fight fight fight fight for this love,' Inga sang.

'Don't give up your day job, will you. No, there's no need to fight. He will always have a place in my heart. He's moved on and I have to respect that.'

'And there are just so many men and so little of the time.'

'You saying I'm a slut or something, Inga Gowenska?' They both laughed. 'Talking of sluts,' Gordon continued. 'Can you babysit on Thursday? I thinkit's time that little ol' me had some fun.'

'I'm signing up for Weight Busters on Thursday,' Mo announced as she and Joan marched around the park. 'It's the only way I am going to lose more weight: shame myself into it. You up for it?'

'Ooh I don't know,' Joan grimaced.

'Oh come on, if it's too awful we can just stop going. And I've chosen one in Micklehurst, so we are unlikely to bump into anyone we know.'

'I've heard that if you put on even a pound they make you strip naked and beat you with cheese straws,' Joan sniggered.

'Maybe we should make a film of that and sell it at the school fete – imagine old Preachy Knickers' face,' Mo said.

'She'd probably want to star in it with those knockers.'

They both giggled like schoolgirls. Cissy joined in from her pushchair.

'Here, let me take her.' Mo took the handles. 'Increases the heart-rate, evidently.'

Rosie, Clark, Kent and Skye shrieked as they did relays down the slide. 'It's good to see you laughing, Mo.'

'It's good to laugh. Although on a serious note, Joanie, I'm actually in a dilemma.'

'Oh, what is it?'

'Well, it's good that Ron has stopped drinking but I was foolish thinking that it would be plain sailing. He's so agitated at night and when he does eventually go to bed, his sleep is so disturbed that he wakes me all of the time. He still has night sweats and I know he's really trying not to be, but he's so bloody moody. I've been cooking him lots of nice food to compensate for the lack of alcohol, but he pushes it away saying he's not hungry half the time.'

'Oh, Mo.'

'And do you know what the worst thing is?'

'Go on,' Joan urged.

'I am sick and tired of looking after him. I just want someone to worry about me and Rosie for a change. One day, it would be just so lovely to come home to a cooked meal, a bunch of flowers or even just a bloody cup of tea.

I've been treading on eggshells for years now – and yes, I know that alcoholism is a disease, but he's hurt me, Joan. He's hit me. He's scared Rosie and I've just about had enough.'

'Is the Escape Fund still going?' Joan enquired.

Mo started pushing Cissy faster at the thought of her son failing her. She let out a big sigh.

'There is no Escape Fund. Charlie took it.'

'Mo, I can't believe you sometimes.'

'Oh no, I didn't give it to him. He took it without me knowing and then upped and left back to London. It probably paid his rent somewhere or got him a few eighths of pot.'

Joan felt herself squirm as Mo went on.

'My Charlie may be a pretty face, Joanie, but with one bat of those long lashes and a flash of that perfect smile, he could strip a girl bare of both her clothes and her wallet. I've lost count of the times that I've had to bail him out.'

'I would never ever have guessed. He always treated me so well,' Joan said, chastened and only now realising the enormity of her own misdemeanour withthe young lad.

'He was living rent-free and you were cooking his dinners, of course he did,' Mo replied curtly. 'But you love 'em unconditionally, don't you? He's not a bad kid really and he's still only young. Let's hope knowledge and experience will teach him some respect. Because a good clip round the ear and countless heart-to-hearts haven't worked before.'

Both ladies were becoming quite short of breath as they started their third lap.

Joan was more than happy to keep pressing about Charlie. The more distance between him and everyone, the better now. Perish the thought of him ever telling all.

'Have you tackled him about the money yet, then?'

'No, he's changed his number. Ffion was obviously getting too clingy.'

'Chip off the old block, eh?' Joan winced, 'Sorry, Mo, that was out of order.'

'Actually, I can't agree or disagree. Ron isn't Charlie's dad.'

'Oh – my – God!' Joan exclaimed in slow motion. 'Bloody hell, Mo Collins, you're a dark horse.'

'It's not something to shout about, is it really. I've kept it to myself until this year. But I know I can trust you, Joan.'

Joan felt slightly sick.

'So, he is a chip off the old block really, I guess,' Mo concluded after telling Joan the whole story. His dad had been a tearaway. A beautiful, dark-haired lovable rogue.

'He had the face of an angel, but the mind of a devil,' she said dreamily. 'But how I loved that boy. I've never ever known sex like it. Full body-and-soul stuff. I know we were only young but the passion was incredible. In fact, I cannot believe that at seventeen I was sensible enough to let my head rule my heart and make the decision to tell Ron that he was Charlie's father.'

'Have you ever thought of contacting him?

'God no! I've got enough drama in my life without opening up another can of worms. Sometimes I think it's better to keep quiet about certain things and I know for sure this is one of them.'

Mo went on ruefully, 'Charlie would never forgive me and I couldn't bear to ever lose him, as much as he drives me to distraction sometimes.'

Joan went quiet.

'You OK, Joanie?'

'Yes, fine – was just thinking. You're right. Sometimes it is so much better never to tell. You only salve your own guilt by opening up to others, and that is selfish. If there's no need to hurt someone else, then don't.'

It started spotting with rain.

'Come on, kids,' Joan shouted across the park to the

143

children. 'Home time.'

Mo smiled down at a now – sleeping Cissy. 'Thanks for listening, Joan.'

'Hey, that's what friends are for.' She squeezed Mo's arm and prayed that Charlie Collins would never ever divulge her own dirty little secret.

Chapter Fourteen

'P Day tomorrow isn't it?' Mark announced over breakfast.

'Yes.' Dana couldn't actually believe that Mark, being a typical man, had actually remembered the date.

'Do you feel any different?'

'Boobs are a bit sore and I'm feeling a bit tired, but nothing different to usual really.' Dana played it down. She actually did feel a little bit nauseous this morning and the excitement was welling inside of her. She couldn't wait to confirm her pregnancy. She had enjoyed every little twinge she had felt with Tommy. Such was the love she had felt for her unborn child, she had even delighted in seeing her slim tummy expanding day by day.

Mark got up, stood behind her and wrapped his arms around her tiny waist. He kissed her on the neck. 'I just know that you are.'

'Yuk.' Tommy dropped his spoon in to his cereal bowl with a loud clink. 'Why don't you get a room.' And with that he got up and skulked to his bedroom, leaving both Dana and Mark open-mouthed.

The next morning, Dana awoke at 5a.m. Later, reliving this moment over and over in her head, she could scarcely believe she had actually managed to get to sleep. Deep down, she just knew she was pregnant and the test was merely a formality.

She thought back to when she did the test for Tommy. It had been such wrong timing but she had been so in love with Mark, that she knew that whatever happened, everything would be OK.

IVF was a funny phenomenon. There were no surprises. Everything was regimented. You knew the day of conception exactly. You knew the precise day to do the test. There could be no surprises on your due date.

She opened the white box that was already set on the side of the sink and pulled out one of the two tests. She had ummed and aahed about getting just one test but it was only an extra pound for a second go so she thought she might as well – just in case she couldn't wait until the correct day of testing.

She reread the instructions, held the stick in the warm stream of strong early morning pee, pulled up her knickers and began the longest wait a woman ever has to face.

These days there wasn't even the uncertainty of a faint blue line. No need to hold the white plastic wand of fate up to the light, no need to wait just a minute more to see if the line got darker, the longer you left it. No, these days the words NOT PREGNANT screamed out from the test. Relief if that was the desired state. Devastation if it wasn't.

Dana sat on the side of the bath. She felt numb. She felt sick. She felt desperate. All that anticipation. All that excitement. She has been so sure that she was expecting a girl. They had even chosen a name – Scarlet Elizabeth.

Her sobbing was as loud as the pain in her heart.

'Oh darling,' Mark opened the door, knelt down and nestled his wife's head to his chest. 'Why didn't you wait for me before you did it?'

'I was just so sure,' Dana blubbed. 'I'm sorry I'm so useless – and what a waste of all that money.'

'Don't be so silly. You are not useless. We have one beautiful son together and Sidney loves you too. If that is what our family is to be, then that's it.'

Dana wished she could look at things so clearly but she couldn't. All those injections, scans and invasive procedures, for what?

She longed for another baby and nothing anyone said could change her mind.

Emily Pritchard – Head of PTA, Netball Coach and Mother of Joshua P seven, chief swot and playground kisser – noticed Dana's husband dropping young Tommy off.

'Pregnant at last, is she?' Emily sneered with no grounds at all for her comment other than school-gates gossip.

Mark Knight was horrified. 'No, Emily, not pregnant, just unwell and I'd rather you kept personal comments like that to yourself in future.'

The unpleasant woman teetered smugly back to her convertible as Tommy waved wildly to his dad from inside his classroom.

Alana had also overhead the comment and had jumped at the word pregnant. Still no word from Stephen either. Thank God he was due to return to work tomorrow. She would drive to his office if necessary.

'All set for tonight?' Joan patted Mo on the arm.

'For three months of misery eating just dust, you mean?' Mo laughed. 'I am eating as many biscuits and crisps as I can today before the weigh-in so at least next week I'll be in with a chance of losing something.'

'Oh, Mo.'

'Oh nothing, Joanie. I am so up for the big dress drop challenge, but just give me one little day of pleasure as I know it's going to be hell on a bread stick.'

Inga stood at the end of the school drive and kissed the twins on their foreheads. 'See you later. Remember we are at Joshua's tonight as I am babysitting you all.'

'Cool,' the girls piped up together.

'So your agreed goal weight is ten and a half stone then, Mo – smashing, smashing.' Sally, the weirdly rather large

Weight Busters team leader, with thick, long dark hair and even thicker eyeliner, had a very enthusiastic voice.

'Smashing, smashing,' Joan mocked behind her back.

'And yours is, now what shall we say.. .ten stone, Joan? Realistic and smashing, yes smashing.'

'Smashing,' repeated Joan. 'We really are raring to go, aren't we, Mo?'

Mo was feeling decidedly queasy after all the goodies she had consumed at work and nodded slowly, trying not to burp.

'Now ladies, I suggest you stay for the meeting so you can pick up any hints and tips from our other lovely Weight Busters. Welcome to the group,' her voice went up an octave, 'and remember, ladies, what are wheat and fats?'

'The foods of Satan!' everyone in the room shouted together.

Joan looked at Mo and made a face at this comment. Blimey, maybe they did beat you to death with bread sticks if you went off course.

They chatted quietly as they sat in a semi-circle of chairs waiting for everyone to be weighed. The actual recipe sheets they had been given didn't actually look too calorie sparing, maybe this wasn't going to be as hard as Mo thought.

Feeling slightly bored, Joan looked over at the weigh-in queue. The only man in the room put his socked feet onto the scales. Mo craned forward to take a closer look. No! It couldn't be, surely! Her heart did a 100-mile dash around her ribs, causing her to heave in a deep intake of breath.

Those velvety brown eyes, with to-die-for lashes, were now set in a much fatter face but were still framed by that recognisable black curly hair. Even steely, smashing Sally Curtis was getting giggly at his obvious flirtation.

'Joan, we have to go.'

'Eh? Why?'

'Now!' Mo's voice sounded alien.

Joan had to wait until they were safely on the train back to Denbury before she could get any sense out of her obviously troubled friend.

'So come on, what the deuce is wrong with you? I mean, I know they weren't all our sort of people but I think it would have made sense to stay.'

'It was him. Standing there, bold as brass.'

'Who, Mo?'

'After twenty-four years. I can't believe it. I really can't believe it.'

'Are you sure you haven't been eating some sort of opiates with your cakes today?'

'Joanie, it was Charlie's dad!'

'Oh my God, how weird is that? I thought he lived miles away.'

'To be honest, I hadn't even thought about his life now.'

'It's quite lovely really,' Joan added. 'I mean, what's the chance of bumping into your childhood sweetheart after all those years?'

'Sweet is not the word for Charlie Lake. And if I was going to bump into him again, it would have been nice to have happened somewhere more romantic than a bloody fat club.'

Mo turned to her friend. 'I'm not joking, but even after all this time my heart literally leaped.'

'Aw, maybe you should have spoken to him, not run a million miles an hour to get away from him then.'

'No. I can't talk to him. I mean, what would I say? He knew nothing of Charlie and I can't just make idle chat with the man. I could so see my boy in him, it was ridiculous. So bloody typical that he's the only man with all those women. He hasn't changed – still a womaniser, albeit a fatter one now.'

'So, does that mean that after all this effort we won't be

going back to Weight Busters next week?'

'Hmm. I've got a week to worry about it now. Let's get home and eat some dust – I'm starving.'

'Come on, Mo, it's not that bad. Mushroom omelette and salad we can have tonight, that's all right.'

'All right? That's smashing.' They both laughed. 'Thanks for always supporting me, Joanie.'

'I believe that's what friends are for. Now, no cheating, you.'

Mo pushed open the lounge door – no sign of Ron. She was so used to seeing him slumped drunk on the sofa, it felt strange.

She went straight up to Rosie's bedroom and there he was sitting by the little girl's bed, stroking her hair and reading her a bedtime story. He looked up and smiled a smile Mo had not seen for quite some time.

Maybe, just maybe she had made the right decision all those years ago after all.

'Mummy, your tummy bug is lasting a long time. Maybe you should go and see a doctor.' Eliska faced Alana as she came out of the toilet after being sick for the fifth time that morning.

'Oh darling, let me give it another day. I will be able to take you to school again though, so that's a good thing.'

'Yeah!' Eliska spun around in the hallway. Since Stephen's harsh words about her parenting skills, and their bonding trip to Lapland, Alana had really been trying to make an effort with her one and only.

Today was the day and she couldn't be sure that it wasn't nerves that were actually making her sick this morning. She would get Eliska to school, she decided, then she would call. She had never missed anyone like she had missed Stephen over the past few weeks, and she couldn't work out if this was a good feeling to have or not. She so

150

hated being out of control. It was so against her grain.

Alana put the kettle on. A ginger tea would settle her queasiness. Talking of ginger, she was probably the only mother alive to be literally praying that the little child growing within her did have ginger hair. She so didn't want it to be the product of a one-night stand with that Italian Stallion at Rosco's. In her own mind, she didn't think that it was a one-night stand with Stephen because she knew him so well and he was, after all, the father of her firstborn. And, in being away from him for so long, she experienced something which she hadn't felt for years. She felt love.

She truly, properly loved this good, kind man. In fact, if she knew one hundred per cent that the baby was Stephen's there would be no doubt in her mind that she would want to keep it. A little brother or sister for Eliska would make her daughter so happy and then the chance of her being with Stephen would be much greater.

The turmoil within in her was so great but until that little bundle appeared, how would she know whose baby it was? She literally had slept with Bruno and Stephen days apart. Oh why oh why did she not think to use a condom? Bloody drink! Bloody stupidity.

And, that was the other thing, to be blessed with getting pregnant naturally in her forties. She touched her tummy. How could she even think of not having this gift of a child?

She poured the hot water over her tea bag, opened her lap top and let out a deep breath. She checked her phone to see if he had rung her, but there were no missed calls. She tentatively logged in and found plenty of emails from SM Public Relations but not one from Mr S. McNair.

How come this man had managed to turn her into a blithering wreck? Alana Murray always knew what to say or do. She looked at a bottle of red wine on the kitchen side – then told herself not to be such a stupid cow. Drink had never been the right answer to anyone's question, especially now.

And then, it happened. The delicious, heart-thumping feeling that only the name of someone you really love showing on your phone screen can bring.

'Alana, it's me. We need to talk.'

Chapter Fifteen

'I've tried most things but never fucked a Daddy before.'

'Ssh, let's not let the whole block know that before we get inside.' Gordon staggered to the door and attempted to put the key in the lock.

Robbie came up behind him and pushed forward so they literally fell into the hallway.

'Quick, get up, I've got to unset the alarm.' Gordon staggered up. 'Strange, it's not on.'

He heard laughter coming from Inga's room. Even weirder, as she was supposed to be at the Pritchards' babysitting at a sleepover with the twins and Joshua.

He ran down the corridor and threw open the door to find a very startled, naked Inga and a red-faced Kenneth Pritchard, husband of Emily Pritchard – Head of PTA, Netball Coach and Mother of Joshua P… tied securely to Inga's bedhead with a pair of pink fluffy handcuffs.

He slammed the door immediately before Inga tore out in her slinky purple dressing-gown.

'Gordon, I eez so sorry. It is only ten thirty, I thought you would be much later and we'd be gone by the time you came home.'

'Inga, I don't care who you bring here and shag as long as the girls aren't here, but my big question is why you are not with Lily and Lola?'

'They are with Emily. Kenny and Emily came home from the party early as she was not feeling well. Lola had forgotten Teddy and wouldn't settle without him, so Kenny gave me a lift to get him and then…'

Robbie was by Gordon's side.

'And then the babysitter shagged the married man – how clichéd.'

At that moment, Kat and Alfie started fighting, and caught Robbie's ankle with one of their claws.

'Ow! You little fuckers. Right – I'm getting myself a drink whilst you sort your domestic out, Gordon.' He sloped off to the kitchen.

Gordon drew Inga to him and kissed her forehead. 'I mean, how H.O.T, is he?! I don't blame you, girl. And imagine if self-righteous old Preachy Knickers found out – that'd be bloody hilarious.'

'She mustn't.' Inga was completely serious.

'As if! Mum's the word, darling.' Gordon began to sober up slightly. 'So, I still don't understand what's happening. Are you going back to the Pritchards' to stay even though they are home?'

'Yep. I said you had friends staying over and there was no room for us as that had been the original plan. So go get your rocks off, baby.' She patted his bum gently. 'I best release my captive and convince him his little or should I say big secret is safe.'

The sex was hard and fast. Gordon needed to unleash his pent-up sexual frustration and the experienced Robbie took charge at every opportunity he could.

When it was over, Robbie jumped up, saying huskily, 'A little more champagne and then there's more of where that came from. I forgot I've got some poppers in my bag too.'

Gordon watched his young lover's naked butt hungrily as he walked out of the room.

Robbie returned with two beers to find Gordon on the phone.

'No, no it's fine, they must come back then. It's OK, I can send a taxi now. Get them both ready and I'll see you soon. Little poppet.'

'What the fuck?' Robbie screwed his face up; his Mancunian accent seemed even stronger when he was drunk.

'Lilly's got a stomach bug, keeps crying for me. She wants to come home. I'm so sorry.'

'It's one a.m., come on. Surely she can just wait it out until the morning?'

Gordon sighed. 'This is what fucking a daddy is like, I'm afraid. Come here.'

'No, you're all right. I'll ring myself a cab. Thanks and all that.'

06.30. The alarm went off in the Knight bedroom and Mark sleepily pressed snooze. Dana was awake already, lying on her side looking at the wall. Tears streaked her cheeks. Mark spooned against her, kissed her cheek and felt the wetness on them. He hugged her tightly.

'Oh, baby girl, I love you so much. Please don't be sad. There are other options, you know.'

She squirmed round to face him. 'I was hoping maybe we could have another go at IVF. I mean, it doesn't always work first time and we were told there is nothing wrong with either of us, so there is a high chance it will work a second time.'

'We have to realistic though, darling. People can try and try for years and it is five thousand pounds a go for the privilege. You never know – it still may just happen naturally. I'm on the zinc now. Those sperm of mine will be like torpedoes.'

'I knew it! I knew it was just about the money.'

'Hey, Dana. Calm down. You know that money is not an issue.'

'Well, it doesn't bloody sound like that to me – and shut that alarm up!'

'You're just hormonal. See sense, woman!'

Mark hit snooze again as Dana shot out of bed and

went to her jewellery safe in the spare room.

'Here!' She threw two thousand pounds in ten-pound notes on to the bed. 'I have my own money, see?'

'Oh right. So... where did you get this? Been squirrelling your house-keeping away, have you?'

'No, Mark. I have a job. A proper job that pays me money. A little bit of independence. I don't want to rely on you for everything.'

'A job? When, where, how?'

'You don't like it, do you, when you can't control me? You really upset me when you said a few months ago that being a mother was just like being an au-pair. I need more in my life than that, Mark.'

'And you think having another baby will give you more? You'll be even more trapped.'

'But it will make me feel complete.' She bit her lip. 'I think.'

'"I think"! So you don't even bloody know what you want. Where is this job then?'

'In the café on the high street. I'm a waitress.'

'A bloody waitress! No wife of mine is going to work in a café. You could have picked something a little bit more upmarket.'

Tommy appeared at the door. 'Mummy, is it time for school?'

'Yes, yes, darling. Get in the shower quickly now, and what would you like for your breakfast?'

When the little boy had scuttled off, Mark said nastily, 'So, does Tommy know?'

'Nobody knows, except for a couple of mums at the school but they are not the gossipy type and it wouldn't bother them anyway. They are all realistic about life. Not stuck up on this posh hill without any money worries to care about.'

Dana began to cry. 'I was actually saving so I could take you away on a lovely weekend break. To prove I wasn't just your au-pair.'

Mark went to hug her.

She pushed him away. 'But now I thought I can put it towards the IVF. It is so important to me, Mark, to have another baby; it is all-consuming.'

'And, that's the problem, darling. If you could take a step back and see what you already have, then you wouldn't need to feel this angst about another child.'

'Arggh! You just don't understand.'

'You're right, I don't and I'm sorry. Do you know what, maybe this job isn't a good thing either. Perhaps you are too tired and stressed to get pregnant. I think you should leave it. You can't deny, it's just not the same in the bedroom anymore.'

Too hurt to even reply to this, Dana pushed past him to go and see to Tommy. He had done it again. He had called her bluff. Taken control. His little wifey could put her pinny on and be at his beck and call.

Surely then, he would want her to have another child so she was tied to the house again. He had put her in a complete head spin. But he was right: their love-making wasn't fun or sexy or spontaneous any more. It was purely functional – and that wasn't right either.

She didn't want to give up her job as much as she did want to have another baby.

She would power-walk to the school after work today, Dana decided. She had to get her thoughts straight.

It seemed weird to have Stephen McNair sitting in her kitchen. She had only ever seen him in the office or in a posh hotel, and here he was an ornament among her real life. Pictures drawn by Eliska on the fridge; a few dirty cups on the side and the washing machine whirring. This reality check didn't seem right. The fragrant perfume and aftershave, the best clothes – the laughing, drinking, fucking and fun that the irresponsibility of an affair

157

brought – it was all missing here.

All missing – but she had never been more pleased to see anyone in her whole life.

'Coffee?' she offered sombrely.

'Yes, please. Black.'

She sat down opposite him. She had put on jeans and a crisp white shirt but had made sure her hair and make-up were perfect. He, also in jeans, and a casual black cashmere jumper, looked absolutely worn out.

'So. Been somewhere nice?' Alana had so not wanted to sound like a sarcastic bitch and cringed at her opening gambit.

'Lani, please just let me talk.'

'Yes, yes.' She put her hand on his and he quickly moved it away.

'Susan is dead.'

Alana gasped. 'Oh, darling – no!'

'She had decided that it wasn't fair for me to live with someone who was so unwell and who couldn't produce a family or even make love with me. She was like that, you see. My wife put everybody above herself and that is why I loved her so much.

'I think she realised that day at Waterloo station that Eliska was mine. She saw the resemblance, understood the situation and wanted to set me free.' His eyes filled with tears and Alana just wanted to comfort him. He got up and began pacing around the kitchen.

'So what happened?' Alana asked gently.

'She arranged to fly out to stay with her sister Cheri in Cyprus. Of course I got the next flight I could and went over to see her, to tell her not be so stupid. To tell her that I had meant my wedding vows with all my heart and was with her in sickness and in health, till death us do part.' A little sob came from his throat.

'Here, come and sit back down.' Alana led him back to the kitchen table. 'She was dead when I got there. Had said her goodnights to Cheri and her girls and then took a massive overdose of her painkillers. And now I feel so fucking guilty that I slept with you. Because if I hadn't, she never would have seen our daughter. God, it sounds so strange, saying that. "Our daughter". A human being created out of anything but love. Just pure filthy lust. I hate myself right now.'

'Oh Stephen, you don't know if that was the reason why she did it. You really mustn't blame yourself – or me. It won't change anything. And Susan is at peace now, no more pain.'

'Don't even say her name. You knew nothing of her,' Stephen snarled. 'You could never even be half the woman that she ever was.'

Ouch. A left hook would have hurt less, Alana thought, suddenly feeling sick and putting her hand to her stomach.

'I really am truly sorry though. What a tragic thing to happen.'

'I must go.' Stephen shivered. 'Do you not have heating in this bloody house?'

'Must you leave?' She went over to the wall and twisted the heating dial. 'I mean, is there nothing else you want to say to me?'

'I wanted to discuss Eliska's maintenance and how we are going to deal with this whole damn situation.'

'I don't want your money, Stephen, I said that before.'

'But maybe now is the time for Eliska to know she has a father.'

'Even if you despise her mother? I'm not sure how that's going to work really.'

'And also I want to shut down all communications as your PR agency.'

'Hmm, that's a shocker. So you don't want to work with me or have anything to do with me, but you'd quite like my daughter to know she has a father. This is all too much for me to take in, Stephen. I really don't think you've thought this through.'

'Oh, come on, Lani. You're as hard as nails, you are. If it's like a business arrangement, you'll work it out somehow.'

Hormones and emotions suddenly started to slush around her body, and big ploppy tears started to fall slowly down her cheeks.

'You actually don't know anything about me, do you, Stephen? The truth is I missed you. I missed you so bloody much, it literally hurt. Every time my phone rang I prayed it was you. I literally counted down the days when you would be back at work. I know I haven't been the best parent or even the best person in the world, but if you were to just give me a chance...'

Stephen was startled by her reaction.

'Give you a chance? What are you saying to me, Lani?'

Alana took a deep breath. 'I think I'm saying that I love you, Stephen.'

'Love! You wouldn't know what love was if it bit you in the fucking arse!' He stood up, furious once more. 'I shall sort out terminating our contract with you and we shall talk again re Eliska when things aren't quite so raw. Goodbye, Alana.'

Feeling a rush of cold air as the door slammed shut, Alana ran to the toilet to be sick.

Chapter Sixteen

'I wish we'd chosen to lose weight in the summer, Joan, it's bloody Baltic tonight.' Mo and Joan, head-torches blazing, were marching around the perimeter road of the park.

'But what do exercise points mean, Mo?'

'They mean pies, duckie – extra pies.'

Joan laughed. 'I was thinking more like maybe an extra banana, but pies does sound a better option.'

'I've been meaning to ask you how it's going at home. Now the party is out of the way, has Colin Barrell upped his sexual prowess?'

'Like a panther now, he is – waits to pounce on me every Friday. It was just a blip. I love my old man, you know that.'

'I so wish I had what you have. I can't even remember the last time I had sex with Ron, but to be honest I'd be horrified if he suggested it.'

'So, you haven't even done it since he's been off the booze then?'

'No, he's still really agitated and has night sweats and I just don't fancy him.'

'Oh, Mo. What are we going to do with you?'

'I really don't know. He is being so good with Rosie at the moment. I got home from Weight Busters and he was even reading her a story and being really loving.'

'Maybe you should just have a passionate affair with Charlie's dad? You said how good he was in bed.'

'Imagine! He's probably married and we are both so fat at the moment it would be like elephants at it – vile. I have trouble getting naked in front of myself let alone anyone else. And anyway, you know I can't have anything to do with him as I don't want him to know about Charlie. It would be unfair on him and my boy, and if I got close to him, he would have to know.'

'Sometimes to find happiness you have to reach out and grab it though, Mo. Life rarely comes to you. You have to find the right path to go down. It just takes some people longer than others, that's all.'

'I've come across too many dead-ends, that's my problem,' puffed Mo.

'Well, you're taking a step in the right direction now by exercising. Yourskin is looking great now, and when Ffion does your hair you look a million dollars.'

'Aw, listen to you. I'll be marrying a Hollywood A-lister yet.'

'Well, I hear Tom Cruise is on the market again.'

'Too short,' Mo snorted.

'Yeah, and you'll have to become religious,' Joan added as they laughed their way to the park gate.

'Hi, Inga.' Emily Pritchard came running up to her outside the twins' classroom. 'Any chance of babysitting Friday night? Kenneth and I are going out for a meal.'

'Er…'

'We will get you home safe as usual.'

'Let me just check with Gordon as I do not know his flights yet.' This was a complete lie. Inga, despite the satisfying prospect of playing with Kenny's huge appendage again, just wasn't sure if she wanted to carry on having sex with a married man.

Dana power-walked up to the school gates. Mark had really upset her this morning but he had also given her a lot of food for thought. Maybe she had just got tied up in the whole second-baby thing. Felt it was what she should do, rather than what she wanted. She nodded to Alana, who gave her a weak smile. Eliska was such a handful as an only child, Dana thought, but that was probably because her mother was a single working parent. Tommy was such a lovely kid and he did have Sidney, who he was very close to and who quiteoften holidayed with them.

She realised how much she liked her job and the independence it brought her. It got her out of just being a glorified au-pair and if she was honest she had always hated housework anyway. Maybe she should just do as Mark said and get a cleaner. Do a bit more for herself.

But did she just like her job because of the lovely boys she worked for? She didn't want to dwell on that thought.

'Mummy!' Tommy flew out of the classroom with Eliska hot on his heels. 'Can Eliska stay for tea? Please say yes! She's got a new Mario Carts game on her console – perleease.'

Alana overheard and wandered over. She noticed how tired Dana looked.

'You OK with that?' she asked Dana. 'I'm happy for him to come back to mine instead, if you like. I'm not drinking so can bring him back after dinner.'

Dana smiled. 'Do you know what, Alana? That would be lovely.'

'And please let me give you a lift up the hill, you look shattered.'

'Actually, a lift to the high street would be great as I've got to get a few bits to get,' Dana said gratefully. Thanks.'

The children excitedly piled into the back of Alana's Audi. 'Well done on the not-drinking.'

'It was time I stopped, eh? I'm so sorry for all the times I let people down.' Hormones to the fore again, she suddenly began to cry. The children were oblivious as they chattered away. Dana was quite taken aback by this rare display of emotion.

'Hey, we all make mistakes.'

'And I know I can tell you this as you have been

nothing but discreet, but I've made another one. I'm pregnant.'

Dana took a deep intake of breath.

'And I'm sorry, but life goes on in mysterious ways. The most terrible thing is I don't know who the father is.'

Dana thought back to the conversation she had had with Tony in the café. If she was in the same situation, which she quite easily could have been, she would want the reassurance.

'OK. I may be completely out of turn and you don't even have to respond to what I'm going to say, but if Bruno in the café was a contender, I know it's not his. I work there, you see, and I put two and two together the night you were late coming here and then I overheard a conversation in the café between the brothers which confirmed it was you.'

She couldn't put her through the pain of knowing Tony had discussed her indiscretion directly with her.

'Anyway. After a mistake he made before, Bruno without fail uses condoms, so there's no way it would be his.'

Alana went completely quiet, until a few moment later, when she asked: 'Where shall I drop you?'

'By Fishers is fine, thank you.'

Alana leaned over to the passenger seat and kissed Dana on the cheek. 'Thank you *so* much. You have just helped me make a massive life decision. I'll have Tommy back by eight-thirty.'

Dana told Tommy to be good and blew him a kiss. Alana wound down the window.

'And Dana? It will happen for you too. I'm sure of it.' She sped off up the road.

Dana enjoyed pottering around in Fishers. It was such a wonderful delicatessen and she delighted in treating herself to lots of goodies she didn't really need. She even went to the chemist and bought herself a new lipstick. She loved having her own money. Mark was working late tonight, so she had until 8.30 p.m. to do exactly as she pleased.

She set off up the hill home. Walking past Rosco's, she noticed Tony wiping down the tables. He ran to the door and unlocked it.

'*Bella ragazza*, what brings you here?'

She kissed him on each cheek. 'Tommy's playing with a friend and Mark's still at work so I'm free to be alone for a while. I was just walking home.'

'*Perfetto*. Let me just get my coat and I will walk with you. If that is OK, of course?'

Dana felt her heart do a little skip.

'Bet you wish your girlfriend was hot like me.' Gordon turned up the radio and danced around the kitchen as he made breakfast for the twins.

'Shut up, Daddy,' Lola moaned. 'And when are we going to meet your new boyfriend anyway?'

Miaowwww! Alfie shot into the kitchen. Kat limped behind with a little splint on her front leg.

'Bless little Katty baby.' Gordon swept the moggy gently into his arms.

'See what happens, Daddy?' Lily said solemnly. 'We go away for one night and the kitten gets hurt. What happened to her anyway?'

'Oh, I don't know. You know what these two are like, they are always fighting.'

Inga appeared in the doorway half asleep.

'Sorry I eez late up. I have headache. But will of course do the school run.'

'It's fine, darling, I'm off today so I will take the terrible two. Here, have some breakfast.' He'd filled the toast rack with a selection of muffins & granary bread.

'I was going to ask you, are you OK to babysit on

Friday night?'

Inga sighed with relief. 'Yes, yes of course. I won't have to babysit Joshua then.'

'Ooh, Daddy's got a new boyfriend,' Lily mocked. 'So, will we get to meet him Friday then?'

'Maybe. Now get on with your breakfast.' Inga went to the sink to refill the kettle.

'Just a one-off then, you and Kenny boy?' Gordon asked quietly.

'I think it has to be. He has a huge cock but then again he is a huge cock – but you can't have it all, I suppose.'

Gordon laughed. 'What are you like?'

'And also what it is you say? You shouldn't take a poo on your own front step or something like that? I need the babysitting money and can you imagine the scandal? Nobody would employ me if the word got out!'

'Well, luckily that will never happen. Kenny boy is hardly going to announce it and if you keep working hard, then I promise I won't either.'

She swiped him with a tea towel as the girls started fighting.

'Right, that's it. To your room go and get ready for school, *now!*' The girls stomped off.

'How's it going with Robbie anyway?'

'He's not a keeper but by God I'm going to enjoy his young bod for now.'

'Good, you bloody deserve some fun. Right, let me stuff a muffin in and I can get moving.'

'Another one dear.' They both laughed.

'Oh, God, there he is.' Mo tried to hide her ample frame behind Joan. 'Shit, we are going to be next to him in the queue.'

'Ssh. It's fine. Let me just stay in front of you.' Smashing Sally was in startling form.

'Ooh Charlie, look at you. I can tell you've been a good boy this week.'

Mo nearly fainted when she heard his cockney twang. Last time she heard that, he was telling her how fit she was behind the potting shed at the care home.

'Well, you did say that sex burned 180 calories every half hour, and that has helped.'

'You saucy boy, you.' Smashing Sally giggled like a schoolgirl.

'My fiancée of course is delighted.'

'See, see?' hissed Mo. 'I told you he'd be with someone.'

'Mo, we are forty-something, not bloody teenagers; there was always a high chance of that.'

'I know – and I also know that's a good thing. I cannot even be tempted now.'

It was Mo's turn; she took off her shoes, socks, jacket, cardigan and necklace and stood on the scales.

'You have a weight loss of 4lbs! Wow, that's smashing Mo, smashing. Well done you.'

'Get in!' Mo shouted far too loudly as she ran to sit down next to Joan, who had also lost a fantastic 5lbs in her first week.

The friends were so engrossed in talk about how much they were going to lose this week that they didn't notice their neighbour until he spoke – causing Mo to nearly jump out of her skin.

'Maureen bloody Stubbings. Well I never! Fancy seeing you 'ere after all these years. I mean, what must it be… at least twenty?'

Mo had lost the inability to speak and let out a slight squeak.

'I'd like to say we 'aven't changed a bit but we wouldn't be 'ere if we 'adn't, eh?' He laughed his big happy laugh. 'You've still got that twinkle, gel, I'll give you that.'

Mo blushed to her roots. 'Charlie Lake. Still holding court with a room full of ladies, I see.' She beamed and kissed him on the cheek. 'It's good to see you. This is my good friend and neighbour, Joan. We are fighting our bread and wine addiction – the foods of Satan, according to Sally.'

Charlie chuckled and shook Joan's hand. 'Pleased to meet you.' Then: 'So are both you lovely ladies married then?'

They held out their left hands in unison. 'Kids?'

Mo shuffled in her seat.

'I've got four and Mo has two,' Joan intervened swiftly. 'You?'

'I'm on my third marriage. Well I say third, I'm getting married to Penny in June to make it number three. So I've got four months to shift this lot.' He squeezed his fat tummy. 'She's twenty years younger, so I'd best do as I'm told I guess, and as for kids, I've got none that I know of.' He winked at Mo, who squirmed again. Surely he couldn't have heard about Charlie junior? She was just being paranoid.

'I had no idea you lived in this area,' Mo piped up.

'Well, why would you?' Charlie said nonchalantly. 'I've just moved down south. Was in Liverpool for a good while. Met Penny on holiday in Corfu and this is where life has taken me. I've lain my hat in a few places but I like it round 'ere. Green and serene. The haves and the have lots.' He laughed again. 'Right, I'm not staying for the boring talk,' he said then. 'I'm off to the pub, me. Penny thinks I'm here till nine so that gives me a couple of hours' grace.'

'What are you like?' Mo smiled.

'Same as I ever was.' He winked at her again and she felt a feeling she hadn't felt for quite some time. 'Fancy joining me, ladies?'

'You're all right, Charlie,' Mo replied.

'And make sure you mix it with a slimline,' Joan added. And then he was gone.

Chapter Seventeen

Dana shivered. Tony took off his scarf and wrapped it gently around her neck. '*Mi tesoro*, keep yourself warm. It is very cold today.'

They started walking up the big hill towards her house.

'It would be wrong if anyone saw us together.' Dana breathed out cold air into the darkness. 'And I can't invite you in.'

'It is dark, my lovely. No one can see us and we are just work colleagues, that is all.'

'Somehow I don't think Mark would see it like that. He has always been incredibly jealous.'

'Then we shall definitely make sure you don't get in trouble.' He herded her through the park gates to their left.

Dana giggled. 'You make me feel twenty-five again, Tony Rosco.'

'But you are twenty-five, silly.'

'I know. I know. But being with an older man makes you act older, do older things. I mean, I can't remember the last time I went out and really let my hair down.'

'Your husband, he is not that old.'

'I know, I guess you just get into a rut.'

'Well if you were mine I would make sure you were happy all the time and our hair would be forever let down.' He shook out his ponytail and kissed her gently on the forehead.

'Here, let's go on the swings.' Tony took her hand and began to drag her across the park.

'I can't see a thing,' Dana screeched.

'It's fine. I have a torch in my bag.'

He held a swing still for Dana to get on and sat on the one next to her. 'And I also have a little warmer for us both.' He handed her a miniature of Amaretto. 'This is the drink of love in my eyes.'

'Well, don't look at me with Amaretto in your eyes, I am a happily married woman.'

'Are you really, Dana?'

Dana loved the way he said her name. Not Dar-nar, the way it should be pronounced but Danna.

'I thought I was – until this morning that was actually.' She took a slurp and started to swing slowly. 'I'm not sure what I want any more. Don't get me wrong – I lead a blessed life. I have a beautiful son, a kind husband and lovely house, and I don't have to work if I don't want to. I have been yearning for a baby because I have struggled to have one, but now I'm not sure if that is what I am really yearning for at all.

'My life hasn't panned out as I wanted it to,' she went on. 'I never really achieved my dreams as Tommy came along when I was just so young.'

'But think on the positive side: when you are just forty, your youngster will be twenty and you will have a new life ahead of you. And you will be able to follow your dreams as far as you want them to go,' Tony chipped in.

'You're right, and even if I was blessed to have another child at twenty-five, I know I am still young.' She started swinging harder. 'Oh. I don't know, Tony. I am content, I guess.'

'But is content really enough? Do you still love your husband, Dana?'

She hesitated. 'Yes, I do, but…'

Tony leaped off his swing, slowed hers, got on his knees and pulled her to him.

'Do you love him enough to let me do this?' He moved her scarf and kissed her gently on the neck. She bit her lip with pleasure.

170

'Or this?' He lifted her face and put his soft lips on hers. She could taste the sweetness of the Amaretto and smell the deep musk of his Italian aftershave. She couldn't resist. It was the softest, most passionate kiss she had experienced in a while.

Did other people still kiss when they were married? she wondered. Because she couldn't remember the last time she had properly kissed Mark. Lately, everything had been purely functional. The act of making a baby without making love.

'Oh my God!' Dana pulled away. 'Look, there are two lights bobbing about over there.'

Tony flashed his torch. 'It's fine, *mia rosa*, it is just two people walking around the outside path.'

'In this weather? We must go. I can't be seen here with you.'

'Dana Knight, you are such a worrier. I doubt if Mark has sent in a private detective, yet.' He lifted her chin and smiled at her. '*Mama mia*, I'm crazy for you, my little Czech princess.'

Robbie had been an angel to babysit Eliska at such short notice, but once she had made her mind up, there was just no stopping Alana Murray.

Since her row with Stephen, he had refused to talk to her. He had terminated the contract with SM Public Relations via Sandra, his PA, and just sent an email saying that he would work out a maintenance sum for Eliska, and maybe Alana had been right that announcing he was the child's father would not be a good thing.

It had been an immense relief knowing that Bruno always used condoms. Bless Dana for being so outspoken and in a way so bloody thoughtful. She had to believe that was true, and to be honest, if Bruno was so free with his favours, it made sense that he should be careful. Especially as he had had a scare once already.

Maybe, just maybe now she had learned her lesson too!

171

Her mind was made up. She was keeping this baby and against all the odds that were currently stacked against her, she was hell bent on keeping her man too.

She had managed to find Stephen's address on an old email from years ago. She had got good at stalking, these past few weeks. Analysing former emails, trying to glean meanings from online conversations they had had. He did care about her – she knew it.

It took her about an hour to drive to Chiswick. She parked on the road alongside a beautifully kept three-storey townhouse. His car was there and the outside light was on. She could see a candle burning through the half-closed shutters in the front room.

Oh, God, what if he had company? She hadn't thought of that. She bloody hoped not, what with it being Valentine's Day tomorrow as well. OK, maybe she should ring him first. Just say "I'm outside – may I come in?" But what if he said no? She had driven all this way. No, that was it. Mind made up, she would ring the doorbell.

She had put on a plain black shift dress with colourful chunky jewellery. She had intended to wear jeans, but her three-month bump was just becoming evident and she didn't want to feel uncomfortable. It was going to be difficult enough as it was. Be nice, she said to herself as the bell rang throughout the house.

'Coming!' Stephen's voice echoed down the hall, as if he was expecting someone.

'Alana? I was expecting an Indian takeaway.'

She had to laugh. 'Well, sorry it's just me, and not a Bollywood actress.'

'Very good.' He had always loved her quick wit. 'You'd better come in.' He waited while she shrugged off her coat and put it on the French antique rack in the hall.

Alana took in her surroundings. Beautiful Victorian parquet flooring led through to a wonderful long kitchen with a modern glass table at the end, set beside patio doors. Candles were burning everywhere, even out on the decked patio area at the back, despite it being just five degrees.

Classical music was playing in the background and an open fire was burning in the decadent lounge which she had walked past to get through to the kitchen. 'You have a beautiful home.' She clocked a lovely picture of Susan and Stephen on their wedding day on the side.

The doorbell rang again.

'Must be the curry, hang on a sec. Glass of wine?' 'No, thanks. Have you got any juice?'

'Alana Murray, turning down wine? Are you ill?'

'I'm driving, Stephen.'

'Hmm. Well, that doesn't usually stop you.'

'I've changed.'

'What – that big suction machine has come and sucked all the spots off, has it?'

'It's having a good old go.'

Stephen started getting his dinner out of the containers.

'Look. I miss you, Stephen. You can't just block me out. I mean, now you know about Eliska, don't you want to stay in my life so you can at least share the joy of her? I even work from home two days a week now so I can do the school runs. We are getting on so much better and I am already considering a decent summer holiday for us both – despite having to take the time to pitch for a new PR agency, of course.'

'See? I knew you would have to get a dig in about that somewhere. Here, have some food.' He handed her a fork and a plate. 'There's plenty here for two.'

'I just don't understand your actions, Stephen. If I did then maybe it would be easier for me to deal with the situation.'

'I've already explained, Alana. I blame myself for Susan's death. If she hadn't seen Eliska, she would never have felt the way she did, I know it. You are my direct link to Eliska so I figure every time I see you, I will always be reminded of Susan and what happened.' He clenched his jaw.

'Oh, Stephen. But I think our relationship is too special to just throw away.'

'Our relationship was sexual, Alana. Period.'

'But we have a child! Surely that counts for something?'

'Everything is just so raw, Lani.' He bit his lip and held back tears. 'I miss her so much. I come back here to our beautiful home and she is everywhere and nowhere, and the pain of that is so intense that I can't explain it. It's like I don't want to be anywhere. I don't mean that I would take my own life. But it's just I am so miserable in the place I am in at the moment and I cannot see a way of getting out of it.

'I hate waking up because I know she won't be here and I've got that whole day of her not being here in front of me, and then when the day is over, that's even worse because I eat alone and sleep alone and after twenty years of sharing that with her, it bloody hurts.'

Alana had tears streaming down her face. How could she tell him about the baby? Or maybe this was the *raison d'etre* he needed to pull him out of his depression.

She got up and walked around the table, stood behind him put her arms around his shoulders. Sobbing, he turned around and pulled her to him tightly, nestling his head in her breasts.

Coming to his senses, he sat up, pushed her gently away and took a large gulp of his red wine.

'God, you're such a bitch, Lani, but underneath it I know you're not all that bad. I also know that you're pregnant.'

It was Alana's turn to stand up, take a deep breath and a big gulp of her orange juice.

'Who told you?' She was flabbergasted.

'Nobody bloody told me, you silly woman. Those gnat bites of yours swelled to baby melons last time and the simple fact, despite you denying it, it is the only time you have ever stopped drinking before in your life. I take it you know who the father is?'

'What do you take me for? Of course I do.'

Stephen banged his hand down so hard on the table it made Alana jump. 'Stop playing your stupid fucking games with me this time. Just tell me – is it mine or not?' She had never heard him so angry.

'Y...y-yes, it's yours,' she whispered. 'How far gone are you?'

'Almost twelve weeks. I have the scan booked for next Tuesday at the private clinic in Thewkesbury.'

'So still plenty of time to get rid of it then?' Stephen said matter of factly. Alana bit her lip and ran her hands through her hair.

'Don't tell me you hadn't thought of that option because I know you so well, Alana Murray.'

'I actually made up my mind today that I wanted to keep it and that's why I'm here. I felt you should know. I realise the timing is bad as you are grieving. But, with or without you, I've been blessed enough to be given the chance of the gift of life again and I am going to take it, with arms outstretched.

'I know I haven't always been the best mother to Eliska, but things are going to change from now on. This is the new start I needed.'

Stephen put his hand to his head. 'I just can't believe I could be so naïve twice. But, it takes two to tango, I guess. Look, I need to get my head around this. Please – just go. I'll be in touch.'

Alana went to say something and thought against it. She had known the news wouldn't be taken with outstretched arms and hugs and kisses. But, he hadn't told her to piss off totally and that was as good as she was going to get for now.

Stephen saw her to the door. He looked at her tummy. 'Drive carefully, eh?'

She smiled up at him. 'I will.'

Chapter Eighteen

'Clark! Will you please do as you are told and bring your dirty washing down.'

'Cissy, no! Squidge is patient but don't steal his biscuit off him or he will bite you.'

'Skye, you can't wear red socks to school, no.'

'Morning, love.' Colin Brown appeared at the breakfast table in his suit. 'Whatever is Kent doing upstairs?' Joan asked, harassed.

'He's still in the toilet, I think.'

'Right, you lovely lot, breakfast, come on,' she bawled. 'Or we'll be late.'

'TFI Friday, my sweet, oh and Happy Valentine's Day. I couldn't get us a babysitter, so next best thing. We shall have a takeaway curry instead.'

'You old softy – sorry, I had completely forgotten. I love you to your bones – you know that.' She kissed her husband on the cheek.

'Right, must go. See you later, you lot. Be good for your mum.'

'See ya, wouldn't wanna be ya,' Clark piped up.

'Daddeeeee.' Cissy waddled over to him and gave him a squashy kiss.

'Bye, Skye.' Colin mucked up her hair. 'Bye, Kent,' he shouted up the stairs. 'Bye, darling wifey.'

'Can we swap places for the day, please?' Joan laughed.

'I will help you tomorrow, darling I promise.'

Inga ran the twins up to the classroom, reddening slightly

when she saw Kenny Boy. It wouldn't have been quite so embarrassing if she hadn't just opened a Valentine so obviously from him with just the words inside I want to fuck you till you scream. I mean really, where had romance gone? But seeing his bottom in his tight designer jeans and his quirky beanie hat, she actually was quite up for it again.

He came bounding over to her and stared right into her eyes. 'Emily mentioned Friday night to you, I take it?'

'She did, Kenneth,' Inga replied politely. 'I can't make it, I'm afraid, as Gordon needs me.' She lowered her voice. 'But, I can be home naked in ten minutes for me to give you a Valentine's Day treat you'll never ever forget.'

'We'll have to be quick,' he replied, already hardening in his tight jeans.

'I'm good at quick – oh, and at screaming,' she murmured seductively. Loving the power she had over weak, wet Ken.

She swiftly turned around and bumped straight into Alana, who was rushing up the drive with Eliska.

'So sorry. Oh, hi Alana.'

'No worries. All OK with you, Inga?'

'Yes, yes. Thank you.' God, what was wrong with her? Inga thought. She had never known her ex-boss to be so polite.

Alana was indeed in a good mood. Well, in a mood of hope anyway. Hope that maybe, just maybe, Stephen would want to be with her eventually. Mind you, she had not heard a word since the night she turned up at his house. He had wanted time, and she would be patient and give it to him. She knew it was the only way. She had, however, sent him a single red rose for Valentine's.

Joan rushed her brood and Rosie into their various classrooms. Cissy was sleeping in the cat basket on the front of her bike, despite the fact she was now far too big for it and her legs hung down precariously. Joan had on her long list of things to do – buy a proper bike seat.

She was seconds away from the Late Book as Mr Chambers appeared. He wore a red bow tie today. He smiled broadly on seeing his favourite mum.

'May I wish you a Happy Valentine's Day, Joan. The sun is out too. You'd best get your shelf ready for three more cards later.'

'Great stuff. You have a good day with all those terrors too. At least they can go outside and play in this weather.'

Tommy scooted in under Mr Chambers' arm.

'I shall pretend I didn't notice you, Tommy Knight,' he called out. 'Right, in I go. See you later.'

Joan got on her bike and headed off home; rounding the corner, she had to slam on her brakes as Kenneth Pritchard screeched away from the school, nearly knocking her off.

What an earth could be so important to have to drive that fast? she thought.

Joan got back home from the school run, put Cissy down for her morning sleep and made herself a cup of tea. She had got used to replacing her customary biscuit with a piece of fruit and was on a mission to get this weight off her by the summer.

She started to go through the washing pile, sorting whites and emptying pockets. She got to the pair of jeans she had been wearing the night of Weight Busters and pulled out a business card.

Strange. She didn't remember putting that in there. She screwed up her face and had a good look. On one side it said Charles Lake, Private Detective and a mobile number; on the other, in scribbled handwriting: Maureen's friend, call me without her knowing, please.

She sat down and took a slurp of her now lukewarm tea. Oh, God, what if he fancied her? I mean, he was such a womaniser. What on earth could he want to speak to her about? Should she ring Mo and just tell her? No, because if he did fancy her, that would just be so terrible. She had only just cleared her head of sleeping with her friend's son, for goodness sake! Joan had managed to absolve herself of that terrible guilt by realising she was deeply in love with her husband; she also knew that her friend might disown her if she knew.

It was a terrible thing to admit, but she was actually glad that Charlie junior had stolen the Freedom Fund and cleared off out of sight, out of mind and out of ruining her life and those of the people around her. What a mess.

Right, decision made, she would phone him after lunch. If it was anything to do with him fancying her, then she would tell Mo straight away. She couldn't bear any more deceit.

The doorbell rang. 'Delivery for Mrs J. Brown,' the young delivery driver stated, handing over a bouquet of a dozen old-fashioned, beautiful-smelling deep red roses. Happy Valentine's Day, love, read the accompanying card.

'Silly old sod,' she said under her breath, knowing they couldn't really afford to do this. But he had done it every year since they'd got together, and Colin was a creature of habit. And, for this, she was actually eternally grateful.

'Charlie, Charlie Lake? It's Joan here – Maureen Collins' friend.'

'Joan? Oh, yes. Thanks, gel, for calling me back.'

'How can I help you?'

'Now seeing as you are so close to young Maureen, well, I wondered if maybe we could meet up.'

'What for?'

'I want to talk to you about Maureen. Maureen and her boy.' Joan crinkled her face up. He knew about Charlie!

'Can't we just talk on the phone?'

'No – it's not the time or the place at the moment. You live in Denbury, right?'

'How did you know that?' Joan quizzed, then suddenly

remembered he was a private detective and shut up.

'Details, details,' Charlie senior blustered. 'How about I meet you in Rosco's at ten-thirty tomorrow? I've got to meet another client soon after in Denbury anyway. Maureen will be at work then – right?'

'Um, I'm not...' Joan spluttered.

'Right, see ya then, gel. It won't take long.'

Dana parked round the back of Rosco's. Her heart was beating faster than usual. She had never cheated on anyone in her life. The kiss she had shared with Tony had just felt so perfect in the park the other night, but deep down she knew that what she was doing was wrong. She was a one-man woman. Having an affair just wasn't in her remit.

Once they had been disturbed, she insisted that Tony just walk her home.

She had not had any contact with him since.

Now she took a deep breath, walked in the back door and took off her coat.

Bruno was in the back room sorting stock.

'Morning, bella.' He kissed her on both cheeks. Dana prayed that Tony had managed not to share what had happened with him. It seemed as if he had been discreet, since Bruno said no more.

She put on her apron and walked out into the café. It was already heaving so she set to work clearing tables. Tony, behind the counter preparing coffees, blew her a kiss and gave her a cheeky wink.

Her heart did a loop the loop and ended up in her mouth.

Why could your head never take control of this beating muscle of love? she thought. I mean, it wasn't even that big! Her mind was made up: she would talk to Tony in their 'lull' break. All this had to stop. She was acting like a teenager. I mean – snogs on the swings. At her age!

'Lull break' time came quickly. Tony took off his

apron and insisted that Dana close her eyes and hold her hands out. She opened them to find a heart-shaped pink meringue with the words *Pazza di Te* in white icing. Crazy for you.

'I knew you couldn't take a rose home. So, you can eat this, then my love will be inside you all day.'

'Tony Rosco, what are you doing to me?'

'Nothing yet, but I so want to be.'

'We can't.'

'But I know you feel the same, Dana.'

There he was again, saying Danna, and not Darna. She melted a little bit more.

'I'm not a bad person, Tony. I just can't cheat on Mark and I have Tommy to think of too. I'm not that woman who can jump into bed with someone then go home and pretend life is normal. I mean, earlier this morning, I was trying for a baby with my husband. This isn't right. Maybe I should stop working here.'

Tony's face went white. 'No, no that can't happen. I could not bear the thought of not seeing your beautiful face three times a week.'

'With Bruno recruiting, you could get another pretty face in within seconds. He could make sure it was not a married pretty face too.'

'But that is the problem, *mia rosa*, you are so much more than a pretty face.'

'Flattery and pink meringues will get you everywhere, but we have to be realistic, Tony.'

He walked to face her. 'Just one more kiss then.'

'Not here.'

'So where and when?'

Bruno came charging into the back room.

'*Adesso*, brother! Do you want to retire to Tuscany or no?'

Dana rushed to get her apron. She would have to leave. The temptation for this beautiful man was too great. But was temptation alone enough to ruin Tommy's life for ever? Enough to change her lifestyle completely? Maybe it was, because to be honest, Mark was the last thing she was throwing into the equation.

'Ooh, a daytime Valentine's fuck, how delicious, Daddio.'

'Glad you can accommodate me. I'll be skipping up those plane steps with a smile on my face later.'

'If I have my way, you'll be crawling.'

'Promises, promises.'

Gordon ushered Robbie towards the bedroom. One of Lily's dolls was face up in the hallway and Robbie caught his toe on it. He kicked the toy in anger and its head flew off.

'Hey, what are you doing?'

'Sorry, I stubbed my toe on the bloody thing.'

'Get naked this second and I might forgive you.' Robbie slammed the bedroom door behind him.

Two seconds later, Kenneth Pritchard tiptoed slowly down the same corridor, sweat dripping from his brow.

Joan wished wholeheartedly that she hadn't agreed to meet Charlie Lake in Rosco's. I mean, what was she thinking of? It was all completely innocent, she was sure, but it just didn't feel right somehow. Whatever happened, she would be telling Mo all about it later. The deceit of sleeping with Charlie junior still hung over her, but she knew that was something that could never be divulged for the sake of her marriage and friendship.

Charlie was already sat at a table in the corner when she arrived, drinking a black coffee and reading the *Daily Mail*.

He stood up when he saw her. 'Joan, how lovely to see you again.'

Joan ordered a skinny latte from Bruno.

'So, Charlie, what's all this about then?'

'I just wondered how Maureen was, that's all.'

'Why the sudden interest?' Joan felt very protective of her friend.

Charlie screwed up his plump face. 'To be honest, it's not really Maureen I'm interested in, it's the kid. I randomly bumped into someone in my new local who had gone to the same care home as us all those years ago, and he said he had heard on the grapevine that Maureen had had a baby not long after our little dalliance.'

'Oh, right.'

'Once you said you both lived in Denbury, I started putting out my feelers out to see if I could find out anything more. I mean, everyone wants to know if they have a kid out there, don't they?'

'Mo has been with Ron for years, so you've had a wasted journey, I'm afraid, Charlie. And I'm not sure why you are asking me anyway?'

'Because if Mo had wanted me to know, then she would have told me.'

'And you think her best friend would spill the beans? I don't think so. Sorry, Charlie, I must go.'

'With thirty thousand pounds at stake, I thought she might.' Joan nearly choked on her latte.

'Thirty thousand pounds! What? Why? I don't understand.'

'Look, I'm ill,' Charlie said roughly. 'I don't know how long I've got. I'm writing my Will, and if I have a kid, it's only fair they get some of my inheritance.'

He blew his nose. 'Think about it, Joan. Please. Mo needn't even know – but my conscience will be clear. She must have struggled with that decision back in the day, and I want to do right by her and by my son. If he really is my son that is.'

He stood up. 'I'll be in touch. And Joan… obviously there will be a drink in it for you.'

With that he waddled his fat body out of the café door,

leaving an open- mouthed Joan to settle the coffee bill.

Mo ran up the steps to the doctors' surgery, noticing that her breathing was so much better now that she was walking so often. She also noticed that her clothes were beginning to feel looser. She must take a trip to the charity shop and get some new ones. Ffion had coloured, cut and blow-dried her hair the night before, so she was feeling good this morning.

'Morning, Mo. Your hair looks great today,' Dr Delicious offered, walking through to his treatment room.

'Bloody good stylist she has, that's why,' Ffion trilled in her Welsh accent.

Then she breathed to Mo: 'He definitely fancies you.' Mo raised her eyebrows as this standing joke.

'This is a surgery, not the set of *TOWIE*, thank you, ladies.' Grim Lynn obviously hadn't got a shag at the weekend.

Mind you, nor had Ffion. 'Mo. What's going on with the Denbury Dish count? I mean, there hasn't been a new one for quite some time.'

'So now my Charlie is off the menu, are you not back seeing Bruno from the café?'

'No, he's old news now. I think I may have to move to London – at least then I'll get a better selection.'

Mo laughed. 'You're bloody hilarious, you are. Life is not all about men, young Ffion. Concentrate on getting your beauty certificate first. Then you can wax lyrical about them as much as you like, at the same time as waxing backs, sacks 'n' cracks.'

'Ha, I like that, Mo. If any of the buggers annoy me I could wax their eyebrows off too. Now that'd be funny.'

Mo tutted.

'By the way, you look gorgeous today, Mo. I can definitely notice you are losing weight.'

'Aw, thanks, Ffi. I feel so much better too.'

'And how's that husband of yours been treating you?'

'All right, actually. Now he's off the drink he's a different person. I've never known Rosie so happy.'

'Well, that's good. But how about you, Mo – are you happy?'

'Oh, it's not all about me, Ffi,' Mo blustered.

'Mo Collins: please don't be so selfless. It's a lot about you. Please tell me you will think about your own happiness too one of these days.'

Mo looked at her screen and began typing.

'I take it you've had no word from Charlie either?'

Mo stopped what she was doing. 'No, love, I will let you know if I do. But, the pattern is that he usually waits a good few months when he has done something wrong, then reappears when he needs me again. Right, we'd better get on before the grim one starts moaning again.'

'She's in that supplier meeting now, I think.'

'Oh, good. Forgot she had that. I need caffeine. I'll shoot down to Rosco's and get us a proper coffee. What do you fancy?'

Mo had a quick look in Fishers window as she power-walked down to the café and her mouth watered at the selection of chorizo they had hanging in the window. Although her life was not perfect, she didn't feel so bad. At least she didn't have to deal with Ron's violence any longer, and as she had said to Ffion, Rosie was happy – and that counted for such a lot.

She put her hand on the door to Rosco's, and as if propelled by an electric shock, suddenly jumped back two metres. For there, sitting bold as brass drinking coffee together, were none other than her best friend and Charlie Lake.

She began to shake slightly. What on earth did they have to say to each other? It was on their doorstep so it was obviously nothing sinister, was it? OK, what should she do? She really didn't want to speak to Charlie. No, it would be just too embarrassing a situation. Joan would obviously call her anyway, she must have just bumped into him. Yes, that was it; it must have been a chance meeting. But, what in God's name was Charlie senior doing in Denbury? Something didn't feel right and she didn't like it, she didn't like it at all.

Chapter Nineteen

Alana walked into the private clinic in Thewkesbury, with its high-tech TV screens advertising the next best thing in prams and baby clothing, registered her arrival and took a seat amongst the reassuringly expensive plants and pictures. She poured herself a fresh coffee from the jug on the side and began flicking through a brand new *Vogue* magazine.

It was a week since she had seen Stephen. A very long seven days without any contact whatsoever. But, she knew that if there was any chance at all of him coming round to her way of thinking, she just had to let him be. She was still working, but it was no longer her priority and that suddenly felt good.

What was important, here and now, was the happiness of Eliska and this little bundle inside of her. However, Alana Murray was used to getting what she wanted – and what she wanted most of all was to be the partner of Mr Stephen McNair.

'Alana Murray?' A nurse smiled and ushered her through to the scan room. 'Hi, I'm Annabel; I'll be doing your scan today.' The lady at the helm of the scanning equipment introduced herself.

Suddenly there was a kerfuffle at the door. The familiar Scottish accent made Alana's heart set up a kerfuffle all of its own.

Then in he walked. All six-foot-four of handsome, reliable man. He put his coat calmly on the back of the door and sat in the chair that Annabel pointed out to him.

Saying nothing, he picked up Alana's hand and kissed

it. It was the sweetest kiss she had ever received in her whole life.

The gel felt cold on her stomach. She couldn't wait to meet the new little person inside of her.

'You wanted a 3D version too, is that right?' 'Yes, please. How exciting is this?'

Stephen squeezed her hand and tears filled his eyes. In the midst of his grief, a new life. It was ever the way of the world.

They could see the form of the baby in all its black-and-white glory. A blurry face, tiny little hands and skinny legs.

And then they could see the sombre face of Annabel. Hear her calling for Dr Lovitt.

They learned that the baby had died in the womb at around ten weeks. Its heart had just stopped beating. This was a relatively common occurrence and they would probably never know why. Alana would have to have a small operation to remove the foetus from her womb. She would be able to go home that evening and would need 'a lot of love and care'.

'Will you be here when I come out?' Alana asked Stephen tearfully outside the operating theatre.

Unable to speak, he just nodded and kissed her forehead softly.

Dana put her shopping bags down and her key in the front door. It was Saturday and Mark had insisted she go for a facial while he cleaned the house. Unheard of!

She had to admit she had rather enjoyed the pampering and had been totally sold on buying all the products the salon had used on her as they had smelled just so good. Maybe she could get used to this 'kept woman' lifestyle after all. She just hadn't given herself a chance. She had made a point of getting a taxi up the hill so that she didn't have to walk past Rosco's. The temptation to see Tony was so strong but her morals were stronger and she had to do right by Mark. He deserved more.

Mark heard the key and opened the door wide.

'Mrs Knight, please do let me take your bags. I have run you a bubble bath and there is a glass of champagne on the side.'

'Look at you treating me like a princess!'

'Nothing less than you deserve, *ma cherie*.'

His French talk reminded her of Tony's Italian love notes and she couldn't decipher whether she wished she was with him or just felt plain guilty.

'It's awfully quiet in here – where's Tommy?'

'With my mum for the weekend. So it's just me and you, kid. Now go and get in that bath so I can prepare dinner in peace.'

Dana lay in the huge bubbly bath and put the Jacuzzi jets on. She began to think of Tony – his smell, his kiss, his full-on feelings for her – and started to stroke herself. She imagined what it would be like to make love to him and realised it would most definitely be explosive. She couldn't deny she wanted to fuck him. But maybe that was it, just a quick fuck and fumble with someone new. After a lot of years of marriage and sex with the same person, maybe that's what everyone wanted? A no strings attached, filthy sexual encounter with someone extremely hot.

She began to finger herself slowly, then imagining doing it every which way she could with Tony, more frantically until she climaxed so hard she cried out.

'Are you OK, darling?' Mark called up.

'Yes, yes, fine. I put the cold on instead of hot.'

She sank down into the warm bubbles to catch her breath. Wow, if that was the fantasy version, imagine what it would be like in real time.

She parked that thought and began to wash her hair.

'Mr Lake?'

'Who's asking?' 'Mark, Mark Knight.'

'Oh hello, Mr Knight. I removed the device from the café as you requested last week but I'm obviously on call 24/7 if you need anything else.'

'Thank you very much. I won't be requiring your services further. Please email me your invoice as agreed and I will settle by return. Good evening to you.'

'Good evening, Mr Knight.'

Mark rubbed his face and went over to the calendar on the kitchen wall. He double-checked that the big letter 'O' was written on today's date and headed up to the en-suite to shower.

Dressed just in the lacy cream underwear she had bought today, Dana stuck her head forward to dry her hair. Mark came out of the shower with just a white towel around his waist and took in the beautiful figure of his young and very pretty wife.

He turned the hairdryer off at the wall. 'Oi, you.'

Dana sat up. 'Oi, what.'

Her now rampant husband dropped the towel to reveal a huge erection. He lifted her off the dressing-table stool and threw her on to the bed.

'I was going to wait until after dinner to do this to you, but you look so hot I can't wait.'

Dana laughed and looked up at Mark. He was still as toned and fit as when she had first met him, and she couldn't deny that she did still fancy him. She was still feeling horny from her Tony masturbation session in the bath too.

It was the first time in a while that Mark 'fucked' Dana. The sort that you do when you first meet and want it every second, every minute, every hour. He made her reach heights she had barely reached with him before and when they had finished, she lay sweating and panting on the bed.

'And there's more where that came from.' Mark kissed her on the lips. 'Now, I shall just go and get some champagne for my little angel so she can get her breath back.'

Dana scissored her legs and arms on their huge round bed in snow-angel fashion and grinned. There was one thing that she hadn't thought about once during that marathon sex session and this pleased her greatly. The fact that she was ovulating.

Mr Chambers was at the classroom door checking which parents had arrived for home-time when Robbie caught his eye.

'Hey, how's it going, Will? I'm fetching Eliska today, Alana's not very well – she only just called me.'

'OK, fine – and in answer to your question it'll all be better in half an hour,' Mr Chambers replied, nearly getting bowled over by an enthusiastic escapee.

'Oi, what's the rush, Joshua Pritchard?'

When Inga spotted Robbie, she hid behind Joan. He was so forthright she dreaded him mentioning anything at all about her compromising position the other night.

He saw her as he was leaving.

'Any chance of taking Tweedledum and Tweedledee out tomorrow night? I've got a pleasant surprise for your boss and an empty house would be good.'

'I'm babysitting anyway, aren't I? So yes, let me see… maybe I could take them to Pizza Express.'

'I meant all night.'

'Oh, Robbie. It's not always that easy with kids, things take a bit of arranging.'

'Well, try and arrange it then,' he replied sharply. 'How's Barbie's Ken doing anyway?'

'Ssh.' Inga was mortified.

'Imagine if Barbie Doll were to find out – she'd be pulling her hair extensions out in anguish.' Robbie tipped his head back with laughter.

That was it. It was all too close, too real. As much as the quickie had been amazing the other morning, it couldn't happen again. She wanted a boyfriend, not a temporary fuck.

'Inga, darling.' Emily Pritchard – Scorned wife, Head of PTA, Netball Coach and Mother of Joshua P, seven, chief swot and playground kisser – was upon her. 'You didn't let me know if you could babysit tomorrow.'

'Oh Emily, I am so sorry, Gordon needs me to babysit the girls, but I think I may be taking them to Pizza Express so Joshua could come with us, if you like?'

'Great, super, that may just work as Petula is having a sleepover at Jemima's. Thanks ever so, Inga. You really are a brick.'

'Who teases your husband's prick,' Robbie whispered in Inga's ear. Inga felt like punching him.

'Call me in the morning,' Emily shouted imperiously as she headed towards her car.

'Do your worst, bitch,' Robbie sniggered. 'Call me, too. Young Gordy deserves a treat, you know that.'

Mr Chambers assisted Joan's brood by helping find their lunchboxes and coats. 'You look tired, Joan.'

'No more tired than usual,' she replied wearily. 'Just a few things on my mind. Nothing that can't be sorted though.'

'Good, good. Remember I'm always here if there are any issues with the children.'

'I appreciate that. Thanks, Mr Chambers.' 'Call me Will.'

'Thanks, Will.'

Joan got on her bike. God, she could do without her children's teacher fancying her now, although it was rather flattering.

The boys started play-fighting in the road, while Rosie

ran alongside Skye without a care in the world. Thankfully Mo was at the surgery this afternoon.

Joan couldn't think straight since this morning. How was she going to approach Mo? She didn't want her to think she was being underhand. Oh, why hadn't she just told her in the first place? Level-headed, sensible Colin would know what to do. As soon as he was home she would discuss it with him then ring Mo. Mind you, the 'drink' Charlie senior had mentioned would come in handy at the moment.

'Come on kids, homeward.' She raised her voice as they continued to ignore her. 'Today, please!'

Mo was at Joan's front door waiting for them when they turned the corner. She pulled Rosie to her and gave her a kiss. 'Good day, darling?'

'Yes. Look – I made this in pottery for Daddy.' She revealed an earthenware mug-type creation with the word DAD written inside a pink heart.

'That's lovely, well done.'

'You finished early,' Joan said brightly. 'Right, let's get this lot in and the tea on.'

Mo couldn't believe the first thing that she said wasn't about Charlie senior. Her suspicions were raised even further. Come on, Joanie, tell me. Please keep our friendship real, Mo urged in her mind.

Joan put the kettle on and looked at Mo playing with the kids. The poor woman had been through enough. Should she really worry her now with Charlie's recent antics? If it was Colin, would she want to know? Yes, of course she bloody would! How could she be so stupid? Mo was her best friend and whether good or bad, she should know what her devious ex-lover was up to. Mind you, she did still wonder how much 'the drink' Charlie senior would be offering her if she did cough up.

195

Once snacks and drinks had been issued to the young hungry mouths, she made a fresh pot of tea and sat at the kitchen table with Mo.

'I have something to tell you, Mo.'

Not even caring now what she was going to hear, Mo shut her eyes with relief.

'I found a business card from Charlie senior in my jeans pocket after Weight Busters.'

'Go on.'

'He's a private detective, evidently.'

'He always was a nosy bugger.'

Joan interrupted. 'Anyway, to cut a long story short, he said to call him. I did and we met this morning. He had said it was about you and Charlie junior.'

'Oh my God, Joan, so he knows! Oh no!'

'No, wait, he doesn't know. Get this. He asked me the question and of course I avoided the answer.'

'I don't understand, Joan. Why come to you and not me?'

'He was of the opinion that as you hadn't told him in over twenty years, why would you suddenly do so now?'

She took a deep breath. 'And, I hope this doesn't upset you – but it's quite sad really. He's ill, Mo. Said he doesn't know how long he's got and is writing his Will. If Charlie is his, he is going to leave him thirty grand!'

'Oh bless him, that's awful, Joanie. Oh, how that conniving son of mine could do with the money to get him on his feet. It might even make him sort himself out properly. I mean…thirty thousand pounds!' She raised her eyebrows. 'That would be a decent deposit on a house and more.'

'Yes, it would. But then I started thinking, Mo. Would he really be bothered to lose weight if he was dying? I mean, there's vain and then there's vain.'

Mo laughed. 'Mind you, he always did love himself, even at seventeen. And how on earth did he know that we

196

would be there? Maybe he is a really good private detective.'

'Mo, he saw us there the first week; it's not brain science that we would be there the next.'

'Oh, what am I going to do? If I had never seen him again, then I wouldn't even have this dilemma. Is thirty thousand pounds really worth the upset? Money is, after all, the root of all evil. Just imagine the scenario of that son of mine knowing the truth. Young Charlie wouldn't take the news well – about the dad bit, at least; he'd love the fact that free money was coming to him. Charlie would then have great delight in telling Ron. Rosie would then have to go through another massive upheaval and trauma, with shouting and rows and violence; it would just be too terrible for us all.'

'Mind you, if money was involved young Charlie might keep his mouth shut.'

'"Might" isn't good enough. I couldn't bear the time bomb. And he would still hate me for not telling him in the first place.'

Mo took a slurp of tea.

'Why didn't you tell me when you found the card, Joan? I feel a bit miffed about that. And even worse – when I saw you together in Rosco's, I was mortified. You should have just told me everything.'

'Oh Mo, I'm sorry. I am so stupid sometimes. I didn't know how to play it. I thought maybe I could avoid you getting hurt by this man, who is obviously a bit of a charlatan.'

'Oh Joanie, always tell me. There is nothing else you are forgetting to tell me, now is there?'

Joan thought back to her previous antics with Charlie junior and felt sick. 'Or course not!'

'Good. Look at the size of these shoulders: they can take anything, you should know that by now.'

Joan went to the sink and started washing down the

kitchen surfaces. She let it go that the kids were running around like elephants upstairs.

'So, how did you leave it anyway?' Mo added.

Joan wiped her hands on a tea towel and sat back down.

'Well, the cheeky bastard said there would be a drink in it for me if I did tell him the truth and that he would be in touch.'

'What a prat! It makes me glad I didn't stay with him now. Bloody game- playing. OK, let me sleep on it. What worries me is, is there any other way he can find out if it doesn't come from me or you?'

The two woman sank into a thoughtful silence.

Chapter Twenty

Alana awoke in her own bed to the sound of hushed voices downstairs. She felt a bit groggy and remembered Stephen giving her a sleeping tablet as she was just too fraught to sleep. She got out of bed, put on her dressing-gown and headed downstairs to the kitchen.

Stephen was on his laptop at her kitchen table. It made her feel warm inside to have him so close to her.

'Hey, what are you doing up? I was just going to come and see if I could get you anything. How are you feeling?'

'Sad,' she said in a childlike voice and burst into tears. He got up and held her to him tightly.

'Where's Eliska?' she asked in a panic. 'What have you told her?'

'She's absolutely fine, Lani. She stayed at young Tommy's last night. We haven't told her anything. We wanted to consult you first.'

'We?'

'Yes, we.' Isobel Murray walked in to the kitchen, duster in hand.

'Mother!' Then to Stephen: 'What's she doing here?'

'Lani, don't be like that. Stephen was kind enough to call me and tell me what had happened. I'm here to help.'

'Please don't be upset with me or your mother. I didn't know where to turn and thought she should know you were having an operation, and then she just turned up late last night.'

'OK, but no funny business, Mother, or you can go home.' Alana didn't feel she could cope with this latest development right at that moment.

199

Stephen kissed her on the forehead 'Look, I have a meeting this morning, so I have to go back into town. I will call you later, I promise. We have lots to talk about when you are feeling stronger.'

Grabbing his briefcase off the floor, he was gone.

'Please let me try and care for you, Lani. Just for a few days. I know I've been a shit mother, but you need me now and I want to prove I can give you some love back.'

Alana sat down at the table. 'Eliska has never even met you, but at least she does know you exist. I told her that you were on a big life adventure. She has seen pictures and you have been a subject for one of her "show and tells" at school. Glamorous Granny travels the world and all that. Little did they know, hey? Glamorous Granny too wrapped up in her own one-way love affairs to see the reality of life and accept her out-of-wedlock granddaughter.'

'Stephen is obviously the father? Just looking at her beautiful photos shows that. Scottish too, can't believe you didn't tell me that. Perfect!'

Alana refused to comment. 'So do you know what time Eliska is back then, do you? Seeing as you seem to know more of what's going on in my life than I do today.'

'This Dana seems like such a lovely girl – I suggested to Stephen that he ring her. She offered to have the bairn another night if you'd like that. Said she would pop by after school and pick up any clean clothes she needed.'

'Yes, Dana is a lovely non-judgmental lady. But no, let's ring her. I want to see my little lady and it will be really exciting for her to meet her granny.' She emphasised the word granny.

'Oh Lani, does she have to call me Granny? Can't she just call me Isobel?'

'Just put the kettle on, Mother, and do something bloody useful for once.'

'So let me get this straight, you are taking the girls and

Joshua to Pizza Express so I can have the house to myself with Robbie if I want to?'

'If that's OK with you, Gordon?'

'Of course it is, but I think we're going out anyway.'

'OK, well, I will try and stay out until at least eleven. My friend Martyna – you know, the one who au-pairs on Bramwell Hill, near Dana – says she is home alone with the children so we can go and watch films and eat popcorn round there afterwards if we want to.'

'Fine, that's lovely. I know they will have fun with you whatever.'

'How's it going with Robbie, anyway?'

'Yeah, it's OK. I realise he is a bit of a player but you know me, I'm a heart- on-sleeve boy. I am a bit worried that I am falling for him ever so slightly.'

'Well, try not to, Gordy. I think as you say he is out for the fun and I would hate to see you get hurt.'

'Look at you giving me the advice, Miss Marriage Wrecker you. I normally wouldn't condone it under this roof but just the fact that it's Preachy's husband is too bloody hysterical. I can't abide that woman.'

'Well, you won't be seeing him here again, Gordon. I have come to my common senses, is that how you say? He is so boring. I would like a nice new young boyfriend, please. Can you send one by magic?' She laughed her tinkling laugh and clicked her fingers.

Gordon smiled. 'Good call, Inga. It can only lead to heartache in the end and better to leave it now when no suspicion has been raised. It can just be your little playground secret and God knows how many of those are lurking around those school gates, eh?'

'Exactly. It eez a den of iguanas, no?'

Gordon kissed her on the cheek lovingly. 'Iniquity, I think you mean, my lovely friend. Now, where are those girlies? I need to get them bathed and ready for you to take out.'

At that moment, Lola came rushing in, looking upset. 'Molly's head won't go back on, Daddy.'

'Oh, sorry Lo, I meant to fix her. Give her to me and I'll superglue it.' The kittens were running havoc in the toy box.

'Kat's back to her usual tricks, I see, now her paw is better,' Gordon commented.

'And Alfie keeps farting,' Lily added, holding her nose.

'That's nice. Did you teach him all he knows?' Gordon said cheekily, grabbing her and tickling her.

'So, Daddy do we get to meet Robbie tonight then?'

'You may do actually – depends what time you go to Pizza Express.'

'Good. He has to be as nice as Daddy Chris or Mummy will be cross, remember.'

A lump hit Gordon's throat at the mention of two people so dear to him. 'Of course I remember,' he said huskily, then pulled himself together. Now get undressed the pair of you, the bath's running.'

The twins were arguing about clothes when the doorbell rang.

'I don't want you to wear a red top, I'm wearing a red top,' Lily screeched.

'But's it's a different design!' Lola screeched back.

'And it goes with my glasses too.'

'Oh, all right. Daddy always gives you what you want. You're a spoilt little cow.'

'Oi, ladies! Let me answer the door and when I get back I want you to be friends again, all right?' He ran to the front door.

'Evening.' Gordon opened the door to a smirking Robbie. 'What you been up to? You look sneaky.'

'Guilty as charged. I'll tell you in a minute.' He then grimaced theatrically as he heard the twins screaming at each other.

'I thought you'd be used to this in your Bebops world?' Gordon asked, rather hurt by his attitude.

'I am, that's why I like to get away from it in my personal life.'

'Yeah. I get you,' Gordon acknowledged, taking in Robbie's revealing red jeans and tight black T-shirt and suddenly feeling remarkably horny.

'Here, open this.' He threw him a beer. 'I'll go and sort them out.' He went into the girls' bedroom and shut the door behind him. They were both still wearing their red tops. Stalemate.

'Now, you wanted to meet Robbie, and Robbie is here. He is also wearing red jeans. Obviously, a very trendy colour at the moment. So, why don't you just stay as you are – you both look beautiful. I get that you want to be individuals and not wear the same and that's totally cool by me – you know that. But your tops are very different and you have different coloured jeans on, so come on. Inga is going to be ready to leave in ten minutes.'

'Does he look like Chris then? Your new boyfriend?' Lola asked.

'Oh, it's you. We know you already,' Lily announced as she paraded into the kitchen.' You're Eliska's manny.'

'Indeed,' Robbie replied. 'Manny, eh? That's funny.'

'Not that funny,' Lola interjected. 'Anyway, my mummy said you have to be as nice as Chris or you are not allowed to see our daddy again.'

Inga walked into the kitchen and grimaced at Gordon as Lola said this. 'Oh, did she indeed,' Robbie said rather stiffly. 'Well, let's hope I pass the test then.'

Gordon bit his lip and mouthed, 'Sorry.'

Inga intervened . 'Right – come on then you two, we need to leave. Joshua will be waiting.'

'What do you mean, no?' Robbie couldn't understand why Gordon was turning down the line of cocaine he'd prepared on the coffee table whilst Gordon was in the toilet.

'It's just not what I'm about, that's all.'

'I'd have thought in the airline game, it's all party, party, party.'

'Well, it is sometimes, but that doesn't mean everyone has to take drugs.'

'Go on, try it. It'll make you feel horny. I can guarantee it.'

'Look, Robbie. I have kids, who will be home later. I am flying in the morning. I can't.'

'But you're happy to get pissed?'

'I said no, all right?' Gordon got up and went to the kitchen to get himself another beer. He was no prude but he wasn't a drug-taker either and never wanted to be.

'I need a fag,' Robbie said. 'Can I have one in here?'

'No, you'll have to go outside or lean right out of the bathroom window.'

'God, you're really no fun tonight, Daddio.'

'Come on, let's get a cab to the station and go into London then. We can party till late.' Gordon tried his best to appease his now coked-up and super-lively companion.

'No, let's just stay here. A party in your pants is just fine.' Gordon laughed. 'You're like a naughty schoolboy.'

'And ain't that the attraction,' Robbie smirked. 'You know you want it.

'Who's Chris anyway?'

'My long-term ex.'

'What happened?' Robbie's Mancunian accent seemed stronger all of a sudden.

'He couldn't cope with the kids. No, that's a lie – he couldn't cope with the whole family bit, although he loves the girls.'

'Yeah, can see where he's coming from. Don't know how you do it. I can just about tolerate them for my job, but that's it.'

'I had no choice but I don't regret a single day of having them.' Gordon suddenly thought of his beloved sister.

'Well, you're a better man than me. I like my freedom too much to be bogged down with all the baggage and ties that come with kids.'

Gordon looked at a smiling photo of him, Chris and the girls at last year's trip to Legoland. He had not been able to take it down.

'Do you know what, Robbie? I want you to leave.'

'What?'

'Please leave. It's not all about sex, is it? We are poles apart. I'm wasting your time. It's been fun but I can't do this anymore. Sorry.'

'Come on, Gordon, let's just have fun tonight then? I'll get us another beer, eh? We can talk about it.'

The doorbell went. Gordon went to answer it and walked back into the kitchen followed by a tall good-looking man with shoulder-length hair and stubble.

'John, what the fuck are you doing here?' Robbie snapped. 'You said…'

'I said I probably wouldn't want a lift until at least midnight, mate.' John looked completely confused as Robbie virtually frog-marched him down to the door of the block of flats, leaving it swinging open and a totally confused Gordon left in the doorway to his flat.

Robbie lit a cigarette the minute he was outside. 'What the fuck?' John asked.

'There ain't none of that, that's for sure. He already refused a line and has told me to go. I think you trying to suck his cock as well would tip him over the edge.'

'Shame, he's well cute.'

'Isn't he? But so's Mickey Mouse and to be honest we'd have more fun at Disneyland. Can you just wait a sec? I'd better nip up and say goodbye.'

'See you in a minute. We can polish off that gram

together.'

The door was shut when Robbie went back upstairs. When Gordon opened it, he had already changed into his joggers.

'Didn't realise you were a pimp as well as a drug dealer?'

'He's my flatmate – just got confused, that's all. Look, I'm sorry, Gordon. Sex aside, I do really like you. Have a think about us and give me a call, eh?'

Gordon rubbed his face. 'Yeah, I'll call you. Sorry about tonight. Lots on my mind.'

Robbie smiled and brushed Gordon's neck with his hand. 'He's not coming back, mate.'

Shutting the door gently, Gordon got himself a beer, put on the TV and lay on the sofa. With Chris, life had been so easy. God, he loved that man and he knew that Chris had loved him too. A life of sex, drugs and rock 'n' roll might be what Robbie wanted, but he was over thirty now and it just wasn't for him. He was a dad and wanted to settle down and lead a comfortable, uncomplicated life.

Realising he no longer even had a number to reach Chris on, he got up to go to the loo. When his beer slipped from his hand and smashed into pieces on the wooden floor, he promptly burst into tears.

'Cancer, you say?' Mo repeated calmly. 'Are you sure?'

Noah Anderson nodded slowly. Ron gripped his wife's hand tightly as the doctor continued, 'The results from the endoscopy were conclusive, I'm afraid.' Mo could feel a burning in her throat. Just as her life had taken on a slight sense of normality, here it went again – seconds out, round thirty, another blow to deal with.

'It's OK, Ron duck, we need to see what we've got to do to make you better now.'

'Do you want me to explain further?' Dr Anderson put in.

'How long have I got?' Ron asked matter-of-factly.

'Well. There are four stages of tumour in oesophageal cancer.'

'Just tell me, Doc.'

'T4 means the tumour has grown into other organs or body structures next to the food pipe.'

'Just tell me how long I've bleeding got!' Ron suddenly shouted. Mo looked horrified at his outburst.

Unfazed, Dr Anderson replied, 'Mr Collins, you are at the T4 stage, I'm afraid, and the prognosis is not good. I would say you are looking at a year at the most.'

Ron managed a weak smile. 'Expensive business this drinking lark, isn't it?'

'Yes.' Noah looked to Mo, who was gulping back her tears. 'Yes, unfortunately it is.'

Tony was waiting at the back door as Dana pulled into Rosco's car park.

'I never thought you were coming back. We had to get a few of Bruno's temps in and everything. Could have all won Miss World, but thick as shit.'

Dana kissed him on the cheek and luxuriated in his recently applied aftershave.

'I've had the most terrible flu, I'm so sorry to let you down.' Dana cringed inwardly, she was such a terrible liar.

The truth was, Mark had suggested she take some time out as she looked so tired. He also had told her that today he wanted her to give in her notice. She had promised him she would, but had no intention of doing so. On Friday it was the end of term so she would be having a two-week holiday for Easter anyway. She would try to persuade him to let her carry on whilst they were off.

'It's so nice to see the sunshine,' Dana trilled as she put on her pinny. 'And you.' She smiled at the handsome Italian and was annoyed to realise that her feelings just hadn't gone away. Tony said nothing. 'You OK? Not like you to be so quiet.'

'I'm fine. Just a bit sad already that you will be gone on Friday and not be here for two weeks for the Easter holidays.'

'I shall come back all brown and lovely as we are going to Majorca.' Dana was doing her best to pretend that 'the kisses' hadn't happened. But she felt as if a string was joining her to this gorgeous man and she just couldn't cut it, not just yet.

'We are having an Easter tea-party for all our locals on Thursday. Free cakes, a glass of fizz – you know. Eggs for the kids. It goes on till six so I was hoping you could maybe stay and help, and join in the fun too, of course?'

'Tommy breaks up at lunchtime on Friday so I'll have to shoot off right on time, then but Thursday – yeah. I should be able to get a play date for him. Mark is playing squash so he'll be late back.'

Tony smiled broadly. At least he would have a few extra hours with his little Czech princess.

Isobel Murray had headed off to the supermarket. Alana hated to admit it but she was actually being a great help and Eliska adored her. Stephen had been called away to Sweden on business for a week so she was welcoming the company.

Dana had also been a complete brick and with her now softer approach, Alana had at last, she thought, found herself in an unlikely friendship with the young mum.

Eliska came running into the conservatory, where Alana was to be found feet up on a pouffe watching her recent obsession, *Countdown*. Her company had agreed willingly for her to take a month off to recover from her loss, and she couldn't believe how much she was enjoying the freedom. It made her realise just quite how burned-out she was. And that in being that way, and so unhappy with it, had turned her into a person she didn't want to be.

Her daughter was closely followed by a lively Tommy and a tired-looking Dana.

'Hey, how you doing?' Dana asked as the children tore out of the French doors and into the spring sunshine to jump up and down on Eliska's huge trampoline.

'I'm actually feeling OK, thanks. I'm supposed to be back at work next week and really don't want to. Never ever thought I'd say that.'

'Do you think you will try for another baby with Stephen now you are feeling better?' Dana asked innocently.

Alana laughed. 'Us trying for a baby? We haven't even established our relationship yet. It's going to take him a long, long time to work out what he wants, I reckon.'

'He might surprise you, Alana. Men are useless on their own. Women are so much stronger. You wait – he'll keep going back to that big empty house of his in London and realise his heart lies here with you and Eliska. Yes, just you wait and see.'

'You should write romance novels, Mrs Knight.'

'Actually, I meant to ask you, now you're on your feet again, would you mind awfully having Tommy after school tomorrow? The boys have asked if I can work late at the café tomorrow; they are having an Easter treat afternoon and could do with the help.'

'You and your boys.' Alana cocked her head to the side. 'Why is it I see your face light up when you mention your workplace?'

Dana reddened.

'Dana? Have I hit a nerve?'

'No, no,' the young woman blustered. 'Well, they are good-looking and I do think Tony does have a soft spot for me.'

'You think?' Alana quizzed, her intuition with men and relationships coming to the fore.

Dana laughed. 'Let's just say if I wasn't married...'

'Well, from the little I can remember, his brother was bloody good at it.'

'Alana! I can't.'

'Which means you've thought about it. There is nothing wrong with fancying someone else if you are attached, it's only natural. It's when you act on it that it gets tricky, and by God I've learned a few lessons in my life by being so naughty when I shouldn't. That's probably why I'm still single at forty-two.'

'Did you love any of them?'

'The ones I had affairs with, you mean?' Dana nodded.

'Yes. I love Stephen now and I hate to say it out loud but the fact that his wife is no longer around is fate in my eyes. He would never have left her – and I could never have left him alone. My feelings are just so strong. Before Stephen, yes, I fell completely in love with a married man. Saw him on and off through my twenties for years. Had so many lonely Christmases, holidays, et cetera. He had kids. I got the usual flannel that when they were both at boarding school, we would be together. He never left his wife.'

'Oh, that's awful.'

'Yes, awful, but what a silly cow I was, thinking he would leave her. They rarely do – leave their wives, that is. Men just like the sexual buzz. Like to know that they've still got it. He was twenty years older than me. I mean, why wouldn't he want the affair? So my advice to you, Dana, if it's worth anything at all, is if you want extra-marital flings, make sure it's you doing the buzzing. A no-strings fuck with an unattached sexy young man…what's the harm if nobody knows?'

'And what if it's more than just sex?' Dana asked quietly.

'Then you've got to weigh up what you really want out of life and whether it's worth the complete turmoil it will cause by following that path. You've got a good life going on up there on Bramwell Hill, and Mark may be older but he's still a handsome man – and by what you tell me, a very good husband and father.'

Alana put her arm out and squeezed Dana's. 'I'm always here if you need a chat. Oh, and I nearly forgot.' She stood up and went over to the sideboard. 'Here.'

She presented Dana with a beautifully wrapped gift.

'It's not much, but I just wanted to thank you for all the help you've given me. Not just with Lissy but with…' she stopped.

Dana couldn't believe that Alana Murray actually had a tear in her eye. '…with everything to do with what happened with the baby and Stephen.'

Dana kissed her on the cheek. 'I've done nothing really and you shouldn't have, but that's lovely of you. Thank you. Can I get you anything before I go?'

'God, no – look at me. I'm absolutely fine. Getting used to all the attention. I will ask Mother to collect Tommy as well tomorrow and pack his uniform and we can take him to school on Friday too. That will give you a bit more time with Lover Boy.'

'It isn't happening,' Dana stated adamantly.

'Well, just in case it does.' Alana winked.

'You really are terrible.'

'I know. But as Mother always says, quite possibly to my detriment: "We are only here for a long weekend so we might as well enjoy it"'

Chapter Twenty One

'What time have we got you until then? Forever, I hope,' Tony flirted on their lull break.

Dana laughed. 'Actually a friend of mine has Tommy and Mark isn't home until after ten, so I haven't got to rush back.'

'*Bene, bene.* I shall kidnap you then in the flat upstairs and feed you grapes and pour champagne over your naked body.'

'Tony Rosco! NO!'

'No, what?' Bruno sauntered in and kissed Dana on both cheeks. '*Ciao*, Dana. Thanks for helping today. Now *fratello*, bring these cakes through, can you please?'

'Saved by the cream horns,' Dana grinned as Tony carried the box through to the café.

The boys' kind gesture of an Easter treat for their local clientele was really well received. Dana loved the generosity of her Italian employees and after just one glass of fizz she actually felt quite giddy.

She was clearing tables and putting more cakes out when Tony brushed up behind her. 'I have saved the biggest cream horn for you for later.'

Dana could feel her heart start to beat a little faster. Her intentions had been just so strong, that nothing would ever happen again between her and Tony. She had to stick to them.

Undeniably, sex now with Mark had gone up several pegs. She had put to the back of her mind about having a baby and was just enjoying it whenever she could, which had been quite a lot, to be honest – now that Mark was so into it too.

She did love her husband, but as Alana had so rightly said, that didn't stop you fancying other men. It was just what you did with that 'fancy'. She had been brought up with strong values of what was right and wrong. And to sleep with someone else was obviously a complete no, no. Then the devil would get on her shoulder and tap at it. But who would ever find out if once, just once, she slept with Tony? She wasn't hurting anyone on his side, and Mark need never know. Just one little fling and then she would settle with Mark and Tommy in her lavish lifestyle up on the hill. It was almost as if the more sex she was having, the more she wanted!

There was no denying Tony was a fit lad and had a lot of admirable qualities, but his focus now was the business, not settling down with a ready-made family – she was sure of that. Also, both he and Bruno had said they wanted to go back to Italy when they had enough money. The brothers shared the flat upstairs. Somehow she couldn't see Tony moving out and playing Happy Families with her, despite his declaration of how much he thought of her.

No, she had to keep her conscience clear. How could she possibly wake up next to Mark every day, knowing she had cheated on him? It was a good thing that she was going on holiday. She could clear her head of this folly.

She recognised Mo from the school coming in with the young Welsh girl from the surgery.

'Hello, there – Mo, isn't it?'

'Oh hi. You're Tommy's mum, aren't you? I kept seeing you in here and couldn't put my finger on it.'

'Looking forward to the holidays?' Dana politely chit-chatted.

'Not really. We are not going anywhere. Ron – my husband, that is – has cancer. So we need to be at home.'

'I'm so sorry – I didn't know. It's like having a cold

these days though, isn't it, the big C. They seem to have people in and out like a conveyor belt with loads of new treatments.'

'Sadly, it's not as easy in his case.'

'I'm so sorry. Look – here's my mobile.' Dana scribbled the number down on her pad. 'If you need any help with anything, lifts for Rosie, or to the hospital – anything – please do give me a call, eh? It must be so hard, not driving.'

'You little love, thank you!'

'Right, let's get you a couple of glasses of fizz.' Bruno was already by their side.

'*Bella, bella*, Foxy Ffion – how are you, my darling?'

'Always better when fuelled by a little fizz,' she flirted.

'Your wish, my lady, is my command.'

Mo laughed. 'You two. Get a bloody room. But refill my glass first.'

The place was empty by six and Dana hung her pinny on the peg in the back room.

'Do you want me to take it home and wash it?' she asked Tony as he came through to join her.

'No, I want to take you home and lick you all over.'

'Tony Rosco, it isn't going to happen. I am so sorry. It just can't.' 'But stay and have another drink with me and Bruno, please.'

'OK, just the one though as I'm rubbish with champagne, it goes straight to my head. And we wouldn't want you taking advantage of me now, would we?'

The flat upstairs had a beautiful roof garden, which couldn't be seen from the outside. The fence surrounding it had fairy lights and lanterns, and a spotted parasol sheltered the four chairs which were sat around an ornate French antique table.

'It's lovely up here. Bet it's beautiful at night when the fairy lights come on. I didn't expect this at all.'

'What, did you think it would be a real lads' pad, I guess?'

'Yes, I did, to be honest. But I love your flat too. You have good taste, you Rosco boys.'

Bruno stuck his head around the door to the garden, saying, 'I'm off to the pub with Ffion and then probably for dinner, so don't wait up.'

'OK, bro. Have fun.'

'Yeah, see you in a couple of weeks, Bruno, and don't do anything I wouldn't do.' Dana blew him a kiss.

'What wouldn't you do, Dana? Go on, tell me,' Tony urged, pouring her another glass of champagne. She was already light-headed but didn't want to stop.

'I wouldn't sleep with a married man and wreck a marriage.'

'I see. Sleeping with a single man is OK then. You can do that, *si*?'

'Oh, Tony. You just do something to me and I know I shouldn't be here, but I so want to be. And, I do so want to kiss you again, but it is just too dangerous.'

'I'm not asking you to leave your husband, Dana, but you do something for me too. It's hard to explain. You are like this drug and when you are not around I want you even more. I have got my head around the fact that this may not go anywhere, but just to have you here and alone is the most beautiful moment.' He got up and leaned down to kiss her.

He was so tender and so loving, and Dana melted into him. He pulled away, picked up her glass of champagne and poured it into a plant pot.

'And I don't want you drinking this and feeling you are doing something that you don't want to be doing. As much as I would love to make love to you, it has to be your decision alone. I would fuck you without stopping until Christmas if I had my way. You are just... just so fuckable.'

Dana loved it when he spoke like this. But what the hell was wrong with her? She was getting all the sex she needed, Mark was giving her loads of attention. She wanted for nothing.

She stood up and brushed her skirt down straight. 'Are you leaving?' Tony asked softly.

'No.' She roughly ripped the tie from his ponytail and let his hair go free. 'I'm hopefully coming.'

It was the best sex that Dana had ever had in her life. She screamed in pleasure time and time again. Tony just wanted to please her – and please her he did. Every which way but loose. When they were spent she lay back on the pillow in complete ecstasy. Tony went to speak and she put her fingers to his lips. He pulled them away.

'*Pazza di te*. That is all I can say.'

She snuggled into him and within minutes they were both sleeping.

BANG, BANG, BANG!

'What the...?' Tony sat upright, waking Dana. 'Shit, Dana, it is midnight.'

'I'm frightened – what's that noise?'

Tony ran to the window. 'Please don't tell me that your husband has a black Porsche.'

'Oh my God. What am I going to do?'

Suddenly Bruno came rushing in. He threw some keys at Tony.

'You, fire escape. Give it five, then drive up the road in the van until I call you. Dana, get dressed quickly and just get on the sofa and keep your eyes closed. *Now*!'

'Where's Ffion?'

'God, woman, she's not the issue – come on, get dressed and leave the talking to me.' He was whispering now.

BANG! BANG! BANG!

'All right mate, I'm coming.' Bruno shouted.

Mark pushed his way into the café. 'Where the fuck is my wife? And more importantly the little shit with the ponytail?'

'Hey, calm down. If you mean Dana, which I think you must, she is upstairs. Had a few too many champagnes so I suggested she sleep them off on the sofa. She must have forgotten to text you as she said she was going to. Come on up and have a drink. She was so worried about driving that she'll be pleased to see you.'

Mark leaped up the stairs two at a time, adrenalin making his heart race – only to find his wife looking dishevelled but fully dressed, on the sofa under a grubby duvet.

'Hey.' Dana yawned and rubbed her face, then sat up. 'I'm so sorry, darling. It's so not like me to be at home when you get back. We just had a little bit of an Easter party, that's all. I should never have had those three glasses of champagne. God, I feel ill. My head is banging.'

'Well, I was worried sick,' Mark said, his anger beginning to fade. 'You could have let me know.'

'I'm so sorry, I meant to text you but must have crashed out. You know what I'm like when I drink champagne. Never again!'

'And where's Tommy?'

'He's staying the night with Eliska – he's fine.'

'So it's just you two here then?'

'Yes, my girlfriend Ffion has gone home now. And Tony, "the little shit with the ponytail" as you call him, is out with his.'

'Oh right, well, sorry for the commotion. I was just worried about Dana, that's all.'

'Well, you needn't have been. You've got a good wife here, mate, don't forget that. The fact she didn't want to drink and drive is commendable and she's worked her socks off for me here. Now go and enjoy your holiday, the pair of you.'

Dana grabbed her bag and shoes and dutifully followed her husband back down to the café and out of the front door, saying a sleepy 'thank you' to Bruno as he locked up.

That was it now. She had had her cream horn and eaten it.

After a post-mortem with Bruno and a very large Amaretto, Tony sat on his bed, head in hands.

Poor Dana, he knew she would be getting such shit now. Sometimes, maybe it was better to hang on to the glorious intent rather than going through with the action.

Her husband must have had an inkling, to mention him like that – and if she had any chance of saving her marriage, which is what he thought she did want in the long run, he would have to leave her alone now.

He would also never give her the worry of knowing that one of the condoms they had so carefully used had split.

Chapter Twenty Two

Mo was glad that this end of term was not culminating with a boring assembly but a picnic for all the kids on the playing field. Thankfully, April had given them a beautiful sunny day for this.

Robbie was there helping Mr Chambers set out the picnic tables and he waved to Inga as she approached. She waved back but thought she must text ahead to Gordon to warn him he was here.

To be honest, she was glad that Gordon wasn't seeing him anymore. There was something about him that she just didn't like – the way he spoke to her for one. As if she was just some sort of home help when she knew that within the Summers family she was so much more than that. In fact, she had never felt happier and had even started seeing a lovely guy her own age whom she had met at the local pub a couple of weeks ago.

Isobel Murray, wearing a huge floppy sun hat and even larger designer glasses, walked alongside Alana up the school drive. They were chatting away amicably. Mr Chambers had noticed the difference in Eliska since Alana had been off work and it pleased him greatly. He'd also noticed the change in Alana and realised she wasn't a bad person at all. She was just a stressed working mum, and not everyone was lucky enough not to have to work full time and bring up children, especially in this current austere climate.

'Who does that old bag bloody think she is – Sophia Loren?' Robbie commented to Will Chambers.

'Maybe I should have arranged a Glamorous Granny

competition, instead of just Guess the Weight of the Cake,' the teacher retorted, smiling.

'I'm just popping round the back for a fag,' Robbie stated and he walked towards Inga, saying, 'How's little Miss Au Pair today, then?'

'I eez very well, thank you, Robbie.'

'Gordon not coming up today then?'

'Yes, he is. His flight should be landing around now, so he's coming straight here.'

'How is he?'

'Yeah, he's fine. Seems really happy at the moment. The single life suits him, I think.' She paused. 'Leave him alone, Robbie. Two schoolkids is enough in that flat.' And with that, she walked over to Dana who had just arrived, leaving a seething Robbie to walk off and have his cigarette.

Dana smiled as Inga greeted her.

'You look tired, honey – are you OK?'

'Fine, fine. Just lots going on at home at the moment.' Dana thought she was going to be sick.

Inga noticed what looked like a slight bruise on her cheek but it was covered with so much make-up she chose not to say anything.

Dana walked over to one of the picnic tables and put her face to the sun. Tired? She had never been so tired or upset in her whole life. Mark had gone mad at her. He had told her that he had parked outside the café one day and seen the way Tony looked at her – and that had from then on sparked off his jealousy. When she didn't come home and he saw her car parked outside the café last night, he had thought there was something going on.

Thank heaven for Bruno intervening or things could have been a lot worse. He had virtually dragged her to his car, shouting, and even when they got outside the house he carried on. The more she denied anything, the more he kept on saying he didn't believe her. It was when she said the fateful words, 'Well, if you are going to keep on accusing me of doing it, I should have bloody done it anyway,' that Mark had lifted his hand to strike her. She didn't know if he would have or not because she had ducked, slipped and ended up hitting her cheek on the corner of a kitchen unit. God, it had hurt.

But what hurt more was the fact that he had even raised his hand. In all their years together, Mark had never ever been violent.

She had, however, been unfaithful and was now in complete and utter turmoil. She didn't blame the way Mark acted; she probably would have been a lot worse if it was him, but today she hated him and she wasn't sure if they could get back to how it was. Especially with her knowing what she had done.

The sex and closeness to Tony had been amazing and the thought of waking up next to that beautiful man every day was making her now consider whether her marriage with all its material benefits was enough.

'Mummy!' Tommy came bounding towards her. 'Me and Eliska slept in a tent in her conservatory last night, we ate so many sweets and Mrs Murray had to tell us off for being noisy. But it was such fun.'

She hugged him so tightly he started squirming like an irritated kitten.

'Mummy, get off me, will you.' He ran off onto the playing fields as she tried to stop the tears from flowing.

Alana came over and saw her face. 'Shit, you look rough.'

'Thanks for that. I'm OK. Flying to Majorca tonight. Two weeks of sunshine with my beautiful family.' Dana smiled weakly.

'So?' Alana enquired.

'It's not the time or place here, Alana, but it's not good.'

'You can always phone or text me when you are away,

OK?'

Dana nodded as the whirlwind that was Isobel Murray joined them.

'So when do we get our food then?' she asked loudly in her strong Scottish accent.

'Mother, we bring our own. What do you think this cool bag is for?'

'Oh, I thought that was just the wine, darling.'

'Any news from Stephen?' Dana enquired.

'No, I haven't seen him to talk to for weeks now. First he was working away a lot and now he's spending Easter with Cheri, his wife's sister. They jointly owned a property over there and he's helping her with the legalities. I'm hoping he'll be home during the second week of the holidays as I could really do with some sun and some fun too. And also, to bloody see where we are going, if anywhere.'

'He sounds like such a good man, Alana – he will be straight with you, I know he will. The only thing with being with her sister is it will drag it all up again, so be ready for that.'

'Yeah, I know. It's not going to be an easy fix. But what is? Thank heaven for romance novels, eh? At least we get to read a happy ending now and then.'

Dana laughed. 'Have you really got wine in there?'
'Beautifully disguised as apple juice, yes.'

'Perfect. Hair of the dog is required, I think.'

Emily Pritchard – Scorned wife, Head of PTA, Netball Coach and Mother of Joshua P, seven, chief swot and playground kisser – was suddenly among them. She was wearing the shortest summer dress, with a V neck that revealed her ample bosom to the world.

'Hello, ladies. What a joy to be able to show a bit of flesh.'

Mo overheard and looked at Joan. 'A bit of flesh? She might just as well have worn a bloody bikini. Look –

there's an empty table. Let's go and set up camp.'

They spread out their food and looked to their youngsters who were all running around in the top playing-field.

'So any word from Charlie senior then?' Mo asked.

'I was just going to tell you that I had one missed call from him yesterday – and that was it. I won't call him back as agreed. But if he doesn't happen to catch me unawares it will be the same answer: Charlie is Ron's. How is he today, by the way?'

'Oh Joanie, it's terrible. It is so hard for him to eat even with the sleeve thing they have put in him. He has lost so much weight. It's ironic really that here we are trying to get thin, and all he wants to do is get some food in him and put on weight.'

'And how's Rosie?'

'You know what kids are like, she knows he's ill but of course I haven't told her yet just how serious it is. She sits on the bed and chats to him if he can't get up and he reads to her every night. I tried to get hold of young Charlie last night, haven't got a working number for him, so emailed his Hotmail account and just hope he picks it up. He has a right to know, despite how little he thinks of his father. Oh Joanie, what a mess!'

Joan rubbed her friend's shoulder. 'Come on, Mo, you can do this. When I used to go to church a few years ago, the vicar always used to say, "Everything will be all right, you know. It always is." And do you know what, Mo? It will be. At the moment, I bet everything seems dark and you are on this constant treadmill, fighting life and what it's throwing at you, but you will find peace – I know it. You bloody deserve it, girl. You are a diamond of a person.'

'Aw, that's the nicest thing to say. Thanks, love.'

Gordon came scooting up the drive, waving frantically to Inga. Noticing Robbie talking to an animated Emily, he lowered his hand and slipped quietly down on a seat on the table next to Inga.

'What's he doing here?'

'Helping Mr Chambers out.'

'I could really do without talking to him, to be honest.'

'Just sit here with me, darling. There is no love lost between us so I doubt if he'll come over for a while anyway.'

Mr Chambers rang a bell and called all the children inside. Each class emerged wearing Easter bonnets they had made in class that morning and sang a song to the waiting picnickers. Then he lifted his megaphone, told everyone about the Guess the Weight of the Cake completion, cranked up some pop music and said, 'Enjoy!'

'God, he's not in the mood today,' Gordon quipped. 'Mind you, after a whole term of a hundred plus kids, nor would I be.'

Inga laughed, not noticing Emily Pritchard – Scorned wife – approaching. 'Maybe this will take the smile off your face, you marriage-breaking slut.'

And, in true slapstick style she slammed a paper plate full of trifle right into Inga's pretty little face.

– Summer Term –

'(24/7) – once you sign on to be a mother, that's the only shift they offer.'
Jodi Picoult

Chapter Twenty Three

Joan was puffing as she changed her third bed of the day. She was just getting clean sheets out of the airing cupboard for the fourth when her mobile rang.

'Joan?'

'Yes?'

'Charlie Lake here. I have a cheque here for five hundred pounds with your name on it if you're ready to tell me if I am the father or not.'

'Charlie, even if you had a cheque for five thousand pounds I still have nothing to say to you, and I would be grateful if you don't even consider contacting Mo at the moment, if that is on your agenda. Ron is dying, you see, and she has enough stress without you upsetting her further.'

'That's awful.'

'Yes, it is. He has cancer – it's a terrible business.'

'Well, I'm sorry to have bothered you. Take care, Joan. Good morning to you.'

Joan looked at her now dead handset and screwed up her face. Charlie Lake really had sounded sincere then. Maybe he wasn't such a bad man, after all.

Mo had decided she didn't want Ron to go to a hospice to end his days. His Marie Curie nurses had been exceptional and she took on all of his care when they were not around. Dr Anderson had been superb and had given her all the time off she needed.

She had just dropped off Rosie at school and was putting some bedsheets in the washing machine when there was a knock on the door.

'Charlie, my darling. I can't tell you how pleased I am to to see you.' She burst into tears and her son hugged her tightly. His floppy fringe had now been cut into a much smarter, shorter style and he was dressed in his trademark skinny jeans and trendy T-shirt.

'How's he doing?' he asked when Mo had calmed down. She just shook her head. 'Not good, darling, not good.'

'I got him these.' It was a batch of old West Ham football programmes from the seventies.

'Oh Charlie, he'll love those! Remember the times he used to swear at the telly when his mighty Hammers were losing?'

'He's not gone yet, Mum. Can I go up?'

Ron was propped up in bed watching the television. Charlie took a deep breath and walked over to sit by the bed. He could hardly recognise his dad. The cancer had stolen his drink-induced pot belly. He was instead a small, frail, skeletal figure. His breathing was very laboured and his skin like parchment.

'Hey, Dad.' Charlie's voice wobbled slightly.

'I thought you were never bloody coming.' Ron attempted a smile and put his hand out to find Charlie's. He squeezed it as hard as he was able. 'I'm so sorry, son.'

Charlie couldn't hold back the tears as his father told him, 'I love her with all my heart, you know, and I have been trying to make it up to her, now I'm off the drink.'

'I know.' Charlie spluttered. 'She told me in an email. She does love you, Dad. I mean, she wouldn't still be here now, would she?' The young man sighed. 'And I'm sorry too for hitting you. But I had to.'

'You did, and I will be forever grateful to you for doing it because at least I had a few sober months to show those girls of ours how much I do care. Look after 'em, Charlie. I know you're not a bad lad, really. Look after 'em.' And with that, Ron closed his eyes. There was a moment of peace, but then Charlie could no longer hear his father breathing...

'Mum!' Charlie screamed. 'Mum!' She ran up the stairs.

'He waited for me,' Charlie sobbed. 'Dad waited for me.'

'I couldn't just ring you, I had to come in.' Dana had got up at 630 a.m. and knew that the Rosco boys would already be up preparing for the morning's coffee rush. She had told Mark she was going for a morning jog and would be back in time to get Tommy ready for school.

Bruno carried on cleaning the coffee machine.

'It's fine, Dana. I knew you wouldn't be able to stay.' He came round from behind the counter and gave her a hug.

'Thanks so much for what you did,' she said shamefacedly.

'I was saving my little brother's arse as much as yours.'

'I know, and I'm sorry.'

'Don't be sorry – be kind to him. He's upstairs just out of the shower if you want to go up.'

The sight of Tony at the top of the stairs with a towel round his waist took her breath away. His long wet hair was dripping down his smooth, muscly chest.

'You look so beautiful with a tan,' he said.

He put his arms around her and Dana breathed him in. Even without aftershave she just loved his smell.

'I take it you have come for your P45? I can swap it for a T69 if you like?' He laughed.

'Tony, this is serious.'

'I know, *bella*, but if I don't joke I might cry. Did he believe you?'

'Yes, in the end. But I do have to go.'

'I know.'

'It's so hard, but I think it's more about Tommy and trying to make a go of it than anything else.'

'I understand.'

She exhaled loudly. 'You, you are just so amazing though, Tony Rosco, and I fancy the arse off you. And I can't believe I am using my head here and not my heart. I am so sorry.' She started to cry.

'Oh darling girl, do not cry. It is fine. All I want out of this is for you to be happy, hey?'

She bit her lip and nodded, tears still streaming down her face. 'I'd better go.'

'You hear me? Be happy,' Tony repeated as she disappeared round the bend in the stairs.

He walked out on the roof garden and lit a cigarette. Bruno came out to join him.

'All right, bro? She's got you right in the heart, hasn't she?'

Tony took a large drag of his cigarette and nodded.

'But when Fabia comes over this week I still think you should make a damn good go of it.'

'But Fabia is not Dana.'

'No, but she is equally hot, would never cheat on you – and she worships the floor you walk on.'

Bruno scooted off downstairs, leaving Tony deep in thought.

The Indian waiter delivered another large gin and tonic to Gordon. 'I really can't believe this is happening.'

'Nor can I, and I am so sorry.' Inga bit into her poppadom.

'I do understand though. I mean, the thought of facing the wrath of Preachy Knickers every day. I have to say it still makes me laugh that she came at you with a custard pie.'

'I know,' Inga laughed hard. 'But it's terrible too. I am such a slut. That poor woman. Hardly anyone saw her do it, I don't think, and as I quickly went to the bathroom to get cleaned up, there was no real big scene.'

'You must fill me in,' Gordon said eagerly. 'With you going away over Easter I've missed out on the goss. So, any word from Kenny Boy since?'

'I thought I told you, he sent a massive long text saying how sorry he was but he would obviously not be seeing me further and was making a go of it with his wife. They had been having problems anyway and are now going to Relate.'

'I can't believe he told her in the first place. I guess it was him and she just wasn't assuming?'

'He must have had a massive guilt trip. I mean, how else would she have found out? His life will be a living hell now.'

'So tell me about this Marcin then?'

'He's Polish like me, very tall, very sexy and I like him a lot.'

'So, when is our last goodbye?'

'It's going to have to be this weekend. His building contract starts on Monday, he has sorted us a studio flat to rent, and his boss needs me from then too.'

'Good timing though, in light of the situation. I will miss you so much, my lovely, and so will the girls.'

'I'm only going to be thirty miles away, so we will still see each other. I will make sure of that.'

'How many children will you be looking after?'

'Just the one – it will be like a holiday.' Inga laughed. 'So what are you going to do about looking after the girls?'

'I've got a week off, which is good. Then, I'm thinking about asking Robbie. At least Lily and Lola know him already.'

'Really? Are you sure?'

'Oh, don't. Why are you saying it like that?'

'There's something about him, Gordy. I can't put my

finger on it, but I really don't like or trust him.'

'That's the trouble. I quite fancy putting my fingers in him again.'

'You are so vile, Gordon Summers, but that is why I think I love you just a little bit less than Marcin. Please, think carefully,' she added, genuinely worried. 'Maybe use Robbie as a stopgap, but that is all.'

'You are so wise for your young years sometimes, girl.'

'Not so wise to sleep with a married man and have to move counties, is it?'

'We all make mistakes and learn from them,' Gordon said kindly.

'So please don't make one with Robbie.'

'I promise I won't. Now come on – let's order a bottle of wine and stuff our faces with tandoori chicken.'

'I forgot how much I loved it here.' Alana tipped her head back into the London sunshine and took in the river view.

'It is lovely, isn't it? We haven't done this for such a long time,' Stephen added.

'It's almost a date.' Alana smiled at her tall, auburn-haired companion and couldn't quite believe they still hadn't had sex even though they could now do so without guilt.

'It's also nice to be able to talk without your mother either listening or butting in,' Stephen said. He ordered drinks from the hovering waiter.

'Don't be hard on her. I hate to admit it, but despite her mad old foibles she has been a complete brick. See, another thing in my life I have you to thank for.'

'Bloody amazing, me.' Stephen chuckled.

'You are,' Alana said quietly.

'You might not think so in a minute.'

'Oh no – what? Just tell me, Stephen. I've been waiting to have the conversation about us and Eliska for so long now.'

The waiter delivered the drinks to the table and Alana took a large swig of her gin and tonic.

'OK, I'm not going beat about the bush here.' Stephen looked her in the eyes. 'I'm moving to Cyprus.'

Alana felt as if acid had just been poured through her veins. Stephen saw the pain in her face.

'No, no. I don't want to leave you both. I want you to come with me. Start a new life.'

'But...'

'Hear me out on this one, Alana. My plan was always to retire at fifty out there anyway. Susan's sister has a few villas that she rents out, but it is getting too much for her, so I have bought three of them from her. The intention is to live in the best one and live off the rental income from the other two. SM Public Relations will stay alive, my second-in-command is to become the MD and I will just advise and be involved in the big stuff.'

'Wow, that does sound like a-dream-come-true stuff, but where do I fit in?'

'You fit in with me, Alana. Taking this time away from you recently has given me a chance to have a long, hard think. I will always love Susan, and you'll have to bear with me on the grief front, but you've changed. Since losing the baby and taking time out from your work, you have shown me a different side to you. And I like it.' He leaned over and took her hand. 'In fact, I love you, Lani.'

Tears pricked her eyes.

'It is a big decision for me,' she said quietly. 'I mean, what will I do for work? And what about uprooting Eliska from school, and her quality of life in a different country?'

'You can help me with the villa rentals or see what else suits you. If you work within the tourist industry, being an English speaker is fine. And knowing you, you'll be bi-lingual before you know it. There are a lot of schools for ex-pats – and what better for a little girl than to learn a new language and culture. She's young enough to adapt and such a sprightly little thing, I'm sure she'll love it.'

Alana took another large swig of drink. 'I don't know what to say.'

'"Yes" might be good,' Stephen told her.

'When are you thinking of going?'

'As soon as possible, so I can be around for the main holiday season. I already have a tenant moving into the Chiswick house at the end of the month.'

'I need to think about it. It's a massive upheaval. I mean, I have my house to think about too, plus schools for Eliska. And my job, of course. And yes, even Mother. Plus, I'm forgetting one small point. We still haven't told our daughter that you are her father. She adores you now.'

'So, it's a perfect time to tell her. To begin our new lives together. And I will, of course, help you with everything. You are not alone now, angel.'

When Alana looked pained, he said gently, 'Anyone would think you'd had bad news. Not the offer of being a kept woman in a beautiful foreign country.'

'I've never wanted to be a kept woman, you know that,' Alana snapped. 'Sorry, wrong words – you know what I mean though. Come on, let's order some food, have a nice time, and you can think about this later.'

Alana drained her glass. Wasn't this what she had been longing for? A life with Stephen McNair. But now it was on a plate in front of her, she just wasn't quite sure.

Chapter Twenty Four

'I am so sorry for your loss.' Dana caught Mo as she was just walking through the school gates.

'Thank you, Dana. Ron went a lot quicker than we all thought he would. So he didn't suffer too badly.'

'Here, this is for you. When all has settled, you can take a little bit of time out for yourself.'

It was a voucher for the beauticians at the top of Denbury High Street. 'Aw, thanks Dana, that's lovely of you.'

'And my offer of any childcare, et cetera. is still there, so don't be a martyr.'

'I won't – and thanks again.'

Emily Pritchard, custard-pie thrower, swanned up the drive wearing one of her minuscule summer dresses.

'Well, he was a drinker, you know – overweight too, so what did she expect?' She spurted over to one of the other mothers dressed for the catwalk. Joan was pushing her bike behind her and overheard the spiteful remark. She was so angry that she made sure the front wheel went straight into Preachy's leg.

'Arrggh! Oh my God, you clumsy cow, that really hurt – and if that rubs off my fake tan...'

'Oh, shut up whining!' Joan snapped. 'At least Mo's husband kept his cock in his trousers.'

Gordon had overheard this and gave Joan the biggest kiss. 'You go, girl. When is the funeral, by the way?'

'Tomorrow. Why, are you thinking of going?'

'No, not at all. I was going to offer to see if Mo needed any help with any school runs.'

'You are a love, Gordon.'

'I do my best, Joanie, I do my pitiful best.' He waved his arm in the air camply.

'Sorry to hear you've lost Inga.'

'I know, we all miss her so much. But she's found love and she needed to get out of here, you know that.'

'So what are you going to do when you fly now?'

At that moment, Robbie appeared up the drive with Eliska. 'There's just the man,' Gordon added. 'I'd better grab him. See you later, sweetie.'

'Hello, stranger.' Robbie smiled sexily. 'Hello you.'

Eliska ran off to the playground to meet Joshua P.

'So to what do I owe this pleasure? I mean, last time you virtually kicked me down the stairs.'

'Slight exaggeration, but yeah, sorry. I was caught in a moment that's all, and have kinda been missing your kissing. I want to talk to you about the girls too.'

'I'm around tonight, say the Featherstone Arms at eight?'

'Yeah, that's fine. I'll sort a babysitter. See you later.'

Dana sat on the side of the bath and felt the terrible irony of it all. After all these years of wanting another baby, now she wasn't sure if that was what she wanted at all.

Mo put her handbag on the kitchen table and flicked the kettle on. She couldn't have coped without Dr Anderson's help and support. He had not only guided her through the whole funeral process, she would be eternally grateful that he had also lent her two thousand pounds for the funeral costs. Which, he said, she could pay back at just fifty pounds a month, interest free.

In fact, she had been overwhelmed by everyone's love and generosity. Even Charlie had taken the week off from his new job and was helping around the house.

She went upstairs to see if she had anything smart and

black lurking in the wardrobe. She had a black hat if nothing else. Her hat box was on the top shelf. She jumped up to push it to the edge so she could reach it, and in doing so knocked it flying down on the floor. The hat flew onto her dressing-table, along with a white envelope addressed: To my beautiful wife.

Sitting on the bed, she hungrily ripped open the envelope.

My dear darling Mo,

Unless you've decided to wear your black hat for some other occasion, which I very much doubt, you are reading this because I am no longer with you and haven't had the chance to say this to you face to face.

Quite simply, I love you – and even through our darkest days I always have. Our life wasn't a bad life to start with and I hope I made you happy back then. The regret I have for how I behaved when I did lose my job is immense, and do you know what – I deserved to die young for the way I treated you. And knowing that I have left you no money to carry on with now makes me feel physically sick.

You are quite simply a beautiful woman, Mo. You always have been. Size 8 to18. Some of the things I remember I said to you in my alcoholic state were just so cruel, so unthinkably cruel. All I can say is, I am truly, deeply sorry.

And now to our kids. The beautiful little Rosie and the handsome rogue, Charlie. I know that Rosie wasn't made in a love-filled haze by any means, but the joy that little girl has given me has made my short life worth every second. I don't have to say 'look after her' because I know that you are the best mother any child could ever wish for; one of the many other reasons I loved you so much.

Now, to Charlie. This is the hard part but I didn't want to go to my grave with you not knowing, and I hope it makes you think more of me than you probably do.

I have always known he wasn't mine. Even when he was a little bump in your tummy. It would have been an immaculate conception – even I as a mere bloke worked that one out. But I loved you, Mo, loved you so much that I wanted to take you and your baby on. I couldn't bear not to have you in my life and after all you had been through growing up, I knew you deserved and needed security and love.

Tears poured down Mo's cheeks as she read on.

And when that beautiful little dark-haired boy appeared, it didn't matter that he wasn't mine. All I knew was that he needed a dad and that was going to be me, to the best of my ability. You may/may not know who the father is, but my blessing is with you Mo. If you want to tell Charlie that I wasn't his dad and encourage him to find his real father, then that is fine by me. He gets the best of both worlds then, eh? And who knows, you might just find love again too.

Find happiness, Mo, and love and a person who will look after you properly. I failed you but I always loved you, loved you with all my heart.

Yours forever, Ron x

Mo wiped her eyes roughly with her hand, folded the letter and tucked it into her knicker drawer.

That was it. She would get herself through the stress of the funeral and then tell Charlie the truth. There were to be no more secrets in this house, and if he did take off, she would just have to trust the strength of a son's love for him not to stay angry with her forever.

It was a really warm April night and the beer garden at the Featherstone Arms was heaving.

Gordon waited nervously for Robbie to appear with

their drinks.

'So, if I get you right, you are asking me to be a sort of housekeeper for the girls? I ain't no au pair, love – my dressing-up days are long gone,' Robbie told him.

'Not a housekeeper, but if I could put in your diary when I am flying and you could be available to do school runs, feed the kids and babysit when I'm not around, that would be such a help. It would, of course, be a stopgap until I can get another au pair as I know you have a busy life. I won't go through Bebops and can pay you cash. And I wouldn't expect you to move in.'

'Hmm, and what might my extra benefits be – and you know I'm not talking holiday pay.'

'You're a bad man, Robbie.' Gordon had a sudden thought. 'Do you know what? I don't even know your surname, and that's outrageous. I know the intimate parts of your body but not who you really are.'

'Who's the slut now? It's Williams, anyway.'

'Shut the fuck up!' Gordon exclaimed. 'You are joking.'

'No, my mum had a thing for him and that was it – she married a Williams and called her firstborn Robbie. Just a shame I don't have his money.'

'So, what do you reckon?'

'Let's give it a go. As long as I know in advance, which you say I will, I can organise any other work and fit stuff around the Youth Centre.'

'Brilliant. The girls are with their grandparents tonight, so I have a free house too.'

'Ooh – payment in kind in advance! I like that idea. Sod eating, let's get these down us and go back to yours.'

Mo woke to the rain bashing against her bedroom window and the awful realisation that today she was cremating her husband. Somehow it always seemed worse sending someone off in the rain and she hoped it would brighten up by eleven.

She had given Rosie the choice of whether she wanted to come or not but Rosie was insistent that she wanted to be part of the day. She realised it would be sad but she wanted to be there for her mum, and she said that she could hold her big brother's hand in case he was sad too.

The Collins family looked a very sad, but smart trio as they left the house and got into the funeral car that was waiting for them to follow Ron in the hearse to the crematorium.

The service was short but very nice, even though there weren't that many good things that the vicar could spout on about Ron's recent life. Charlie was a complete angel throughout, looking after his mum and guiding Rosie through the service and wiping her tears away with the tissues he had brought.

Joan and Ffion looked on at how caring he was being and a little piece of each of their hearts melted.

When Charlie got outside, he suddenly cracked. He knew that Joan was travelling back with his mum and Rosie, so he gave her a kiss and said he would see her at the pub where the wake was being held, once he had pulled himself together.

However, once out of their sight, he walked out of the church gates and straight into a pub immediately opposite the church to get a badly needed drink.

'A large JD and Coke, please, mate.'

'And I'll have the same,' a young Welsh accent trilled behind him, handing a twenty-pound note over the bar.

'Ffion! What are you doing here?'

'I was at the back of the church showing support to your mum. I'm so sorry, darling.'

Charlie downed his drink in one. 'Shove another one in there, please, mate.' He wiped his eyes and moved over to sit at a table in the corner.

Ffion joined him. 'You were so brave. I can't imagine

losing either of my parents.'

'I know my dad was a bastard at the end but we made our peace.' He bit his lip to stop further tears. 'And we had such a happy house when we were little. Oh, Ffi. This is so shit and poor Mum, she's got no bloody money. I'm going to help her now and stop being such a bastard myself. And I did love him, deep down. I really did.'

'That is just so lovely, considering he wasn't even your real dad.' Charlie felt as if he had just been shot in the heart.

'What did you just say?'

'Yeah, your mum told me that she was pregnant when she met your dad.' Charlie wished he had been shot in the heart.

'I guess I was lucky we all made it work then, eh? Right, let's get to that wake. I mean, what would my dad think, me not drinking to his health?'

'Mother! Mother! Where are you?' Alana threw her keys on the side. The TV was on and the kettle had just boiled.

She could hear loud screeching in the garden. She went to the conservatory and there was her sixty-seven-year-old mother and her six-year-old daughter running though the sprinkler which was in full flow. She laughed out loud, keeping in the shadows so she could watch with joy for longer.

That was another thing: how could she take Eliska away from her granny now that they had just met and were getting on so well? Her daughter had never been happier – and was it her right to pull her away from all that she found familiar to start up a new life with Stephen?

She walked outside and the naughty twosome stopped still as if to prove they had been doing nothing, although the fact they were soaked to their pants somewhat gave the game away.

'I don't know what you're stopping for,' Alana said,

turning up the hose on the side of the house so that she could join in the fun.

She hadn't had such a laugh in years. In fact, she had forgotten what real happiness felt like, until lately.

'Thank you,' Alana said to her mother as they sat in dressing-gowns having a cup of tea at the kitchen table later. Eliska was up having a bath.

'For what, dear?'

'For coming back and loving us.'

'Not exactly difficult to do, Lani,' Isobel Murray replied in her usual no-nonsense manner. 'Now I really must get bathed if the bairn has finished. I mean, look at the state of my hair!'

'Have you got a sec before you go up, Mother?'

'Sure, my darling. What's the matter?'

'It's a dilemma, but shouldn't be a dilemma.'

'Go on, spit it out, girl.'

'Stephen has asked if I will move to Cyprus with him – I mean me and Rosie, of course.'

'And will you have to work?'

'No. He's semi-retiring and says I can help with his business over there, or if I want to find something for myself, of course.'

'Good God, girl, book the tickets now. What the deuces are you waiting for?'

'I'm worried about Eliska, uprooting her and also leaving you now that we are all getting on so well.'

'Look, let's break it down. The schools will have a lot of ex-pat kids. It is a holiday resort so there will be lots of English speakers to make friends with. And I've always thought that living in new countries rounds you as a person.'

'Stephen said all of that and his wife's sister lives there with her kids, so she can help me with schools, I guess.'

'See? And I can manage the house here, if you like. Or even better, darling, you know that wherever I lay my hat is my home. I could even get a little villa in the sun near you to help babysit.'

'Stephen's business actually is villa rental.'

'Well, there you go! What's not to be excited about, I say.'

'And what about my job?'

'You were saying yourself how much you liked not working, the month you had off. Go, Lani – have some fun with a decent man who loves you. You've worked hard. You deserve it. And you mark my words, that little one will love it and love you for it when she's older, I promise you.'

'Oh, I don't know.'

'What's really your concern, Lani?'

'I think I'm a bit scared.'

'Of what in particular?'

'Of not being in control, of being cared for. Of Stephen never loving me as much as his wife. It all just seems a bit too much. I don't think I can do it.'

'Oh, love. You mustn't throw away this chance of happiness because of your stubborn, single-minded nature. You can always come back if it's not for you, but do you know what? You don't find many Stephen McNairs in this life, and if I were you, I would grab him with both hands and not let him go.'

Chapter Twenty Five

Ron Collins' wake was over in an hour. Mo didn't want it to be a boozy affair, considering that was what in effect had destroyed her marriage and killed her husband.

Charlie had told Ffion to her dismay that he didn't want her to go with him and that in his eyes they were over for good. Well, sod him; he was a nasty piece of work anyway so why would she want him in her life? She let him go and went back to the bar to have one for the road.

'Penny for 'em?'

'What?' Ffion said to the rotund dark-haired man at the bar. 'I said "a penny for 'em" – your thoughts, that is.'

'Oh, sorry – I was miles away. I've just been to a funeral and my sort of ex has just been an arse. Didn't I see you in the back of the church?'

'Nah, it must have been someone who just looked like me. Let me get this for you – can't see a pretty girl like you in distress. I'm Charlie, by the way.'

'Not another one – that's his name.'

'Oh dear. So why's this young Charlie being an arse then?'

'I don't know really. I just mentioned that he was coping so well, considering it wasn't even his real dad, and he went all narked on me.'

'He's probably feeling very emotional and doesn't know how to get it out, like most lads.'

'It is a really sad but also romantic story, actually. His mum met someone while she was in care and felt he couldn't provide for her and a baby. She really loved him too.'

'Yeah, that is a sad tale. You give the lad a break, pet. He'll be fine once today is over, I bet you.'

With that Charlie Lake went out to the smoking area lit a cigarette and grinned broadly.

When Dana picked Mark up from the train station, he seemed tired and agitated.

'Nice day doing nothing in the sunshine?' was his opening gambit.

'Well, it was your choice to stop me working.'

'Don't even go there when I'm in this bad a mood. Where's the boy anyway?'

'He's at Eliska's.'

'So you can't even look after your son when you're not working?' They pulled onto their drive.

'Mark, what is wrong with you?'

'Let's just get in. I've had a bad day, that's all.' She handed him a beer from the fridge. 'Thanks.'

Dana poured herself a Diet Coke and sat at the kitchen table.

'I've got something to tell you.'

'Go on, but be quick as I've got a conference call with the US at seven-thirty.'

'I'm pregnant. The baby is due on Valentine's Day too. See? All that sexy lovemaking did pay off.'

Mark went to the kitchen calendar and started flicking through the pages.

He came back to her calmly.

'So, you did sleep with him then?'

Dana squirmed on her seat. OK, so she had to deny it. She and Tony had used condoms every time. There was no way it could be his.

'So did you?' Mark shouted at the top of his voice. 'No. No, I didn't. It's your baby, Mark. I promise it is.'

'Dana Knight. I have loved you for so many years with all my heart. Please be honest with me – I have to know.

You owe me that at least.'

She started to cry. 'The baby is yours.'

'Now, I am no doctor but I have lived with you for the past two years as a baby-maker and that is all. On this fucking calendar, every four weeks we have five O's for ovulation and five P's for period days. I know everything about your lying cheating sexual organs! So don't you now be saying this is my baby because I know it is that dirty Italian's. And don't think you can get out of it by saying we slept together during your ovulation period, because I know that I was so damn angry with you, I didn't touch you for at least a week.'

'It is your baby.' Dana repeated.

'And I guess this isn't your voice either then?' He fiddled around with his phone until a recording of Tony and Dana could be heard quite obviously discussing the fact they had kissed in the back room of Rosco's.

'You've been spying on me!'

'Well, not me personally – I paid someone to do it. I knew you were up to something, you conniving little cow. No wonder I didn't want you to work.'

'And maybe if you hadn't have been so controlling, I wouldn't have done it.'

'Done what, Dana, a little kiss? No, you fucking shagged him that night I came to the café. I am not as stupid as you think I am. Brother Bruno and his cover story! As if I believed a second of it! I just thought I'd give us a little time. Make a baby together, us two – and be happy again. But no, you've spoiled it all. By going behind my back with a young boy who probably doesn't care an ounce for you and just wanted the sexual buzz of fucking a married woman.'

'It wasn't like that! He really likes me. And I like him too. But not enough to leave our marriage, Mark. I have so much with you and I couldn't upset Tommy or leave this beautiful house.'

'But do you know what, Dana? You are going to have to, because in that little soliloquy you didn't say that you loved me, and for you to do be able to do that so freely with another man, I don't think you can.' He smashed his beer bottle down on to the draining board. 'You profess to not liking the spoils of my job and all that it brings, but you're lying about that too. Go back to being an au pair earning a pittance a week. Me and my boy will be just fine.'

'As if you'd get custody,' Dana jeered, but inside she was trembling.

'I've already looked into it.'

'Who's lying now?'

'Go to Lover Boy, tell him you're having his child. You'll see how much he likes you then.'

With that, Mark stormed upstairs with his laptop leaving Dana to go to the calendar and pray that he had got the dates wrong.

Mo had literally just said goodbye to Joan at the gate when Charlie arrived. Rosie had gone upstairs to change out of her smart funeral clothes. He looked ashen.

'I'm so glad you're home, son. I have something really important to tell you and I don't think you're going to like it.'

'What – she rung ahead, has she?'

'Sorry, I don't you know what you mean.'

'Ffion has rung ahead and told you that I know?'

Mo felt as if her already breaking world was now completely collapsing. She had been in such a bad place when she had told the young girl all those months ago, and since then she had completely forgotten about it.

'Oh Charlie, love. No, she hasn't rung ahead and no, I shouldn't have confided in her.'

'No, Mum, you should have fucking told me. You know – your son – the one this is all about. I'm just finding it so hard to even get my head a little bit around it

250

all. The fact that the man who I have called "Dad" for my whole life, is not my real father. I mean, how does anyone ever take that in? It's just like being told I'm adopted. And every other fucker knew about it but me!' He punched an angry fist into the palm of his other hand.

'Only one other person in the world knows, I promise you.'

'Who's that?'

'Joan − and she would never tell anyone. She is the most honest and loyal person I know.'

'Sometimes, Mother, I think you should really worry about who you trust.'

'What do you mean?'

'Oh, it doesn't matter. So, the million-dollar question, do you know who my dad is then?'

'Of course I do!' Mo was near to tears.

'And does he know about me?'

'Now, Charlie, I am going to be really honest with you. He doesn't know about you, but he was at a Weight Busters meeting that me and Joan went to recently and has been trying to find out if he is your father. Hang on. Wait here.'

She ran upstairs to get the letter from Ron. 'You must read this.' Charlie digested every word slowly and carefully. Mo started to cry.

'My God. What a pair, my parents. Poor Dad and poor you, having to both hold that secret for so long.' Charlie went over to her, gave Mo a massive hug and started to cry too.

'I didn't want to hurt him or you, and he didn't want to hurt any of us,' Mo spluttered.

'I don't want to meet him − my real dad, that is. I don't want to know anything about him. My dad in my eyes, although far from perfect, was Ron Collins. I may change my mind when I get older, who knows. But please can you tell Joan and Ffion to keep their mouths shut in future and that's the end of it.'

'I thought you would hate me.' Mo was still sobbing.

'How could I hate you, Mum? You have never done anything but right by me. It is only because you are my mum that you don't hate me. I'm a bastard and have treated you so badly in the past, but I promise that I will make it up to you. I swear on my late father's life.'

Joan was in her front garden, doing a bit of weeding, when Charlie clicked the gate and walked up the path.

'Hi, love, what are you doing here?'

'Are you alone?'

'Colin will be back from work in twenty and the kids are out the back – why, what's up?'

'I know about my dad not being my real dad but I don't want to know anything about my real dad, if you get me. Mum will say all this to you so obviously pretend you don't know.'

'Oh love…'

'Don't say any more – I can't even talk about it and that's not why I'm here. I'm here because of what happened between us. Firstly, I wanted to apologise for my actions. I mean – what was I thinking of? It was just wrong.'

'OK.' Joan knew he was itching to carry on.

'It's just all these secrets – and look what happens when they come out. It's going to take me forever to get my head round Dad, so I guess what I'm saying is that can we keep what happened between us, between ourselves, please? It's nothing to do with me or you, just Mum. She's suffered so much in her life, and the betrayal she would feel from us both if you eventually told her would be too great for her to bear, I think. You are without doubt too good a friend for her to lose, especially over me.'

'Oh Charlie, I would never ever tell anyone, and I promise you that. I know we didn't kill anyone, but yes, what we did was wrong. No, I will rephrase that. What I did was wrong. I'm the married one, for God's sake. Colin is my soulmate, and your mother is indeed my best friend. I should never have jeopardised either of those relationships.'

Charlie hugged her. 'Thanks, Joan.' He walked towards the front gate, then turned around. 'You old cougar, you.'

'Not so much of the old!' Joan giggled and carried on weeding.

Chapter Twenty Six

Lily would not stop whining the whole way up the drive about not wanting to go to after-school club.

'You love Running Club, Lily, now just stop moaning.' Robbie raised his voice so much that Lily started to cry.

'Daddy always lets me off clubs if I don't want to go.'

'He does actually,' Lola piped up in her sensible voice.

'Well, I'm sorry, but today I have plans until four-thirty so you will both have to wait.'

'I want my daddy,' Lily carried on.

'And so do I,' Robbie replied. 'He could sort you spoiled brats out. Now get into class please, and I'll see you later.'

He caught sight of handsome Charlie holding Rosie's hand as they walked up the drive and did a silent wolf-whistle.

Dana, wearing her dark sunglasses, walked slowly up with Tommy and saw Alana saying goodbye to Eliska.

'Are you rushing off to work?' she asked.

'No, not today. I am working from home, but I've time for a coffee if you want one. We could stop off at Rosco's.'

'No, not there,' Dana said quickly.

'Meet me at mine then. I'll have to chuck you out about ten if that's OK?'

'OK, great. See you in a minute.'

'Kettle's on, get yourself at the kitchen table, girl,' Alana instructed her friend.

'God, if this table could talk we'd have enough material

for a blockbuster,' Dana said, and attempted a smile. When she took off her glasses, Alana noticed her swollen eyes.

'Oh darling, you've been found out, haven't you?'

'It's worse than that. I've been found out – and I'm pregnant.'

'Shit!'

'Yes – and by God, has it hit the fan.'

'Do you know whose baby it is?'

'Well, I thought all along it was Mark's. Tony and I used condoms the whole time, but Inspector Knight looked on the calendar where I always put an "O" for ovulating and put two and two together. He was right – we didn't have sex that whole ovulation period. Me and Tony were at it hammer and tongs: maybe some leaked or who knows, the condom may have burst. I was so into him I wouldn't have noticed.'

'So it was good then?'

'Bloody amazing.'

'Hmm…well, I did tell you his brother was hot to trot too.'

'God – imagine, we could have had little Italian cousins between us.' Dana laughed. 'Hark at me joking when my world is about to bloody fall apart. Seriously though, what do I do now? It has to be Tony's baby.'

'What has Mark said about it all? Has he chucked you out?'

'We're in separate rooms and he says he can't see how he can rebuild things with me.'

'I hate to say it, but you can't blame him.'

'Alana, please don't say that. He has already said he is going to get custody of Tommy. If he does, I don't know how I'll carry on. I don't want to lose my son,' she wept.

'Oh love. That is terrible! Could Tony support you, do you think? I mean, they both live above in that flat, don't they?'

'Yeah. The café is a little goldmine, but I know they are investing for their future. However, Tony really does adore me and I'm sure I can persuade him to help me. I mean, Italians love their kids, don't they?'

'But listen, we're not thinking straight here,' the ever-shrewd Alana chipped in. 'Mark will have to you give you an allowance for Tommy, and if you get divorced, he will have to pay up.'

'I stupidly signed a pre-nup.'

'Oh Dana, that's not in the rules.'

'I know, I know but I was so young – and as for a child allowance, what if he does take my boy? Alana, I can't bear to think about it. What a fucking mess. And the sad thing is, I'm pregnant and I should be so happy but I don't think I've ever felt so bad in the whole of my life.'

'He may come round. Go home tonight and thrash it out. Say how ridiculous you have been and that you want him to forgive you. Blame it on the drink, blame it on anything you like. You need to stay there for a while whatever, and sort things out or you'll be on the bloody street.'

'He's not that unreasonable.'

'He might be, as you've done the dirty on him – and God forbid he does take Tommy. With no divorce settlement, you're going to be a single working parent

– and that isn't easy, I can tell you.'

'OK, right. I'm going to go home now, clean the house from top to bottom. Get flowers, his favourite meal and do my best to save this marriage and myself.'

'I've got to get on, but before you go, I need to tell you my news quickly,' Alana said. 'Stephen has asked if I will move to Cyprus with him – give up work and just be with him.'

'Wow, that's amazing! So when are you going? '

'I haven't made up my mind if I am, yet.'

'Alana, you have to go. A massive life-change like that

with the man you love – it's what dreams are made of. If
you don't go, I shall.'

Alana laughed. 'I've got two weeks to decide so that I
can get Eliska into a new school over there in time.'

'I will miss you, honey, but I think you have to go.'

Alana looked flustered. 'I know, I know. Right, I must
get on. Text me later if you can, and let me how it goes.'

Charlie Lake insisted that he and Joan meet up again.
Unbeknownst to him, Mo was coming along too.

The women were sat armed and dangerous with two
skinny lattes when he arrived.

'Maureen? What are you doing here?'

'Well, I believe we are discussing me and my son.'

'Forgive me,' he said immediately. 'Firstly, I am so
sorry for your loss. Are you OK?'

Maureen sighed deeply. 'I'm fine, thanks, but do you
know what? Losing Ron has made me look at the big
picture and I'm not lying any more. Charlie is your son.
He knows now that Ron was not his real father, but he has
said he doesn't want to know anything about his real dad.
In his eyes, although Ron was far from perfect, he brought
him up to the best of his ability, and sees no point in
meeting someone who is going to be a nigh-on stranger.'

'I understand, I guess. He's a fine-looking lad, just like
his father used to be.'

'How do you know that? You've never met him!'

'I sneaked into the back of the crematorium – wanted to
see him with my own eyes, and as soon as I did, I knew.
He looks so like me when I was a youngster.'

'I can't believe you did that! But yes, he is a handsome
boy.'

Charlie carried on. 'And then weirdly, I went to the pub
opposite and some Welsh girl was in there on her own and
started telling me the story of how sad it was that young
Charlie's dad was not really his, and then I really did know

for sure.'

Joan and Mo looked at each other with raised eyebrows. Ffion the canary had been singing again!

'So what is wrong with you then?' Mo asked. 'Joan tells me you are not well too.'

'Now this is the worst part: I am going to be honest with you now. There is absolutely nothing wrong with me. Just seeing you the other day and thinking back to what fun we had and how much I did care for you, Maureen... I wanted to know. I mean, we are not getting any younger and then seeing what happened to Ron – I would hate to get to my deathbed and wonder if I had a son. I'm getting married again as well, ain't I, and I know Penny wants to start a family, so I would get caught up in that...'

He paused, then raising his voice slightly continued, 'It was wrong to have pretended I was ill, and I am so sorry. Especially after finding out that your husband was dying. But forgive me for just wanting an answer.' He took a slurp of his coffee. 'Do you think, Maureen, there is any chance me and young Charlie could be friends?'

'Look, he has said he doesn't want anything to do with you, for the moment anyway. He's just lost his dad, so let's respect his wishes, eh? You know what life is like. When things settle down and even when he becomes a dad himself, maybe then he'll think differently.'

'Such a shame. But you're right – I can't just blunder my way into the boy's life. Anyway, I'd better go. Penny is waiting for me at home for my suit-fitting today, although I see no point as I've still at least a stone to lose.' He stood up and kissed both ladies on the cheek.

'Be lucky.' He winked and then he was gone.

Joan and Mo sat there in quiet disbelief for a moment.

'Do you know what, Joanie? I can't believe I'm saying this, but I think I made the right choice in Ron, don't you?'

Joan smiled. 'You certainly pick 'em, love, that's for sure.'

Dana checked herself in the mirror as she heard Mark pull up on the drive. Ever since their confrontation he had driven himself to the train station. Dana was wearing the dress he loved her in and had had her hair cut especially. For tonight was the night she was going to save their marriage.

'You look nice – been out shagging someone special?' was Mark's opening line.

He noticed the beautiful aroma of giant pink lilies and went to the fridge to get himself a beer.

'Do you want one?'

'No, thanks. I want to talk, Mark. There's wine cooling and snacks on the outdoor table as it's such a beautiful evening.'

Mark rubbed his head and followed her out.

Dana took a sip of wine and grabbed a bread stick. She had to make sure this wasn't her last supper.

'Why are you drinking? You're pregnant, Dana.'

'I'm just having a glass to settle me. I don't want us to split, Mark. I know we can work this out.'

Mark poured her wine on to the grass.

'So you do care then?' Dana said nonchalantly.

'Of course I bloody care, you stupid trollop. This is just the saddest, most surreal situation. All you've ever wanted was another baby and now I'm sitting here and it's not mine. I would love it if I could see past that fact, but I can't, Dana. I would never trust you again. You know what I'm like and I know it's a big fault of mine. Just seeing someone catch your eye at a party used to set me off. To have to look at a child and know it was conceived outside our marriage – well, I just can't do it.'

'I'm going to have an abortion.'

Mark nearly choked on his beer. 'You what?'

'I said I'm going to get rid of the baby.'

'You don't mean that for a second.'

'It's all booked. I go tomorrow morning. Then we can

260

put the whole sorry episode behind us.'

'Just like that. So the poor little bastard will be gone, but the fact that you are a dirty cheating whore will be with you forever. Dana, I deserve more than that. And do you know what? If you do have an abortion, I will think even less of you. We have tried for years to have a baby and the fact you can cast a little life away just like that to keep you in the life you're accustomed to, is... is disgusting. You're pathetic, you and your silly little games. It would take more than a clean house, fresh lilies and a sexy outfit for me to want you back.'

Storming towards the French doors he turned round. 'It's over and I mean it. I want you out of here by the end of the month. I'll see you right, but Tommy won't be coming with you.'

Gordon put the key in the door; his last flight from Cannes had been delayed and he could tell by Robbie's voice that he had not been amused when he called to tell him.

'Daddy!' Both girls ran to meet him. 'Robbie made us stay for after-school club and we didn't want to.'

Gordon was feeling tired and stressed. 'Don't tell tales, girls.'

'I had to go to the youth club for a meeting,' Robbie said in a surly fashion, coming out to meet him.

'It's fine. Rob. I know you have to stick by your calendar.'

'He left us at the swings when he went to get cigarettes too.'

'Now that is a complete lie,' Robbie burst out on seeing Gordon's expression.

'It isn't. We waited for you for ages.'

Robbie shook his head truculently.

'Get to your room the pair of you, and get ready for bed,' Gordon demanded. Kat and Alfie were meowing loudly for food and started squirming round Robbie's legs.

He kicked out and caught Kat on her back leg and she yelped.

'Rob, there was no need for that. Let me take a shower and we'll have a quick drink unless you've got to go.'

'I've got an hour, that's all.'

While Gordon was washing away his day in the shower, the girls appeared in their pyjamas. Lola was carrying a purring Kat.

Lily stuck her tongue out at Robbie as she made her way to the fridge.

He dragged her over to him by the arm, threatening her: 'If I ever hear you telling tales again I will…' 'You'll what exactly?'

'Daddy Chris, Daddy Chris!' the girls shouted in unison.

Chapter Twenty Seven

It was a tearful goodbye in the Collins household when Charlie had to leave for London to go back to work.

'It's been so lovely having you here, son.'

'I'm going to miss you, Charlie.' Rosie swung on his hand. 'But I'm going to be a big girl and look after Mummy.'

'Good girl.' He gave his sister a big hug and kissed his mum. 'I'll be home a lot more now, I promise. And you'll soon be getting the money back I owe you. I'll work hard and save every penny.'

'There's no hurry with that. We'll manage, we always do. Now, what time train are you getting?'

'It goes in thirty minutes.'

'So you're not going to see Ffion before you go then?'

'No, why would I?'

Mo was pleased. Ffion wasn't a bad girl. Just a bit young and naïve, and in her eyes not really marriage material for an only son.

Joan and her brood bumped into Charlie as he was being waved off down the road. Joan wished him well and hurried into Mo's.

She was so at home there that she flicked on the kettle and lined up cups and glasses.

'Girls, go out in the garden,' Mo said. 'I'll bring you some squash.'

'You all right?' Joan gave her friend a hug.

'Do you know what? Weird as it may seem, I feel at peace. I mean, I've been trying to escape from the silly old bugger and then he dies on me anyway. And now he's gone, I do miss him. But I also feel I can move on with my life properly now.'

'It's only natural for you to miss him. I mean, he has been your life for the past twenty-four years, through thick and thin.'

'True. And even young Charlie seems to have turned over a new leaf. But I won't hold my breath with him.'

'I don't know, Mo, maybe now Ron's gone he will make more of an effort. By the way, have you spoken to Ffion yet? About letting the cat out of the bag, I mean?'

'No, I will when I get back to work on Monday. But to be fair on her, she didn't know it wasn't a secret. I was at a real low when I told her, so it was my own stupid fault. I shall ask her not to mention it to anyone again, though. I mean, the odds of her bumping into Charlie senior too.'

'Yeah, I know – but things happen for a reason, I'm sure of that. Everyone who needs to know knows now, and nobody seems too distressed by that fact.'

'Everyone except Rosie, that is.' Mo got the milk from the fridge. 'She doesn't know yet, but I've decided to wait until she is older and then tell her so she understands properly.'

She offered Joan the biscuit tin and then said: 'Blimey, I've just realised I haven't thought about calories for weeks.'

'And just look at you, sexy lady. You must be at target weight now, I reckon, Smashing Sally will be mortified you've done it without attending any of her classes.'

'I don't want to go again. I lost two stone and gained a strange ex-boyfriend.'

Joan laughed. 'I don't mind whether we go or not, honestly. If we keep up with our weekly walking I'll be happy, as that all helps with the diabetes.'

'I am so broke, I'm actually taking in my old clothes so they fit.'

'Poor you. You look fantastic though, love. Onwards

and upwards now, eh?' They chinked tea cups.

Mo grinned. 'Onwards and inwards, you mean.'

Alana was sat at her home-office desk waiting for a conference call to start when Stephen phoned.

'Hi darling, got to be quick, got a con-call in a minute. How are you?'

'Fine, fine. It was just to say I am booking my flight to Cyprus for a week Friday and wanted to know if you would like me to book for you two, too?'

Stephen's casual, non-pushy approach to the biggest life decision she had ever been faced with made her smile.

'No, no – you go ahead. I haven't spoken to Lissy about it yet.'

'So, you are considering it then?' Stephen tentatively enquired.

'Bugger, that's them ringing through on the other line. Call you later.'

Gordon heard the commotion and walked through into the kitchen with just a white towel wrapped around his waist.

'Chris? What the hell are you doing here?' Gordon's heart kick-started again.

'You owe me fifty quid,' Robbie said, grabbing his bag from the side.

'You don't deserve it,' Chris said angrily.

'Whoa.' Gordon put his hand up. 'Girls, back to your room, please. You can see Daddy Chris in a minute.'

The twins scampered out of the room, hand in hand.

'Just pay me so I can get the hell out of here and you can play Happy Families,' sneered Robbie.

Without a word, Gordon fetched his wallet and took out five ten-pound notes. Robbie stormed to the door, the cash in his hand. He was about to slam it, then poked his head back in, to snarl out one last venomous remark.

'And just for the record, it was me who grassed up Inga

too, the Polish whore. Your sweet little sister would be turning in her grave.'

Chris ran to tackle him, but Gordon held him back.

'He's not worth it. I gave him a second chance. My gut told me not to – but I was a bit desperate. He's a horrible person. He hurt the kitten and now he's threatened my beautiful girls. He's not wrong about Jessica – she would be furious with me. But, sod all that for now and tell me what the hell you are doing here?'

'The door was open, I heard the girls and wanted to surprise you all. Then I heard that bastard threatening Lily.'

Gordon went to say something, but Chris interrupted.

'Let me carry on. Gord, I have missed you so much. And, being away from the girls too has made me realise how much I miss them too. The single life is all right, but if your heart is joined by a cord to someone, that cord won't snap. You can try and break it by taking other lovers. But if it's strong enough, it will always pull you to the heart of the person you should be with. I love you, Gordon Summers. I can't be without you and I am hoping and praying that you will forgive me for leaving and be able to love me back too.'

Tears streamed down Gordon's face.

Chris picked up the huge bouquet of flowers he had brought in and handed them to Gordon.

'White roses, that's a new one on me,' Gordon said chokily.

'They are the flower of light, the "I miss you" rose, the rose of pure intention.

The flower of marriage.' Chris got down on one knee.

'Gordon Summers. You light up my life, you always have. You are a beautiful man inside and out. Will you marry me?'

Gordon knelt down too and hugged him tightly. '*Yes, yes* of course I will.'

The girls came running into the kitchen. Lola saw that both men were crying and burst into tears.

'Oh no, what's wrong? Has someone died?'

'Come here, both of you,' Chris said softly. 'They are happy tears. Now it's group-hug time.'

The girls squealed as Gordon and Chris grabbed them and they all jumped around in a circle hugging each other.

'So, Lily and Lola Summers, how do you fancy being bridesmaids?'

'Who's getting married then?' Lola piped up.

'We are, you doughnut,' Gordon laughed.

'I didn't know boys could get married.'

'They can now.'

'See? I knew it,' Lily told her twin. 'I have been praying so hard for Mummy to send Daddy Chris home to make you happy again, and she must have listened.'

'Yes, darling, she must have listened.' Gordon's tears started again.

'So can you please stop these happy tears and let Daddy Chris cook us some decent dinner at last.'

Chris whisked Lily up in his arms and kissed her.

It was a Sunday afternoon and Rosco's was shut. Dana rang the bell to the boys' flat. A beautiful dark-haired, dark-eyed girl with a shiny black bob came to the door. She had an amazing tan and was wearing a white kaftan covering a designer black bikini. Even her slight pregnancy bump was perfectly rounded.

'Ciao. Can I help?'

'Oh hi, Tony didn't mention that he had a sister.'

She laughed. 'I am not his sister, I am his girlfriend.'

Dana thought she was going to be sick all over the girl's perfectly manicured toes.

'Pleased to meet you,' she calmly carried on instead. 'I work here sometimes, and I just wondered if I could have a quick word with Tony?'

'*Si, si*, what is your name?'

'Dana.'

'Danna,' the girl repeated in exactly the same way Tony said it to her. It made Dana feel even worse.

She shouted in Italian to Tony, who came running to the door as the glorious Fabia went back to her sunbathing in the roof garden.

'Let's go sit downstairs,' he said hurriedly, praying that Dana wasn't going to kick off.

'I don't understand. This had better be good.' Dana was furious.

'Dana, I made you no promises.'

'But you lied – you aren't single at all! Where did you hide her? You said I meant everything to you.'

'You did. I loved being with you, but I had a big decision to make – and you helped me make it.'

'So glad I could be of service,' Dana spat.

'I got together with Fabia when we were just sixteen, so, so young. She came over to live here, in England, but missed the family and Italy too much so went home. She gave me an ultimatum that either I come back to Italy or we split. I was so torn, as I love England. So we had a break. I love our business here and then I thought I loved you, Dana. What happened between us was so sweet. But, when your husband arrived and you left, I thought about it. I don't want a woman who is capable of cheating on her husband. I want someone who is pure and honest, who I can trust and have a large family with. I went home to Italy soon after we had sex because I felt so guilty. And that was when I realised I had made a big mistake. We had missed each other so much, Fabia and I. We had both grown up, and when she told me she was pregnant I just knew she was the one. We are going to get our own place here and make it work.'

'But you cheated on your partner too.' Dana had tears in her eyes.

'Yes, and I will be forever guilty. But we were on a break and our love is strong enough to go on, I know it is, and she will never know.'

'Unless I tell her, of course.'

'And how exactly would that benefit you? I will never be with you, Dana, so please don't cause unnecessary hurt. And if your love is strong enough with Mark, you will save your marriage too. You love your big house up on the hill with all the trimmings. I know you can make it work.'

'He knows, Tony. He wants me to leave and is getting full custody of Tommy.'

'I don't understand. How could he possibly know that you had slept with me? Bruno did such a good cover.'

Dana stood up, ignoring his question. She knew that if she were to say just three words, they would destroy two more lives – so she chose three different words instead.

'Be happy, Tony.'

It was a scorching day in late June and Eliska had jumped straight into her paddling pool after school. Alana sat on a chair at the side with her feet dipped in the cold water.

'I wish we had a swimming pool, Mummy. I love it when it's hot.' 'One day we might, darling, if I keep working hard.'

'I wish you'd marry Stephen, then we could be a real family. He's so funny. I can pretend he's my daddy then.'

Isobel, adorned in a long sarong and huge floppy sun hat, walked over and caught her granddaughter's last comment. She looked knowingly at Alana and sat down on a chair next to her.

Eliska carried on playing. 'When does he go?'

'Next Friday.'

'It's only three weeks until the end of term,' Isobel said. 'They will probably just be drawing pictures and playing. She won't be missing anything important.'

'Mother! Stop it.'

'I have been such a useless mother, I know that, Lani. But if I am to give you just one piece of decent advice, make it this. Follow your heart – that stubborn, locked-up heart of yours. If not for you, for that beautiful girl of ours.'

'Joan? It's Charlie Lake here.'

'Charlie? I thought we'd seen the last of you.'

'I need to see you just one more time, Joanie. And I promise that there is nothing sinister here, but it is really important that I see you alone.'

'Sounds ominous.'

'It's all good, I promise.'

'So why can't you just say what you want to say on the phone?'

'Because I need to give you something. Look, I've gotta go, so I'll see you on Bart Baker's bench in Denbury Park at eleven a.m. on Sunday.' And with that he hung up.

Dana walked with a heavy heart to the park. Who'd have thought that one single moment of lustful madness could cause so much hurt and upset. She sat on the swings where she had sat with Tony and swung gently. She put her hand to her tummy; she wasn't even three months yet so she was well within the realms of getting rid of the baby. She heard screams as some children ran into the recreational area. A mum put her two-year-old in the swing next to her and the tiny tot shouted with delight.

Dana smiled as she got up and went over to sit on a bench in the corner. She had lied to Mark. She couldn't deny an abortion had crossed her mind, but how could she possibly get rid of such a gift after trying for so long. It would be hard, there was no doubting that, but nothing was impossible. She would just have to manage.

There was no going back now so tomorrow she would start making plans to find a flat and a job.

When Mark had told her about getting back with Carol, she didn't even cry. It was then she realised that she was no longer in love with him. It even shocked her, how cold she could be. And, if she was really honest, there was no way she could have slept with someone else if she was in love with Mark. She had never considered it before this year.

But who'd have thought Mark would get back with his ex-wife? Yes, they were the same age and they shared Sidney in common. Evidently, over discussing his woes about his ailing marriage, he realised that he still did have feelings for her. She had never remarried and had always held a torch for Mark. Distressingly, even Tommy didn't seem that upset as he had an instant brother. Mark had agreed to give Dana one hundred thousand pounds in cash and joint custody of Tommy. She knew she was owed more, but she also knew it would be a massive fight to get it. After all, she was the one who had been unfaithful and was pregnant with another man's child.

Feeling sad and lost, she started to walk up the hill. Thankfully, the house was empty. She would pack and make a quick exit, she decided. The thought of a massive goodbye to Tommy, suitcases in hand, would be too much to bear.

Alana had kindly said she could stay with her until she had sorted somewhere to live, so she would go there tonight.

Birds were singing in the trees and the sun shone brightly. It was time for Dana and her little Italian bambino to follow her dreams now.

The airport was heaving with summer revellers and Alana tutted. She normally flew business class and wasn't used to having to deal with the hoi polloi as she called them.

She checked in her small case in and looked up for her gate number.

She saw him before he saw her. Handsome, kind, reliable and sexy. He was reading a newspaper and had a coffee by his side. She went and quietly sat beside him.

'You could have told me it wasn't a private jet.'

Stephen turned to her calmly. 'There wouldn't have been enough room for your shoes.'

He then put the paper back up to his face and slowly pulled it down to reveal his now smiling eyes.

'You've just made an old man very happy.'

'Don't get too excited. I'm only coming out for a week initially. To have a look, check out some schools. See what I might be letting myself in for.'

'If you love it as much as I love you, then we are on to a winner.' Stephen gently kissed her on the lips.

And with that Alana Murray did something she did very rarely. She started to cry. In fact, she started to sob. Stephen held her to him tightly to avert the stares of other passengers.

Then, as if nothing had happened she sat up and blew her nose, adding, 'I take it we will have a cleaner, darling?'

Chapter Twenty-Eight

'Bart bloody Baker,' Joan said under her breath as she searched for the bench in the park. She hadn't realised there were four of them – and it would have to be the one furthest from the gate on this boiling hot summer's day. Reaching it she let out an 'Aw.'

In memory of Bart Baker, chief coach and scallywag of Denbury United 1920-2000.

Talking of scallywags, she could see the rotund form of Charlie Lake approaching.

'I can't believe you picked the bench furthest from the gate,' she puffed.

'Look at me – I need all the exercise I can get, and we can't be seen.'

'You're scaring me now.' Joan looked perplexed.

'Don't be silly. I need your help with something and you are actually the only person I can trust for the job.'

'Blimey, Mr Bond, what is our next mission exactly?' Joan quipped, although she didn't feel comfortable, hiding things from Mo.

Charlie Lake reached into his pocket and drew out a lottery ticket.

'I want you to drop this in front of Maureen. She must be the person who sees it and picks it up.'

'I don't understand.' Joan ran her hands through her curly blonde hair.

'It's a winning ticket. Five balls and the bonus. Sadly there are lots of winners that week, so it's only fifty thousand pounds.'

'Fifty grand!' Joan nearly fell off Bart Baker's memory

seat in shock. 'Look – I still don't understand.'

'When I found out that I was potentially young Charlie's father, I had to find out what he was like, and what sort of person Maureen had become. I wanted to do right by her and the lad, but I knew it would be difficult to just walk in and announce myself. I am marrying Penny and I do live in the next town but I'm a rich man. My first wife was a very wealthy lady with no kids, and when she sadly died young, I came into a healthy inheritance. I couldn't just sit on my fat arse all day, and as I've always been a nosey bastard, I decided to train to become a private investigator and eventually set up my own business. I now employ ten blokes so that too makes me a good living in my own right, thanks very much.'

'Go on,' Joan urged, intrigued.

'Well, it appears Maureen is a fine woman. I've had some of my boys on to Charlie and I know he ain't no angel, but with my genes that was always going to be a probability. But he loves his mum, that's for sure, and that's what matters to me.'

'So why not just give Mo the money?'

'I won the lottery just as I heard about Charlie. I was going to give it to charity as I really don't need any more and I do a lot of fundraising in the local community. Then I had this madcap idea about making someone's dream come true, meaning Maureen's. When she refused to let on about Charlie being my kind, not even for the thirty grand I was tempting her with, I knew I was doing the right thing.'

Joan couldn't get over the fact that they had got this man so very wrong. 'Anyway, after meeting her, I know she won't take any money from me as she is a very proud lady. She would have to explain it to our boy, and as I fully respect her wishes for not telling him yet, this seems the perfect solution. She will, of course, give some to him to get him on a steady path and they will both now be put

274

in my Will so the whole family, Rosie included, will always be OK .'

'But you know Mo,' Joan objected. 'What if she gets all honest and says we should try and find the real winner?'

'Yes, she's bound to do that. We know her so well, don't we! So this is where you come in again. You tell her you will ring the lottery HQ for her and just come back saying finders keepers or something to that effect.'

'You think of everything, Charlie Lake.'

'I know, I'm brilliant.' He laughed.

'Thank you for doing this for Mo,' Joan said, feeling moved. 'Fifty thousand pounds will change her life. It is amazing. I am so happy for her.'

'And this is for you, for doing it.' Charlie handed her a cheque for one thousand pounds.

'I don't want your money, Charlie.' She pushed his hand away. 'I could do with it, don't get me wrong. But just seeing Mo's face when she realises how much it is, will be worth more than any money anyone could give me.'

He put the cheque back in his pocket and handed over the lottery ticket, joking, 'Don't bloody lose it, will you?'

'I will guard it with my life until I see her tomorrow.'

They both stood up and Charlie kissed her on the cheek.

'Well, it's been a pleasure meeting you, Joan, and I'm glad Maureen has got such a good friend in you. I doubt if we'll meet again, but who knows. I pray that in time my son will want to get to know his real dad.'

'If there is such a thing as Karma, Charlie, then I do believe he will.' Joan turned around and touched the plaque on the bench.

'And as for you, Bart Baker, the scallywag – don't you be telling anyone this either.'

They both laughed and headed their separate ways.

Mo walked across the road to the doctors' surgery. The sun was shining and for the first time in ages, she had a spring in her step. Charlie had sent her a cheque for half of the Freedom Fund he had stolen, so she had treated herself to a flowery summer dress from the posh boutique at the end of the high street. Ffion was already in. She had been mortified when Mo gently explained that Charlie hadn't known about his real dad, and that it had been a terrible shock for him, coming on the very day of his father Ron's funeral; chastened and ashamed, the young Welsh girl had promised that if she were ever to see him again, she would not mention it.

'You're early, love,' Mo said comfortably.

'I know – I'm leaving at two today, got one of my beauty exams.'

'Cor, that's come round quick.'

Ffion looked up from her screen and opened her eyes wide.

'Wow! Mo Collins, you look amazing. Those colours really bring out your eyes – and that dress! You have a waist!'

'Aw thanks, Ffi. I have to say I love it now I'm lighter. I feel so much better too.'

'Well, that's the main thing,' Dr Delicious chipped in as he walked through with a pile of patients' notes. 'And Ffion's right, you look very nice today, Mo.'

Even Grim Lynn was smiling as she walked through to her office.

'Must be the sunshine,' Ffion whispered. 'Or she got a good seeing-to last night.'

'Ffion Jones, what are you like?'

'Talking of which, the Denbury total has sprung up a notch. There's a new barman in the Featherstone Arms I've got my eye on.'

'Not many prospects with a barman, Ffi,' Mo said wisely.

'Yes, but plenty of free drinks and lock-ins, that'll do me for now.'

'Ladies, this is a doctors' surgery, not a public house!'

'OK, I take back what I said about the shag,' Ffion trilled.

Dr Delicious rang Mo's extension. 'Have you got a minute please, Mo?'

Mo was glad to be looking good as she walked down to Noah Anderson's room.

'Take a seat.'

'I feel as if I've done something wrong,' Mo said nervously.

'Don't be silly, far from it. I just wanted to let you know how pleased I am with your work. Despite all you've been through, you haven't once let me down and have been as pleasant as ever to the patients. In fact, you are a joy to have around.'

Mo blushed.

'I also need to let you know that Lynn is leaving. Her husband has got a job overseas and she is going with him.'

'That's a surprise. She's like a part of the furniture.'

'Indeed she is, so to that end I was hoping maybe you'd take over being that part of the furniture. What do you reckon?'

Mo was taken aback. 'But as Surgery Supervisor, she must be on at least eight thousand a year more than me!'

Noah Anderson nodded. Tears filled Mo's eyes. 'Dr…'

'Noah, please, Mo.'

'Thank you, Noah. I don't know what to say.'

'Well, I was rather hoping you might say yes.'

'Yes, yes of course I would love to! I realise it will be extra hours, but I will be able to afford to pay Joan now to look after Rosie so that will help her out too. I can't believe this is happening.'

'Well, it is, Mo, and you deserve every happiness. There was also something else I was hoping you might say yes to…' It was Noah Anderson's turn to blush. 'I was wondering if you might want to go out to dinner sometime soon – to discuss your new role, of course.'

'That would be lovely,' she said quietly.

Then pinched herself – ouch – to check that she was still here and had not died and gone to heaven.

Epilogue

It was the end of the summer term at Featherstone Primary.

Gordon and Chris walked hand in hand through the school gates and up the drive. There was no whispering now the initial shock that they were the twins' parents had worn off. In fact, they were the life and soul of the school proceedings a lot of the time. Joan's inkling that Mr Chambers fancied her had proved to be completely unfounded. When Will Chambers found out that two of the school's parents were gay, he was delighted and asked Gordon to let him know if he had any single male friends who might be his type. He was, of course, invited to Gordon and Chris's civil ceremony.

Gordon was pleased to hear that Robbie had been let go from Bebops; although he was still working with the older boys at the youth centre.

Emily and Kenneth followed Gordon and Chris, also hand in hand. A few sessions at Relate had worked for them. In fact, Kenneth had agreed for his wife to have a tummy tuck for her birthday.

Dana, her bump now showing, chatted to Isobel Murray. Isobel was delighted that Dana had made the decision to join Alana out in Cyprus to be her PA. Tommy was to join her for all of the school holidays so she would see an awful lot more of him than she had thought she would.

Joan was sweating with nerves as she walked a little bit in front of Mo. She was so glad it wasn't windy. She Let the lottery ticket fall from her hands and, as if in slow motion, it drifted through the air like an autumn leaf waiting to be caught.

The children ran out of their classrooms, screaming and shouting with the excitement of being free for six weeks of summer holidays.

Before anyone could see, Joan swept the ticket up and put it back in her bag.

Today, Mo felt as if she had won the lottery.

Unbeknownst to Mo, Joan Brown actually had!

Nicola May

For more information about **Nicola May**

and other **Accent Press** titles

please visit

www.accentpress.co.uk

Lightning Source UK Ltd.
Milton Keynes UK
UKOW04f1028210715

255553UK00001B/3/P